MOON

Book 1 of the Fur 'n

C. S. Churton

Other Titles By C.S Churton

Druid Academy Series

DRUID MAGIC

FERAL MAGIC

PRIMAL MAGIC

Fur 'n' Fang Academy Series

MOON BITTEN

CURSE BITTEN

FERAL BITTEN

TalentBorn Series

AWAKENING

EXILED

DEADLOCK

UNLEASHED

HUNTED

CHIMERA

Chapter One

Home sweet home. You know, if you added a little paint, and a crap load of imagination.

I swept my gaze over the farmhouse, very different from the one in my memory. The farm I'd spent my early childhood on had a beautiful grey stone farmhouse with gleaming windows, and a pristine red barn, surrounded by acres of cultivated fields.

This one? Not so much.

I took the two keys from the plain white envelope, and slotted the larger of them into the keyhole, but before I could even attempt to turn it, the door swung inwards, half-hanging from one of its hinges. Great.

I hadn't been here in nearly a decade, and the years had not been kind to Oak Ridge Farm. I crossed the threshold into the kitchen, leaving footprints in the grime coating the weathered stone flooring as I went. Dingy light filtered in through yellowed windows, and the air tasted the way it does when it's been stagnating for years. I leaned over the sink and gave one of the dirty windows a shove, but it didn't budge. Probably sealed shut with years of filth. Great. I gave it up for a bad job and strolled through the rest of the house, trying not to breathe too deeply.

Maybe this hadn't been such a great idea, after all. I mean, sure, free accommodation while I went to uni had *sounded* great, and it was real nice of Uncle Bob to offer me the use of the place – did I mention for free? – but had he seen the state of this place recently? It was going to take a whole lot of work to make the place even remotely habitable. And I didn't like the way the hallways echoed with memories that I'd long since buried. Coming back here had been a mistake.

But university was starting in three weeks, and there was no way I could find somewhere else now. And I couldn't afford it, either, unless I was going to get an evening job, and I would really like to avoid that. Studying law was going to be hard enough without a job eating into my study time.

Three weeks. That had to be long enough to get the place fixed up – or at least, fixed up enough that I didn't have to worry about any animals busting in while I was sleeping, and so that I didn't worry I was going to catch something every time I touched a surface. I was going to need a hardware store – and a whole lot of cleaning supplies. Yeah, I decided, as I stepped back out into the clean air and the fading sunlight. If I could get accepted to study law at University College London, I could absolutely do this.

I glanced down at my watch and sighed. It would have to be tomorrow. The drive up here had taken longer than I'd thought – thanks, motorway traffic – and the store would be closed by now. But I could probably find something to jam the door shut with, and– My eyes came to rest on the old barn, stopping me mid-thought. Maybe I wouldn't need to sleep in the house tonight. Sure, the barn was a bit dilapidated, but it still looked pretty sturdy, and it wasn't cold at night this time of year.

I wandered over to it and rattled the doors. They didn't swing open or collapse at my touch, which in my books was a winner. The door handles were secured with a rusty chain and padlock – proving that crime is a concern no matter where in the country you are – and I used the second key to coax it open, then tossed both the lock and the chain on the floor.

It was dark inside – trees and weeds had long since overgrown the windows – and it took my eyes a few moments to adjust to the gloom. A few dust webs hung from the high ceilings, but at least the floor wasn't covered in the sticky grime, and the air didn't taste like something dead. It was settled, then. I'd grab my stuff from the car, and sleep here tonight, like I had dozens of times as a kid. Then tomorrow, I'd get to work on fixing up the house.

I headed back outside into the fading light. I'd forgotten how quickly it got dark out here. No streetlamps – hell, no streets – for miles in any direction, and when the sun set, the small lights on the farmhouse seemed to cast more shadows than light.

A dark shape drifted across the front of the house and I jumped, then laughed as the shadow moved with me. My shadow. And then the laughter died on my lips as something flitted across the tangled foliage beyond the barn. I froze, peering into the gloom, scanning the near darkness. Nothing but stillness and my own imagination peered back.

I shook my head at my own stupidity and turned for the car. First night back at the farm, I guess it wasn't so unusual to see shadows moving where there ought not to be shadows. An over-active imagination, that had always been my problem. Sleeping in the barn sure was going to be fun tonight.

I hit the fob to unlock my car – city habit – then opened the rear door and leaned in to grab my stuff. I'd brought more than I needed. Much more, probably, but I wasn't planning on heading back to the city until the end of the first semester. Maybe not even then. For now, though, I just needed my sleeping bag and a pillow. And the camping light I'd packed, because maybe I'd gone soft living in the city, but it was just a shade too dark here for my liking.

Gravel crunched behind me, and I jumped back, cracking my head on the car's interior. I blinked through the pain and spun around.

A scream ripped through my throat. Stalking towards me was the biggest dog I'd ever seen. Its fur was mottled, like a husky or wolf, but it was twice the size of any dog I'd ever seen before. Its hackles were up as it advanced on me, teeth bared in a terrifying snarl.

I threw a frantic glance at the farmhouse, but it was too far. I'd never make it. And if growing up on a farm had taught me one thing, it was that you don't run from a feral dog. Especially not one the size of a small horse. My hand groped behind me for the open car door. If I could get inside, I'd be safe.

As if it could read my mind, the dog snarled another warning. It was so close I could feel its hot breath across my skin. It took another step towards me, the movement revealing heavy slabs of muscle beneath its fur. The rising moon glinted on its yellowed fangs. Each paw was the size of my hand, tipped in wickedly curved black claws. I had a flash of those claws and fangs sinking into my body, and my legs trembled under me.

Just get in the car, Jade, I told myself. Very slowly, get into the car.

I followed my own advice, lifting one trembling foot from the floor, and ducking my head slightly.

And that was when the dog leapt at me.

Its teeth seized my leg, slicing through the denim of my jeans and cutting into the skin. I cried out in pain and the sound seemed to drive the animal into a frenzy. It snarled again, worrying at my leg and backing away, pulling me with it. I snatched at the top of the car door, but there was no purchase and the beast easily dragged me off. I hit the ground hard and my forehead smacked into the packed dirt. My vision blurred as tears sprung to my eyes, and the pain in my right leg only heightened as the creature kept dragging me away from the car. I kicked out with my left, slamming it into the beast's face, and the impact jolted all the way up to my hip. The creature didn't so much as blink, and I kicked at it again and again, the whole time my hands frantically scrabbling across the packed dirt and loose gravel, but it might as well have been sand for all the grip I managed to get.

"Get off me!" I screamed at the animal, kicking its snout again. It snarled in response, worrying at my leg and sending scores of agony racing through my calf. I twisted over onto my back and snatched up a handful of dirt and gravel from behind me, then hurled it at the thing's eyes. It blinked and shook its head, the movement tossing me around like a rag doll. I cried out in pain, groping the ground for anything I could use as a weapon – a stick, a rock, anything – but there was nothing. I hurled another handful of grit in its face, but it ducked its head aside, keeping its teeth wrapped around my leg.

What the hell was wrong with this thing? Dogs weren't supposed to act like this. Dogs weren't supposed to be that big, either. My head throbbed as I stared into its gleaming eyes. Pure malice stared back at me. Who would keep a dog like this?

"Let me go!" I screamed. "You stupid mutt, get off me!"

I punctuated my words with furious kicks, each one a little weaker than the one before. Blood soaked through my jeans, and the pain and the head injury were making me dizzy. If I passed out, this thing was going to kill me. I gulped and tried to force the pain to the back of my mind.

I kicked again, but my foot glanced off its shoulder, as effective as a rolled-up newspaper on a T-Rex. I knew it, then. It was going to kill me, and there was nothing I could do to stop it.

I lifted my leg again, and every burning muscle screamed in protest. The beast snarled at me and I snarled right back. If I was going down, I was going down fighting. I hope I gave the damned thing indigestion.

Another snarl ripped through the air, this one from behind me. A whimper of terror from my lips. There were two of them. I twisted my head round, and watched the second dark shape advancing on me, its teeth bared in an identical snarl to the first beast's.

I silenced the tiny sounds of fear escaping from me. I was dead, anyway. Didn't much matter if it was one or two animals. I scraped up another handful of grit. It wasn't much, as weapons went, but if I got close enough, it might ruin his night. Good enough for me.

The beast sunk down onto its haunches and leapt clean over me, slamming into the other animal. I howled in pain as the force ripped the teeth loose from my flesh, and then the two animals were rolling in a tangled mass of limbs and fur, snarling and snapping at each other. I shuffled back across the floor, dragging my bleeding leg behind me. I had to get to the car. I had to get inside – before whoever won the fight came back for me.

I kept dragging myself, biting down on my lip to keep the sounds of pain from escaping. A trail of blood marked my progress, and my head swam. I screwed my eyes tight. *Not now, please.* I had to get out of here. *Then* I could pass out. I swallowed and hauled myself back a few more feet, not daring to drag my eyes from the fighting pair. Neither seemed able to get the upper hand, and the noise of the fight rang in my ears, growing louder and louder with each snap of gleaming fangs.

A third voice joined the cacophony, this one from somewhere off to my left.

"No, no, no," I whimpered. Not more. Where did they keep coming from?

The two beasts broke apart, raising their heads towards the sound of the newcomer. A gunshot rang out, loud and clear, and the two dogs bolted, disappearing across the field without another sound. I swallowed. Guns, dogs, what the hell was going on?

Two more beasts tore across the farmyard, following the trail of the others, their claws seeming to shine silver in the moonlight. Footsteps crunched towards me and I twisted round, then exhaled a ragged breath of relief. Human. He was human.

He was walking towards me, a rifle held across his body, his face shadowed by the harsh moonlight behind him, so that I couldn't quite make out his features. I didn't care. He wasn't a dog, and he wasn't going to eat me. I was safe.

I slumped my head back into the dirt and let unconsciousness take me.

Chapter Two

The pain woke me from my sleep. I twisted with a gasp, the images of my vivid nightmare flashing in front of me, and clutched at my head. I'd hit it when I fell. When the dog attacked me… no, wait, that had been a dream… hadn't it?

I forced my eyes to part. Murky light filtered into the vaguely familiar room, and it took me a moment to place it. The farmhouse. I was in the farmhouse. And a dog had attacked me.

I sat up, and another lance of pain shot through me, this one in my calf. I stared down at it, and saw someone had cut away my jeans' leg, revealing a jagged circle of tooth marks. The dog bite. It hadn't been messing around – it meant to finish me.

The door creaked, and my head whipped round. A figure eased it open and stepped through.

I scrambled back until my back pressed up against the headboard.

"Hey, easy," the stranger said, freezing where he stood. I looked him up and down, taking in his dark, blood-stained clothing, and the rash of stubble covering his jaw. "You're safe now."

"It was you," I said. "Last night, with the gun. The dogs…"

He nodded and took a step closer, leaving the door open behind him.

"Yeah. I scared them off. Don't worry, they won't be back. Looks like they got you pretty good."

He nodded to my leg and I looked down at it again, this time noticing that there was no blood or dirt caked around the wound itself. Jesus, those teeth must've been huge.

"You cleaned it?"

"I had to cut off your jeans. I hope you don't mind."

I shook my head mutely. I'd probably be dead right now if he hadn't come along, so I wasn't going to be complaining about an old pair of jeans any time soon.

"I've got some food cooking in the kitchen if you feel up to it."

I frowned, glancing out of the grimy window.

"What time is it?"

"A little after ten."

"In the morning?"

"If you can call ten a.m. morning," he said, a smile tugging at the corners of his mouth. He was missing my point.

"Look, I don't mean to sound ungrateful, Mr...."

"Caleb. Caleb Morgan."

"Right. But don't you think it might have been a good idea to take me to a hospital?"

"Why?"

I gaped at him for a moment, then gestured down at my leg.

"Uh, I don't know, maybe because I was savaged last night?"

"Look." He folded his arms across his chest. "I cleaned it, and I gave you an antibiotic shot. They wouldn't have done anything different at the hospital, trust me. Except it would have taken them hours to see you, and the infection would have set in by then."

"Oh."

"You're welcome."

"Um… thanks."

He shook his head and dropped his arms.

"Forget it. You had a scare last night. So, do you want some food?"

My stomach growled, answering the question for me – I'd missed dinner while I was on the road last night.

"I should get cleaned up first."

He tilted his chin to the corner of the room, where I recognised the half-dozen bags piled up.

"I brought your bags in from the car. I'll give you some privacy."

He left the room, shutting the door behind him. I listened to the sound of his footsteps receding down the hall, and swung myself off the bed, wincing when I put weight on my injured leg. What a great welcome back to the farm. Maybe I should have looked for a room share close to campus after all. If there were packs of wild dogs roaming around, there was no way I was staying here. One near-death brush was enough for me.

I rummaged through my bags until I found some clean clothes, then pulled a brush through my hair, wincing as I tackled the knots. Gee, it was almost like I'd been dragged through the dirt backwards. Thanks for the warning, Uncle Bob. There was no way I was looking human again until I'd had time for a shower, and there was no way I was chancing that with tall, dark, and handsome in the kitchen. Because he might be hot, but he was still a stranger. *One who saved your life last night.*

I sighed and tossed my brush aside. My hair was a lost cause. I pulled it back into a loose pony, then limped down the hallway, supporting myself with one hand against the wall.

"Hey," Caleb said, when I hobbled into the kitchen. "Let me get you a chair."

He left the hob and pulled one of the chairs out from the table, dusting away a year's worth of dirt with a sweep of his hand.

"You need some help?"

I shook my head and limped over to the table, grimacing with each step. I paused a moment when I got there, leaning on the table, and then slumped into my seat. Caleb watched me silently, then went back to the hob.

"I found some food in your car. Hope you don't mind."

I didn't. I'd done a grocery run on the way up here – eggs, milk, bread, bacon, coffee, the essentials – and right now I felt like I could eat the whole lot in one go. Caleb put a plate of steaming food in front of me, next to a mug of coffee, then grabbed another plate and mug, and claimed a seat on the opposite side of the table, giving me plenty of space.

"So," he said, as I shovelled a piece of bacon into my mouth, and washed it down with the coffee, "I didn't get your name earlier."

I blushed and lowered my fork.

"Jade. Er, Hart."

"Well, it's nice to meet you, Jade, er Hart. What are you doing out here?"

"It's my uncle's place. And surely the better question is, what were you doing on his land?"

"Saving your life, apparently," he said, watching me through amused eyes as he took a bite out of a slice of toast. I flushed again. Damn, he was hot. *And the sort of guy who goes trespassing with a gun, Jade. Get a grip.*

"Do you hunt round here often?"

"What?" He froze, fork half-way to his mouth.

"I saw your gun last night. Do you go hunting round here often?"

"Oh." He shook his head. "Rarely. You were just lucky."

"Lucky. Right." Then I remembered the pure malice in the dog's eyes, and a shudder ran the length of my spine. He was right. If he hadn't turned up when he did, I'd have been dog chow. "What the hell sort of idiot keeps dogs like that, anyway?"

"Sorry?" He cocked his head at me.

"Those dogs, last night. I grew up round here, and I never saw a dog like that before. Those things were massive. Dogs don't get that big. Or aggressive."

He frowned at me, setting down his fork.

"You must've hit your head pretty bad last night. That was just a normal dog. A husky, or something. Maybe I should have taken you to the hospital. You might have a concussion."

"So you're saying it wasn't the size of a small pony? And there wasn't a whole pack of them?"

He chuckled.

"The size of a pony? No. It was just a dog. A mean one, but just a dog. One dog."

Right. Just a dog. I mean, it couldn't have been a pack of pony-sized dogs. This was surrey, not Forks. Dogs

15

didn't grow that big, and they didn't roam in feral packs. Maybe I really did have a concussion. I frowned and rubbed the lump on my head.

"Okay," I said eventually, with a slight nod. "One dog. You're right. Did you get it?"

"Nope. Couldn't leave you. It ran off. I called the animal warden this morning. They're going to keep an eye out."

Great. That was the last thing I needed. An aggressive dog running loose on the farm.

"Do you have anyone who can come stay with you?" he asked. "Any family?"

"It's just me. This place belongs to my uncle, but he's in a nursing home." And clearly had no idea what had happened to his beloved farm in the few years he'd been there. I looked at him sharply, and added, "He said I could stay here."

"Alright, calm down," he said, raising his hands in mock surrender. "No-one's saying you shouldn't be here. I just don't think you should be alone, in case you do have that concussion. There's no-one else? Parents? Boyfriend? Girlfriend?"

"I'm into guys, thank you. And no. My Mum moved abroad a couple of weeks ago, and I left everything behind to come out here to study."

"Okay, it's settled, then. I'll stay the night."

"No, honestly, it's fine," I protested. "I can't ask you to do that."

"You're not asking, I'm offering. And I could never live with myself if something happened to you when I could have prevented it. I'll even help you get this placed cleaned up a bit, get a new lock fitted on that door for you."

I paused at that, because truth be told, you could write everything I knew about DIY on the back of a postcard, and still have room for a 'wish you were here.'

"Are you sure?"

"You bet. Why don't you go take a shower, and I'll head into town and grab what we need to fix the door?"

"Uh, yeah, that'd be great. Thanks."

He drained the rest of his mug, then headed for the door. When he got there, he paused and turned back, pulling a scrap of paper from an old corkboard near the door. He flipped it over and scribbled on it with a dust covered pencil.

"My mobile number," he said, pinning it back on the board. "In case you start to feel dizzy again. There are some painkillers in the drawer, looks like they're still in date."

"Thanks," I said again, as he headed out.

I found the paracetamol, double checked the date, then washed a pair of them down with the remains of my coffee. They started to kick in by the time I was out of the shower, and the sharp pain in my leg faded to a dull throbbing ache. My eyelids were getting heavy again, so I decided to forgo sitting in the dirty kitchen in favour of heading back into the musty old bedroom. Sleeping was a no-go with a concussion, but there was no rule against being comfortable, right?

My eyes flew open with a start, and Caleb was leaning over me, the back of his hand pressed to my forehead.

"Shh," he said, moving his hand. "You're fine. You remember what happened?"

I nodded my head against the pillow.

"Dog attack," I mumbled.

"That's right. Get some more rest. I'll be outside if you need me."

He woke me up four more times throughout the afternoon, once to bring me food, but the smell made my stomach roil and I told him to take it away. The last time he woke me, my leg was burning and I could feel sweat breaking out over my body.

"Hospital?" I croaked, but he pressed his hand to my forehead again and shook his head.

"Tomorrow," he said. "If you don't get any better."

I didn't have the energy to argue. Just that one word had exhausted me. I sank further into the bed and waited for sleep to take me again.

Suddenly, pain erupted all over my body at once, like something was crushing and tearing the life from me.

I twisted, trying to escape it, but every movement seemed to make it worse. My back arched and my head rolled back, and a howl of pure agony ripped from my throat.

The first of many.

Chapter Three

My eyes opened of their own accord, letting the painful light in to sear my pupils. I squeezed them shut again, so that the only pain was the dull ache in every muscle and every joint. Then the image I'd seen filtered through to my brain, and my eyes flew open again.

"Where the hell am I?"

I wasn't in the farmhouse anymore. I knew that, because no part of the farmhouse was a freaking dungeon.

I leapt up from the stone floor, my movement hampered by the metal cuffs around my wrists – *cuffs?* – joined by a short chain, and raced the half-dozen steps it took me to reach the row of vertical bars that separated me from the rest of the barren room. The room was lit with only a bare lightbulb hanging from the ceiling, casting a flickering yellow light that filled every corner of the room with deep shadows. The stonewalls looked ancient but sturdy, and there were no windows, no furniture. I gripped the bars with my shackled hands, a sob of terror slipping from my lips.

One of the shadows moved, detaching itself from the far wall. I gasped and backed away, and the figure came to a halt under the light.

"Caleb! What's going on? Let me out of here."

"It's for your own safety, Jade," he said, and slid a phone from his pocket. "Yeah, she's awake."

"Who are you talking to? What am I doing here?" I rattled the cage door in frustration, but it didn't budge.

"Try to relax. He'll explain everything."

"Relax? Are you insane? And he, who? Explain what?"

I growled in frustration and rattled the door again.

"Let me out of here, you freak, or I'm calling the cops."

"Good luck with that," he said, as I groped for my phone and found it missing. "Trust me, this is for the best."

"Trust you? I'm locked in a cage, you psycho."

"Now, now, Ms Hart," a low, gravelly voice said, as a wooden door at the far side of the room swung open, and a lone figure stepped through. "There's no need for name calling. This truly is in your own best interest."

"And who the hell are you supposed to be?" I snapped, looking him up and down. He was somewhere in his forties, or maybe a little older, with streaks of grey running through his short hair, and a few lines starting to set in his face. His body was lean and muscular, and clothed in jeans and a loose-fitting shirt, with a white tee under it. He shut the door behind him, and came to the front of the cage, just beyond arm's length.

"My name is Blake."

"Well, Blake, if you don't let me out of here right now, my family are going to realise I'm gone and call the cops."

Blake glanced over at Caleb and raised an eyebrow. Caleb answered with a shake of his head.

"No-one's waiting for her. She lives alone. Her family are abroad."

I shot him a furious glare, fear carving through my gut. All that stuff he'd asked me yesterday. He'd been planning this. I was such a damned idiot, I should have called the cops the moment he showed up with a loaded gun!

Blake cleared his throat, and I snapped my jaw shut, redirecting my glare onto him.

"I am a shapeshifter," he said. "And now, you are too."

"Uh, yeah. Of course you are. I think you've got me confused with someone else." I turned to Caleb. "Let me go. Please? I won't tell anyone, I swear."

"You are a shapeshifter," Blake repeated. "A werewolf, to be precise. When you were attacked the night before last, you were bitten. Turned."

"No," I said, my eyes flicking between the two madmen. "It was a dog. Just a dog."

Caleb shook his head.

"No," he said, his voice pretty damned calm for a man who broke into a woman's home and dragged her off to some underground dungeon. "That was a werewolf. Werewolves. Plural. The rest of my pack went after the wolf who attacked you."

"Right. Of course. There's a pack of werewolves roaming round my uncle's farm. Because that makes perfect sense. Tell you what, let me go, and I won't tell the vampires where to find you."

Blake stiffened.

"Vampires are not something to joke about, Ms Hart. Had you spent much time in our world, you would know that. Tell me, how much do you remember about last night?"

I paused.

"Last night?"

I lifted one hand to run it through my hair, but the shackles pulled me up short. My stomach fluttered. I remembered pain, I remembered every part of my body hurting... *like bones were snapping.* A flash of memory: dark fur, snapping teeth, the feel of flesh between my fangs.

I shook my head and ground my teeth together. That. Wasn't. Real.

"Concussion," I said. "I had a concussion. I was seeing things."

Another flash: a second wolf, inside the farmhouse, between me and the door.

"How's your leg, Jade?" Caleb asked, eyeing my right calf.

"It's fine," I snapped back.

…But it shouldn't have been. I was bitten two days ago, but it didn't hurt. At all. I frowned down at it, then rolled up the denim leg of my jeans – noting as I did that I was wearing a fresh pair. The wound had faded to a puckered scar.

"Shifters have accelerated healing," Blake said.

"I…"

I didn't know what to say. What to think.

"Werewolves aren't real!"

Blake turned to Caleb and inclined his head. Caleb pulled his t-shirt over his head, then kicked off his shoes and started unbuttoning his jeans.

"What are you doing?"

"Proving you wrong," Caleb said, and kicked his jeans aside, standing nearly naked in front of me. Any other day of the week, I might have taken the time to enjoy the view, but right now, I had other things on my mind.

"Don't you need a full moon?" I looked up at where sun would be shining if I wasn't trapped underground, and smirked.

"Myth," Caleb said.

"Of course. Full moons are a myth, but werewolves aren't."

I started to cross my arms, but the chain on the cuffs pulled me up short. I exhaled sharply and dropped my hands to hang down in front of me.

"I apologise for the discomfort," Blake said. "I will have the cuffs removed as soon as possible. We had no way to predict how you would react."

Right now, I wanted to react by ripping his damned throat out, but he was out of reach, so I said nothing, shifting my weight from one leg to the other, and watching Caleb warily.

It happened so quickly that if I'd blinked, I would have missed it. One moment he was standing there, near-naked and decidedly human, albeit with a little more chest hair than I like. The next, with a snarl and a snap of his jaws, he was on four legs, shaking out a thick fur coat. His face was canine – no, not canine. Lupine. The face of a wolf. The body of one, too – only more like a wolf on steroids. Muscle clung to his frame in thick slabs, not quite hidden under his fur, and the proportions weren't quite right. His shoulders were too broad, his jaws too wide, his legs too powerful. And he was the size of a damned pony – even bigger than the wolf at the farmhouse. Wolves. I hadn't imagined the others.

He slunk towards me and I staggered back until I thudded into the stone wall at the back of my cell. I raised my shackled hands, but he stopped in front of the bars, and dropped back onto his haunches, sitting.

I sucked in a breath, tried to speak, choked on air, and then tried again.

"You– You're… a werewolf."

I sagged against the wall and stared up at the ceiling.

"What the hell have I gotten myself into?"

"Caleb," Blake said, watching me closely. "That's enough."

The wolf slunk away to the corner of the room, where the pile of clothes lay discarded. There was another snarl and a series of loud cracks that sounded a lot like the time I'd fallen from a tree as a kid and snapped my arm, and then Caleb was standing there with his back to me, fully human again. I didn't even notice his well-toned arse – much – as he stooped to grab his jeans and tugged them on.

"Okay," I said, trying to arrange my body so I looked more like I was leaning casually against the wall, and less like I was cowering against it, wishing the ground beneath me would open up and swallow me. "Okay. I'm… I'm a… werewolf."

I blew air through pursed lips and nodded. That word had a funny taste to it, especially when it was preceded by the words 'I'm a'. I was a werewolf. This was not how I had envisioned my summer going.

"Yes," Blake said. I hadn't been asking, but whatever. I was too freaked out right now to give him any backchat.

"I can turn into a giant dog."

"Wolf."

"Right. Well, that's lovely. If you can just open the door and take these off–" I rattled my chains at him, "– I'll be on my way."

"I'm afraid it's not that simple."

Why, oh why did I know he was going to say that? I made to cross my arms again, remembered I couldn't, and settled for glaring at him.

"Oh? And why not? Is this where you tell me I have to join your pack?"

Caleb snorted.

"Jade, trust me, you're not even close to ready to run with my pack."

"Trust you?" I lifted my chin. "It'll be a cold day in hell when that happens, trust *me*."

"Hold your tongues, both of you," Blake said, sending a sharp look in Caleb's direction. The younger man held his hands up and grinned.

"No offence meant, pup," he said. "It's just going to take you a while, is all."

"Pup?" I all but snarled. "Come over here and call me that."

"She's feisty," Caleb said to Blake. "Have fun training her. If you're done with me, I need to report in with the alpha pack."

"Of course," Blake said, dipping his chin. "Thank you for your assistance."

"Wait, you're leaving me?" I pushed myself off the wall and all my cockiness fell away. "Here?"

"You'll be fine," Caleb said. "The worst part's over. I've got to go track down the wolf that did this to you."

He slipped out of the door, leaving with me with a dozen unanswered questions. I gnawed at my lower lip a moment, trying to decide which to ask first. What slipped out of my mouth, in a tiny voice, wasn't even one of the questions I'd been considering.

"Is there no cure?"

"There is no cure, Ms Hart," Blake said stiffly, "because lycanthropy is not a disease."

"Really? Because I didn't have it until two days ago, when one of you *bit* me. So forgive me for thinking otherwise."

"What happened to you was a grievous crime, and I promise you, the wolf who attacked you will be caught and brought to justice."

"For all the good that's going to do me," I muttered.

"Quite," Blake agreed. "You are what you are, and nothing can change that now. In time, you may come to see this as a blessing."

"Yeah, right. I'm more likely to turn into a donkey."

Blake raised an eyebrow at me.

"Oh, sorry, am I interrupting your big speech?" I swept a manacled hand at him. "Please, by all means, continue."

"Your temper will not be an asset. You have difficult times ahead of you. But with discipline, patience, and determination, you will overcome these trials, as others before you have, and as others who follow shall."

"Wait. I thought biting me was some sort of crime."

"It is," Blake said. "To bite a mundane is against our highest laws."

I put aside the less than flattering term – now who was name calling? – and cocked my head.

"Then why are there so many others? Why will there be more?"

"Ah. Of course. Forgive me. I am not used to explaining our ways to one from the outside world. Being bitten is one way to become a shifter, though it is highly illegal, and almost unheard of. Most of us are born to this life. Lycanthropy goes back more generations in my bloodline than anyone can count. Many of the others who attend this academy can say the same."

"What… academy?" I asked.

Blake smiled and inclined his head.

"Ms Hart, welcome to the Sarrenauth Academy of Therianthropy."

Chapter Four

U m, yeah, that's real nice and all, but I already have an academy to attend. It's a little place called University College London – you might have heard of it."

"I'm sorry, Ms Hart–"

"Stop with all this 'Ms Hart' crap. It's Jade."

"Jade–"

"And you can let me out of here right now, so I can get back to my nice, normal life, and deal with whatever crap your friend dumped on me."

"That's not possible. What has happened to you cannot be undone–"

"Yeah, you said."

"–and there will be an adjustment period. In that time, it is likely you will have very little control. You will be a danger to those around you. I'm afraid there is no question of you leaving."

"No control? Listen, I've wanted to rip your throat out since the moment you walked through that door, but do you see me hulking out into Xena-wolf?"

"The cuffs you are wearing are laced with silver and engraved with arcane symbols. While you wear them, you cannot change forms."

I looked down at the cuffs locked around my wrists, examining them for the first time. About three inches wide, and silver in colour, they fit snuggly around my wrists. They had a whole host of weird symbols carved into them, and if I looked closely, I could pick out streams of silver running through the iron. More than that, I could *sense* it on some instinctive level. Each cuff had two small keyholes, and the short chain that linked them was lightweight, each individual link was thin. It had no engravings – I figure it was just there to make it harder for me to throttle people who try to lock me in cages. As long as I wore the cuffs, there was no changing shape, and no busting out of this cell.

I contemplated that for a moment.

"That's great news. Let me out, and I'll keep the cuffs on and go back to my life like this never happened. Problem solved."

"I would that it were, Jade," Blake said. "But we have laws, and amongst them is that every wolf coming into their power must learn how to control it. Like it or not, you are now a student at this academy, and I will be your… headmaster until you graduate."

I didn't like it. Not one damned bit. But I could see there was nothing to be gained from arguing. Besides, the more fuss I kicked up right now, the more closely they'd be watching me later when I escaped from this hellhole.

"Fine," I snapped. "I'm a student. So teach me, oh great one."

"Your flippancy will not benefit you."

He seemed to think that about a lot of my personality traits, but I really didn't give a damn. Any guy who thought he could walk into my life and tell me what I would and would not do was going to find out pretty damned quickly that there was more to my personality than temper and flippancy.

"Give me your hands."

I eyeballed him, then thrust my hands through the bars towards him, and he reached for them, taking care not to touch the metal manacles. I guess the whole werewolves and silver thing was true. It was as much a part of why these cuffs worked on me as the engravings.

He slotted a small key into one of the cuffs, turned it, and then tugged the chain away. I held still as he did the same to the other cuff, and then he stepped back.

"Hey!" I protested. "I thought you were taking them off."

"Not yet," he said. "I will remove the cuffs in due course. Should you prove capable of self-restraint, that will be before the semester starts."

He didn't sound like he thought that was very likely, which filled me with all manner of confidence.

"Wait," I said, staring down at the cuffs, a dubious feeling starting up in the pit of my stomach. "I'm going to be the only one wearing these, aren't I?"

"The other students will wear a single training cuff to assist their control," he said.

"A training cuff. But not these? Level with me – am I going to be the only freak walking round here wearing these like some sort of prisoner?"

Some sort of prisoner. Who was I kidding? That's exactly what I was. I was stuck here, like it or not – and I'd go with not – until they decided to let me go. *Or I escaped.*

"I would urge you to stay positive," Blake said. "There is every chance you will learn to exert some control over your inner beast before that time comes."

"And how long exactly do I have?"

"A week."

A week. Screw it. I'd be gone from here long before then, anyway.

"You're not going to keep me in this cage for the entire week, are you?"

"Do I need to?"

I shook my head, feigning defeat.

"Look, I get it. I'm dangerous. Where else would I go?"

Blake stared at me for a long moment, and the longer he stared, the more I felt the urge to do something – fight him, back away, hide, I didn't know what. Eventually, he nodded, and some of the pressure building inside my skull eased.

"Good. I will send Dean to you shortly. He will help you get acclimated, and show you to your room."

He started for the door, and I leaned against the bars, watching his retreating back. As he reached for the handle, I broke the silence.

"How long am I– How long do I have to stay?"

He turned to face me.

"Many students graduate within three years. Some take a little longer to reach the required standard. I know that may seem like a long time to you right now, but trust that it will pass in the blink of an eye."

I nodded, and my body sagged as he stepped out of the dungeon, shutting the door behind him. Three years. They wanted to keep me here for three years. Longer, if they decided I couldn't do everything they thought I should.

But they were going to let me out of this cell today. And I would find the way out of here. Semester started in one week? Well, they'd be missing a student when it did. I'd be gone by then. I just had to play along long enough for them to drop their guard.

I paced to the back of the cell and sat, my back pressed against the wall and my knees curled up to my chest. At least I could move my arms now, that was something. Not much, granted, but I'd take what I could get. I wrapped my arms around my legs and slumped my head onto my knees.

After a moment, I hiked my jeans' leg up again, and looked down at my scar, running one finger over the puckered skin. Two days. It had healed from a ragged, bleeding mess to this in just two days. Maybe, just maybe, there were some perks to this whole werewolf gig. Not enough to stick around for, but super healing? It wasn't a bad consolation prize.

I let the fabric fall back over the scar and sat staring at the floor for a long while, my eyes drifting in and out of focus. I couldn't keep track of how much time passed, but I suspected Blake was doing it on purpose, leaving me here to mull things over. Maybe he thought if he left me alone long enough, I'd realise that I didn't have anywhere else to go. Maybe he thought I'd come to the conclusion that three years really wasn't that long, and that I should just go along with it, and make the most of my time here, surrounded by people who knew more about my new curse than I did. He'd have to lock me up for a bloody long time if he wanted me to start thinking like that.

Sometime later, the heavy wooden door creaked again, and a new figure stepped through, this one younger than the other two. He was about my age, or maybe a year or two older, and he didn't bother to shut the door behind him. I straightened, regarding him as he came closer. He had a bundle in his hands, and a look of curiosity on his face, which he quickly buried when he stepped into the light of the single bulb. But I'd been down here long enough for my eyes to adjust to the gloom.

"You must be Jade," he said, stopping outside my cage.

"Must I?" The words came out bitter and left a nasty taste in my mouth. I was supposed to be making them trust me. I sighed and got to my feet. "I mean, yeah, that's me."

"I'm Dean," he said. "Alpha Blake said you were having some trouble adjusting to what happened."

"Alpha?"

"His rank," Dean said. "He's the alpha of the academy. He's in charge of it."

"Oh." I frowned, moving closer to the bars, and recalling Caleb's words. "And the alpha pack?"

"You… don't want anything to do with them," Dean said, looking wary. "It's not a pack, as such. More like… like a council, I guess. It's made up of every alpha in the country, run by the Alpha of Alphas. They're in charge of law keeping."

"They're not good at it," I grumbled, rubbing at my leg.

"What happened to you is rare," Dean said. "Unheard of, really. There's never been another Bitten in my lifetime."

"Not so rare that you don't have a name for it," I observed.

"Everything has a name," he said. I nodded.

"What you're doing has a name, too. It's called stalling." I rattled the bars with one hand. "How about you let me out of here?"

He laughed.

"I think it's called 'conversation', but sure." He pulled a long, heavy key on a wide iron loop from his belt and slotted it into the lock, then paused.

"You're not going to do anything reckless, are you?" he asked.

"Scared of a girl?"

He shook his head and turned the key.

"Of you? Nothing personal, but no. Now Alpha Blake on the other hand – well, you don't get to be alpha of a whole academy unless you're tougher than you look."

I mulled that one over as Dean pulled the door open, then I sashayed through it.

"Aren't you a little too grown up to be scared of the big, bad wolf?"

"Oh, you're going to be a bad influence," he said, his lips curving into something not quite tame enough to be called a smile. "I like you."

I brushed past him and headed for the door. He moved quickly, so quickly that I wasn't sure I'd even seen him move. One moment he was behind me, the next he was in front of the door. Blocking my exit.

"How did you do that?" I narrowed my eyes at him, and he shrugged with practiced nonchalance.

"Stick around, and you'll find out."

I shrugged right back at him.

"I'm not going anywhere." *Yet.*

"Well, if you're staying, you're going to want this."

He held out the bundle to me, and I eyed it suspiciously.

"And what's that supposed to be?"

"It's your uniform."

"Uniform? Yeah, good one." I paused, but his expression didn't change. "Wait, you're serious? What are we, twelve? I'm not wearing that."

"Everyone here wears them."

"Not me." I frowned at him, or more precisely, at his jeans and hoodie combo. "And not you, either, apparently."

"I just got here," he said. "Alpha Blake called me in at short notice. It was all a bit last minute, what with…"

He trailed off, casting a meaningful glance at my leg.

"Yeah, thanks for the reminder." I brushed past him again. "I'm not wearing that, so you can forget it."

He shrugged like it was no big deal.

"Hey, if you want to break the rules, it's your funeral."

"Wait… literally?"

He snorted in amusement.

"For this? Probably not. You might want to watch out for the big rules, though."

"What, like biting a mundane?" I held up a hand before he could answer. "Are we getting out of here, or not? I've seen enough of creepy dungeons for one day."

"This way," he said, and led me out of the room. I crossed the threshold with a shudder. If I never wound up back in there again, it would still be too soon. I'd hated being cooped up even when I lived in the city. Trapped underground in some creepy werewolf academy? No, thanks.

I cast one last look back over my shoulder. Whatever happened, I would fight to the death before I let them put me in a cage again.

Chapter Five

This is it," Dean said, swinging open a door that looked like the last fifteen we'd already passed. Maybe he'd been counting, because I could see no other way to tell it apart from them.

"This is what?"

"Your room."

I peered inside, pleasantly surprised by the presence of windows and the lack of bars across them, and the distinctly non-dungeon-like décor. There was a decent-sized bed, and folded on it were several more sets of the uniform Dean had carried up from the dungeon, as if under some sort of deluded impression that I was going to change my mind on the way. Next to those was a cluster of toiletries that looked somewhat familiar. Sure enough, as I got closer I recognised my toothbrush, washcloth, and seriously indulgent shower gel, amongst other things. I guess Caleb wasn't quite as much of a barbarian as he seemed. He was still a dick, though.

Dean set my uniform on the bed next to the other piles.

"Is there some reason I have a dozen sets of a uniform I'm never going to wear?" I enquired, my voice politely disinterested – because like I really cared.

"Have you ever seen anyone shift?" Dean asked.

"Sure," I said. "Caleb."

"And did you wonder why he stripped off before shifting?"

"Uh…"

"This isn't Disney. Our clothes don't shift with us."

"I don't think Disney ever made a movie about werewolves."

"If you shift fully clothed, they're getting shredded. There won't be enough left to repair."

"Right. That still doesn't explain the uniforms."

"When you get those cuffs off, it's going to take you a while to get the hang of staying human. You're going to shred a lot of clothes while you get control."

"Oh. Wait, this is a mixed sex academy, right?"

"Everyone here's an adult," Dean said. "And no-one's going to be looking, trust me."

"Is that like a catch phrase around here? Because I have trust issues."

I perched on the edge of my new bed, contemplating what a monumental balls up my life had become, and my eyes drifted over the three other beds in the room. Dorm living – exactly what I'd been hoping to avoid by moving into Oak Ridge Farm in the first place. Fate really was a bitch.

"Who am I sharing with?" I asked, jerking my chin at the empty beds. It was too much to hope they'd stay empty for long. Not that it mattered, I reminded myself. I wasn't sticking around.

"That one's mine," Dean said, gesturing to a studiously neat bed in the corner.

My mouth popped open. That settled it. I definitely wasn't sticking around.

"You? I'm sharing with you?"

"Is that a problem?"

Hell, yeah, it was. For one thing, sneaking out just got ten times harder. Dean wasn't going to take his eyes from me. But I couldn't tell him that, so I just shrugged.

"Hadn't expected mixed sex rooms, is all."

"In some ways, shifters are very traditional. In others, not so much. We don't have a whole lot of space at Fur 'n' Fang, and the shifter population keeps growing. I guess somewhere along the way, someone stopped caring about mixed rooms."

"Fur 'n' Fang?" I raised an eyebrow. Dean grinned.

"What, you don't think the Sarrenauth Academy of Therianthropy is a mouthful? Everyone round here just calls it Fur 'n' Fang."

"What's a… therianthrope, anyway?" I asked, sounding out each of the syllables.

"It's someone who can shift into an animal. Or partially shift, but you don't really see that anymore."

"I thought we were werewolves."

"Werewolves – lycanthropes – are the most common, but there are a couple of other species that come here. Wolves are the best, though," he added, flashing his teeth at me.

"Well, I kinda thought being human was the best until this morning, so I'm gonna withhold judgement on that one."

Dean pulled a face. "Human-schuman."

"You seriously did not just say that."

"I did. And I'll say it again. Human-schuman. Shifting is way cooler."

I shook my head in mock-dismay, but I couldn't quite suppress the smile tugging at my lips.

"Just telling it as it as," he said.

"So, what's the plan?"

"The plan?"

I groaned.

"Please tell me we're not spending the next week locked in this room, because I'm already going stir-crazy."

"Oh. No, you're free to explore the castle, or head out into the grounds. As long as I go with you."

"I don't need a chaperone."

"No? So you're not planning to jump the wall and head back to your hometown first chance you get?"

"Hometown? No. Alright then, can you at least give me the tour, if we're stuck with each other?"

"Ouch. I'm not that bad, am I?" A look of genuine hurt flashed through his eyes before he covered it up with a smirk.

"As jailors go," I said, "you could be worse."

"Good enough. Come on, let's take that tour. We can start with the dining hall."

The dining hall was huge – and deserted, apart from us, and a middle-aged guy working from a hatch in the kitchen.

"Dean," the man greeted him with a nod. "I heard you were here early."

"Hi, Mickey." He gestured to me. "This is Jade. She's... new."

Mickey's eyes sharpened, and he searched my face. I guess I was going to get a lot of that. Sucks to be the new kid, but it wasn't the first time and it probably wouldn't be the last. I set my jaw and returned his scrutiny.

"Good to meet you, Jade."

"Yeah. You, too."

I didn't break eye contact and he chuckled, flicking a glance back over his shoulder into the kitchen, at the array of pans lined up by the hob.

"She's a feisty one, huh?" He didn't meet my eye again. "A couple of steaks?"

Dean nodded. "Sure. Jade, what do you want?"

I laughed, then realised he was being serious.

"Oh. I'll have whatever. Thanks."

Mickey turned and ambled back into the kitchen. Dean made to take my elbow to steer me across the room, and I jerked it away, fixing him with a glare.

"Easy," he said, holding his hand up and sounding a little irritated. "Not everyone round here is your enemy. Some of us just want to help you. Most of us, actually, if you give us a chance."

"Well, excuse me if–" I broke off and exhaled, long and low, and got my voice under control. "Never mind. It's been a long day."

"It's going to get a lot longer if you keep challenging everyone you meet," he said, steering us to a table near the back – this time not making the mistake of trying to touch me.

"Challenging?"

"I saw you, trying to stare Mickey down."

"I wasn't just trying. Anyway, he stared at me first."

I pulled out a chair and dropped into it.

"Get used to it. You're the outsider here."

"Gee, thanks."

"All I'm saying," he said, pulling out a chair opposite me, "is if you carry on looking for a fight, sooner or later that's what you'll get – and probably with someone who's more than your match. If you go looking for trouble round here, you're going to find it."

I picked at my nails, letting that sink in a moment. I couldn't fight. I'd never been in a fight in my life. Facing off against stuck up bitches? Sure, I'd done my share of that, but actual fighting? I didn't even know how to throw a punch. And I was in enough trouble as it was. I didn't need any more enemies.

"Alright," I said eventually. "I get it. No more looking for fights."

He quirked an eyebrow at me, and I held up one hand and placed the other over my heart. "I swear."

"I'll believe it when I see it, rebel."

"If you're trying out nicknames, you can stop right there. It's Jade. Just Jade."

"Whatever you say, Just Jade."

I rolled my eyes. I'd brought that one on myself.

Mickey brought two plates over to us, both piled with a trio of the biggest steaks I'd ever seen, plus mashed potatoes, onions, mushrooms… the works. I raised a sceptical eyebrow at the lean figure sitting opposite me.

"Where exactly are you planning on putting all of that?"

"What? Shifting burns a lot of calories. And this is the best steak you'll ever eat."

I prodded one of the slabs of meat with my knife. Blood leaked from it onto the plate, and I eyed the drizzly mess. I was more of a 'well done' kind of girl when it came to steak – on the few times a year I had it – but this was beyond rare. What was it they called it? Blue? Whatever it was, it looked like a good vet might get it going again.

"I can't eat this," I said, shoving the plate away. But my hand didn't let go of it, and my stomach rumbled loudly in disapproval.

"Just try it. Tru– You won't regret it."

I pulled it back in front of me and prodded it again, slicing a small piece from the edge with my steak knife. I paused, wondering if I could stash the potential weapon when we left the hall. Then the scent of the charred meat hit my nose, dissolving all other thoughts. I lifted a small cube of steak on my fork and nibbled at the edge. And then shoved the thing in my mouth and swallowed it whole. Then I speared another.

"See?" Dean said, and I felt a snarl work its way up my throat. He was looking at *my* meat.

"Easy, Just Jade." He'd gone very still. Shit. Was I growling at him? Over a steak? I swallowed the suddenly flavourless lump of flesh in my mouth and set my fork down.

"Dean, I'm sorry. I didn't mean– What the hell is wrong with me?"

I slumped my head into my hands, even as some instinct screamed at me not to take my eyes from him while he was so close to my food.

"Hey. It's normal. The rest of us? We've had our whole lives to learn how to handle these instincts. They're new to you. It's going to take you some time to adjust."

"And what?" I lifted my head to look at him through a few strands of hair that have worked their way loose. "Until then I'm just going to be running around growling at anyone who looks at my food the wrong way? What's next, I'm going to start burying my bones in the yard?"

"Until then," he said, reaching over to place his hand on mine, then remembering himself and pulling back, "people will understand that you're trying to learn control, and they'll cut you some slack. Besides, you're not going to be the only person round here struggling to control themselves."

"I'm not?"

"Pfft. You put a bunch of eighteen-year-olds under one roof, and you think they're all going to be calm? Have you ever seen a freshman dorm?"

I snorted.

"Anyway, you didn't actually try to bite me, so we're good."

"But you'd just heal if I did, right?"

He sucked on his teeth a moment.

"Werewolf healing?" I pressed.

"Not exactly." He set his knife and fork down. "We can heal from almost anything, right? But there are some things we can't heal from. First, anything that kills us. Dead is dead."

I nodded. That one, I'd assumed.

"Second, any wound inflicted by an alpha with the intent to do lasting damage."

"Any alpha… as in, Blake could shred me if he wanted, and I'd stay shredded?"

"Yup. But he wouldn't. Not unless you really stepped out of line."

"Great."

"And the big one, shifter bites. Any shifter. Claws are fine, but if we get bitten, the mark is permanent."

I paused, looking down at my leg.

"And this?"

"Sorry. You'll always have a scar."

"Great," I said, exhaling through clenched teeth. "There goes the bottom half of my bikini body."

Dean looked entirely too much like he was picturing me in a bikini, so I stamped on his foot, and gave him an angelic smile. After that, he suddenly found his food very interesting. We both devoted some time to polishing off our steaks – I was both surprised and disgusted to discover I could clear my entire plate, and probably could have managed seconds – and then lounged in our seats for a few minutes in what could almost have been mistaken for companionable silence.

If, of course, I hadn't been a prisoner here.

Chapter Six

One week isn't a long time to scope out an entire castle and find a way to escape. The first five days had already passed before I had the first inkling of a plan. Dean spent the time feeding me titbits of information about my new shifting power, while Mickey fed me piles of the best steak I'd ever eaten, and the pair of them dropped countless hints about how much being at Fur 'n' Fang was going to help me. The cuffs stayed on my wrists.

It wasn't a deal breaker. Sure, it'd be nice to have at least one of them off so I could have some access to the new, heightened senses I apparently now possessed, but if I couldn't convince Blake to remove them, so be it. I wasn't going to stick around for that.

The wall that ran the perimeter of the academy was made of stone, and it was twenty-foot tall if it was an inch. A pair of iron wrought gates guarded the front entrance, and, near as I could tell, they were always locked. But I didn't need to use the gates. I grew up on a farm. I could climb. And there were a lot of trees here. Some of them close enough to get me halfway up the wall. I'd make it the rest of the way from there.

The landing on the far side was likely to be rough, but shifter healing meant a sprained ankle shouldn't hold me back for too long. Still, I'd need to go at night, so I had as long as possible before anyone noticed I was missing.

I didn't know where we were, but that was fine. It wasn't like I could head back to the farm, anyway. That was the first place they'd look.

I would need to disguise my scent. I'd convinced Dean to take me all round the grounds, telling him that the outside air made me feel less trapped, and he seemed to buy it. It didn't feel great, lying to him, but so be it. He knew I didn't want to be here. As far as I was concerned, that made him just as guilty as Blake.

On one of our many jaunts around the extensive grounds, I'd discovered a compost heap. I was willing to bet that would cover my scent for a while. I'd been able to smell it long before I'd seen it, even with my shifter senses muted by the cuffs. No way would anyone be able to block out that.

I just had to find a way to get out of my room without Dean noticing. And I had to do it soon, because in three days the rest of the students would arrive, and the castle would get a whole lot busier. And then I'd be stuck here.

Tonight. I was going tonight. Dean was already asleep, the cloud cover outside was heavy, and if I didn't go now, there was no telling if I'd get another opportunity this good. I moved my duvet aside and carefully climbed out of the bed. I'd gone to bed fully clothed, pretending to get changed while Dean was in the bathroom. I glanced at him to make sure he hadn't heard my bed springs – there was no telling how good his hearing was – then stooped to grab my trainers. I carried them to the door, not wanting to risk making any more noise than I had to, and crept across the floor, throwing a glance at my roommate with every other step.

Carefully, I eased the handle down, wincing as the metal mechanism scraped quietly, but sleeping beauty just rolled over in his bed, and carried on sleeping. Good. I didn't want to have to fight him if he woke. For one thing, the noise was sure to bring someone down on us. For another, he'd probably kick my arse. Neither scenario sounded particularly fun to me.

I snuck through the door and pulled it to behind me, not wanting to risk the sound of it closing disturbing him. I was in the long corridor lined with identical doors. I figured each of them had to be another room, and I figured each of them had its own bathroom, like ours. That was a lot of assumptions, and I had another. I assumed none of the rooms were locked, or capable of locking – because if they were, it meant ours was, and if our door was capable of being locked, Blake would have done it. And if Blake had done it, well, I wouldn't be standing in a corridor, tugging my running shoes on.

Getting out through one of the other rooms was my best bet. So far as I could tell, the castle had two main entrances – one at the front, and one at the back. They were both kept locked after dark – whether that was to keep the werewolves in, or something else out, I had no idea. I wasn't sticking around to find out.

The dorm rooms were two floors up – probably not high enough that I was going to do any lasting damage, but enough to put an end to my little escape attempt if I jumped. Luckily, I had a better idea than that.

I counted four rooms along, hopefully far enough that Dean wouldn't be able to hear me, then tried the door. I was right, it wasn't locked. The room was identical to mine, except for the notable lack of a sleeping werewolf. I pulled the door shut behind me and crossed quickly to the bathroom. I opened the window, stuck my head out, looked left and right, then ducked back inside and closed it. No good. I headed for the next room.

I tried four rooms before I found what I was looking for. Attached to the wall beside the bathroom window was a water pipe. I reached out and gave it a gentle tug, but it didn't budge. A glance down at the ground told me I was going to be in trouble if it did.

Oh well. In for a penny, in for a pound. Do or die. Now or never. And a dozen other such clichés. I sucked in a deep breath, then swung one leg out of the window. I edged along until I could wrap it around the pipe, still straddling the window, then reached out and wrapped my arms around it. One more deep breath, then I lurched out of the window and clung to the pipe like a circus monkey. I looked down and the ground swam before my eyes. What in the name of ever-loving fuck was I doing? A freaking drainpipe!

I ground my teeth together. It didn't matter. I wasn't staying here as a damned prisoner, just because some feral mutt bit me. I wasn't willing to give up my future for that. I was going to study law, and no pack of overgrown dogs was going to stop me.

I just had to get down this pipe first.

Piece of cake. I'd grown up climbing trees on the farm. Of course, I'd also fallen out of one and broken my arm. Just... don't look down.

I wrapped my feet around the pipe and shimmied down it a couple of inches, then slid my clammy palms down. And again. And again. It was a slow process, and my muscles started aching before I was even a quarter of the way down. I'd spent too much time in the city. I was out of shape. By the time I was halfway down, the half-healed scar on my calf was burning, and I gritted my teeth in pain each time I shuffled downwards. This whole damned thing was taking too long. Dean could wake up at any moment and realise I was gone.

I pushed the pain aside and worked faster. I was three quarters of the way to the bottom when I hit the patch of ice.

My foot lurched and slid out from under me, the jolting motion pulling my other foot loose, too. I scrabbled frantically, desperately trying to find some purchase, every muscle in my arms and shoulders screaming out in protest as they took all my weight. My fingers curled, trying to dig into the pipe while my body swung unpredictably, but there was no purchase, and I could feel them slipping. One of my nails snapped, then another, sending tiny lances of pain through my hands, and I watched helplessly as my fingers came away from the pipe.

I plummeted to the ground and hit it hard, knocking the wind from me. I laid there a moment, staring up at the moonless sky and waiting for the pain to fade. I was lucky. If I'd fallen from much further… I shook my head, and rolled over onto my front, then pushed myself to my feet.

Pain lanced through my right ankle and I cried out, then bit down on my lip and stifled the rest of the sound. I couldn't let them find me now. No way could I explain away climbing down a pipe in the middle of the night.

I tentatively eased my weight onto my right ankle again and hissed in pain. Not broken, but probably sprained. That wasn't good. But not bad enough to stop me getting out of here, either. I hobbled along, keeping to the shadows as best I could, and ignoring the pain each step sent through me.

By the time I reached the treeline, I was panting with the exertion, but the pain had eased off a little. Not enough that I was looking forward to climbing out of here, but enough that maybe I could manage it. But first, I had to disguise my scent.

It looked different out here in the dark, and the trees towered over me ominously. A few animals scurried around in the trees, chittering in alarm at my approach, but I paid them no attention. The only truly dangerous animal here was in the castle, still fast asleep. I hoped.

It took me a few minutes of stumbling around in the dark before I found what I was looking for. The compost heap. I pulled a face, then thrust a hand into it, and rubbed some of the rotting mulch over my arms, torso, and all over the soles of my shoes. My nose wrinkled at the acrid scent, but that could only be a good thing. If it smelled that strongly to me, there was no way any of the shifters would be able to track my scent through it.

Fuck's sake. Seriously. What had my life become?

When I figured I was smeared in enough of the mulch, I hobbled away from the heap, taking care not to snag my bad ankle on any of the protruding tree roots. I was pretty sure the wall was this way. I kept pushing ahead in the darkness, doing my best to keep to a straight line, and eventually I was rewarded with the sight of a tall, dark shape looming ahead. The wall.

How long had I been out here? Twenty minutes? Half an hour? Longer? Too long. I needed to get gone before Dean woke up.

I stared up at the massive stone structure. This was all that was separating me from my freedom. It was tall. Taller even than I remembered, and I wasn't looking forward to scaling it with a bad ankle. But I hadn't come this far just to go back to the castle with my tail between my legs. There were plenty of trees nearby. I just needed to climb up one, then crawl along a branch, and then onto the wall. If I chose a big enough tree, I'd be most of the way to the top. The wall was old, and it had seen better days. The rough stone it was hewn from lent itself perfectly to hand and foot holds, especially further towards the top where it wasn't as well maintained. I could get over it.

I started for the nearest, decent-sized tree, and used a low-hanging branch to pull myself up. A grin spread over my face. This was child's play. I paused to rest on the branch, because once I got high enough to latch onto the wall, there would be no more breaks until I was down the far side. And hopefully that break wouldn't be one of my limbs.

My ankle was growing stronger by the minute. If I focused, I could almost feel the damaged tissue and tendons repairing themselves. It in no way made up for the psycho wolf biting me, but it seemed only fair that it would help me escape from the prison it had earned me a sentence in.

Right, enough resting. I was only a few feet above the ground and time was short. I'd just have to do the best I could with my ankle.

I was just about to move when I heard something below. A snuffling… as though something was sniffing the air. Something big. My heart raced. There was only one big animal that would be in these woods tonight.

I looked down, and there it was, its head only inches from my dangling foot. A werewolf. It snarled at me, and I yelped and pulled my legs up, scrambling back along the branch until my back pressed up against the trunk.

There was a second wolf behind the first, hanging back slightly. Its frame was smaller and its movements less aggressive. Reluctant, even. Somehow, I knew that was Dean. He'd betrayed me. As I'd known he would.

Sounds approached from behind the pair, and I picked out a human form walking towards us. My heart sank. It was Blake.

"I suggest you come down from there immediately, Ms Hart."

"Jade," I muttered under my breath, scanning the tree above me. I was pretty sure the wolves were too heavy to climb. Maybe I had enough of a start that I could get over the wall. They'd had to go out of the front gates, or change to come after me, and by that time I could be away. I set my jaw.

"I'd rethink that plan, if I were you," Blake said.

I snorted. The mere thought of Blake ever being anything like me was absurd. He belonged in this academy. I didn't.

The wolf at my foot snarled again, and I tried to shrink back further against the trunk behind me. Would he actually bite me, try to pull me out of the tree?

Blake held up a single hand, and the sound ceased.

"Watch," he commanded, and I cocked my head to one side as he stooped to pick up a stone, then tossed it lightly at the wall. There was a bright flash of light and the stone ricocheted off, landing a good ten feet away. My jaw popped open.

"The wall is warded – though I must admit it was intended to keep intruders out, not students in. Now, will you climb down, or does Instructor Fletcher need to bring you down?"

My defiance left me in a huff of air, and my calf started throbbing all over again. It was over.

"I'm coming down."

I took hold of the branch and lowered myself to the ground, keeping my weight off my right ankle as best I could, and glared at the alpha.

"Back inside," he commanded, not breaking eye contact.

"You can't keep me here. I haven't done anything wrong – you've got no right!"

"I am the alpha, and you are an untrained shifter. I have every right." He closed the gap between us. "You will stay here, and you will learn to control your power. And we will not have to endure any further escape attempts. Is that clear?"

He glowered down at me, cold rage pulsing from him. I swallowed, and my gaze slid away from his.

"Is. That. Clear?"

"Yes," I muttered sullenly.

"Back to the castle. Now."

I limped along in front of him with as much defiance as I could muster, which wasn't much. Every cell in my body was aware of the three shifters at my back, but I squared my shoulders and refused to acknowledge them. The damned wall was shielded with some sort of magic. I should have known. We were halfway back to the castle before what that meant really sunk in.

I was stuck here.

Chapter Seven

I passed the rest of the night locked in the cell that had been my first introduction to this cursed place. I didn't sleep. I screamed until I was hoarse, I threw myself against the bars until my whole body was bruised, I pounded the walls until my fists were bloody.

How dare they keep me here? I wanted out. I *needed* out. I couldn't be here another minute… and yet the minutes slid by anyway, and I continued to rage and seethe at the sheer injustice of it. I wanted my freedom, and nothing else would sate me. I wanted my damned life back. I'd liked my life. I'd worked hard for it. It was mine.

It was hard to judge how long they left me there, but when a figure finally appeared carrying a bundle in his hands, he looked well rested. It was morning, then.

I glowered at the man from the corner of the cell, not bothering to get up as he crossed the room towards me, running his eyes over the blood smeared on the wall.

"I'm Shaun," he said. "I'm one of the instructors here."

I said nothing, staring at him through sullen eyes. He was older than me – in his thirties, maybe, and he had dark blond hair cut short, and a smattering of stubble covered his chiselled jawline. His smart trousers and gleaming black shoes seemed out of place in a dungeon, though he wore his shirt with the sleeves rolled up to his elbows, like he was aware of that and trying for a more casual look. His expression was sympathetic, but after last night, any questions I'd had about trusting these people were long gone.

"You're Jade, right?"

He paused, and when I didn't answer, he wandered back to the door, picked up the single wooden stool beside it, and re-positioned it in front of my bars. I watched from the corner of my eye as he sat on it with a heavy sigh.

"Jade, I know that you are struggling to adjust to being here."

I picked at the last of the scabs healing on my knuckles without looking at him. I didn't much care what he thought he knew.

"Please understand that we are trying to help you."

"Funny sort of help."

He nodded.

"I know it must seem that way to you."

"It seems that way because it is that way," I spat, lurching to my feet. "I'm locked in a damned cage. Again."

"Alright, Jade," he said, and assumed what must have been his tough love face. Like I hadn't had enough of that recently. "Say the wall wasn't warded and you got over it last night. Hell, say I walked you to the front gates right now, and let you out of them. What then?"

"Then I go back to my life."

"The law degree? At UCL?"

I nodded, and he continued.

"It's a good university. High standards. Lots of pressure. Lots of frustration."

"So?"

He got up and came to the bars.

"Give me your hands."

I eyed him for a moment, wondering what the hell his game was, but I wasn't going to find out from here. I crossed the cell and thrust my hands through the bars. He took hold of my left wrist and inserted a key into the cuff. It fell away, clattering harmlessly to the floor. Then he removed the one on my right wrist.

I snatched my hands back inside the cell before he could change his mind, rubbing at my wrists.

"So," he said. "You're at university, you're under pressure, and you're stressed. What happens the first time someone gets your back up?"

"What's that supposed to mean?"

"I think you know. Forget UCL." He looked me up and down, his forehead creased in scorn. "You're not good enough for them, anyway."

How dare he? I worked damned hard to get accepted at UCL, and I *earned* my place there. My jaws ached to sink into the vein pulsing in his throat and put an end to his bullshit. And then they just ached.

And then every part of my body ached. Then a searing agony was crushing my bones. They broke with a loud crack, and I watched in horror as my hand deformed itself, my knuckles bulging under the thickening flesh, then my nails curved into thick claws, and fur sprouted from my arms. I dropped to the floor, threw my head back and screamed in agony as the bones in my spine cracked and broke and reformed themselves into something longer, more flexible. My face changed shape, my new teeth slicing my flesh as they erupted from gums too small. My next scream was distorted by my elongated muzzle and I collapsed to the floor, writhing and twitching as my hips shattered.

And then, finally, blissfully, mercifully, I blacked out.

*

When I came to, there was not a single muscle in my body that didn't ache, like I'd had the mother of all workout sessions. My head felt like I'd had the mother of all drinking sessions, and even my joints felt bruised and uncooperative. My eyes seemed like the only part of me that didn't hurt, and I slowly pried them open.

I was still in the cell. And I was naked. Someone had draped a blanket over me. It was thin and itchy, but at least I hadn't frozen to death, so that was a plus.

Someone took a breath and I jumped, clutching the blanket to my chest and peddling back across the floor until my back thumped into the cold stone wall behind me.

Shaun regarded me calmly from his stool.

It took me a moment to find my voice, and it came out as a croak.

"I… shifted?"

He nodded to something just inside the bars of my cage. A bottle of water.

"Drink. You'll feel better."

I very much doubted that was true, unless there was either a whole lot of alcohol mixed in with the water, or a whole lot of painkillers sitting next to it. Still, I edged over to it, keeping the blanket over me as I moved. I snatched it up, and drained half the bottle in one go, guzzling greedily until I needed to stop long enough to gasp in a breath. I set it aside and wiped my mouth. Shaun was right. That did feel better. Better enough to start thinking more clearly.

"What the hell just happened? Why did I shift?"

"Your shift is triggered by your emotions. Frustration. Anger. Rage. The cuffs were protecting you from the consequences of your emotions. For what it's worth, I don't doubt you're good enough for UCL, but do you see now why you can't return to your old life?"

"So put the damned cuffs back on! I don't want to shift. And I don't want to be here."

Shaun rose from the stool and took one step forward, towering over me as I sat on the floor, glowering down at me.

"What you want doesn't matter." His eyes pinned me to the spot. "You're not the same person you were a week ago. You have responsibilities now."

I tried to force my eyes to meet his, but I couldn't raise them higher than his chin. I gritted my teeth and tried again, but it was like there was some invisible pressure, some compulsion that kept my eyes averted.

He squatted next to me, and the pressure eased.

"I know you didn't ask for this, but it's yours now, and you have to learn to control it. If you leave here before you can, then it's not a question of if you kill someone, it's a question of when, and it won't be long. I will not let that happen."

"Like you didn't let one of your kind attack me in the first place?"

He straightened with a shake of his head.

"You're staying here until you learn control, so start getting used to the idea."

"Wait." I reached out and touched the bars, my anger ebbing for a moment. Shifting hurt, but that wasn't what scared me. "In *here,* here?"

"Well, that depends on you, doesn't it?" Shaun said. "The semester starts tomorrow, but you're not going to learn a lot down here. So you get a choice. Accept what happened to you, and make the best of it, or keep trying to run from your problems."

My defiance fell away, and my shoulders slumped. My voice came out as a whisper.

"I can't run from this."

"No. You can't. And you don't have to. We can teach you to control it. That's why we're here, and it's why you're here."

"Fine. Give me my clothes and let me out of here."

"You're sitting next to them."

I glanced at the pile of clothes next to the bottle. A folded hoodie sat on top.

"That's a uniform, and I am not wearing it. Where are my clothes?"

He jerked his chin at something behind me, and I twisted round, careful to keep the blanket in place. Scraps of shredded fabric were strewn all round the cell. I recognised a few strips of pale denim.

"You've got to be kidding me."

He shook his head slowly.

"Fuck's sake."

"If you're going to join the other students, you might as well look like them."

Join the other students? I rolled my head back to stare up at the ceiling of my cell, then my forehead wrinkled.

"How the hell did I get blood up there?"

"Your shifted form is quite... agile."

"No shit." I let out a low whistle. That ceiling had to be fifteen foot high.

"Come on, Jade," Shaun said. "It's decision time."

I jerked my eyes back down to him. He was holding out two cuffs. The first, one of the set I'd been wearing since I got here. The second, a single, smaller cuff, similar to the other but lighter and only half as wide. It seemed to shimmer with the faintest green glow as it caught the dungeon's dim lighting, so faint I was sure human eyes would never have detected it.

"Are you staying here, or joining the academy?"

I clutched the blanket in front of me and stood up. I just knew I was going to regret this. I stretched my right arm through the bars.

"Academy."

"Good choice."

He snapped the smaller cuff shut around my wrist and a shudder ran through me as the metal came into contact with my skin. Unlike the suppressor cuffs, it didn't mute my senses, but I felt something almost perceptible change, like the rabid power inside me was being held in check, just enough that I could think clearly.

I stared at Shaun. He stared back. I rolled my eyes.

"Well," I said. "Are you going to turn around so I can put this stupid uniform on, or what?"

Chapter Eight

I trudged from the cell with poor grace, smarting with every step inside my crappy new uniform. It wasn't the clothes themselves that I had a problem with – trainers, black cargo pants, white tee, grey hoodie – but what they stood for. They meant I was staying, and a big part of me was not cool with that. A bigger part of me told that part to shut the hell up, because better a crappy uniform in a crappy room, than a crappy blanket in a crappy cell.

And better a green cuff than a silver one.

"I know it's not easy for you, being here," Shaun said, holding the door open for me. I stalked through it, glaring at him. That was the understatement of the damned century.

"You've got an attitude," he said. "Did anyone ever tell you that?"

"Shockingly, no. Because I didn't have one until I got here."

"Now that I do find shocking."

"Gee, thanks." I shot him a sarcastic smile, then stopped at an intersection in the corridor. "Well, which way?"

"Here's the thing, Jade," Shaun said, squaring his shoulders and stepping in my path. He stared at me, doing that weird thing where I couldn't meet his eyes. "I meant what I said. I want to help. But you've got to help yourself. And this attitude, it's not helping."

"Excuse me if it's been a bit of an adjustment having my whole future wiped out."

"That's what you think?" He leaned back against the wall. I slumped against the wall opposite him and hung my head.

"Well, it has, hasn't it? Do you know how hard I worked to get into UCL? It was all I ever wanted. Now look at me."

I gestured to my crappy uniform and choked on a sound that was halfway between a laugh and a sob.

"I'm looking," Shaun said. "And what I see is a strong, independent and downright stubborn woman, who is going to get through this."

"In a crappy uniform."

"In a crappy uniform," he agreed. "By the way, handy tip for the future, you're not supposed to swear in front of the instructors."

"Uh-huh. I'll try to bear that in mind."

"Most of us are pretty relaxed, but Instructor Fletcher will hold you to the rules."

"Fletcher? Let me guess, Bitey McBiteface who brought me back in with Blake."

A smile tugged at Shaun's lips, and he almost slipped up and laughed.

"Yes, that would be him. And you might want to consider not calling him that to his face."

"You're just full of helpful advice, aren't you?" I wrapped my arms around myself and risked a glance at him through my lashes, trying not to let hope plaster itself all over my face. "Do you really think I can do this?"

"I know you can. I'm not going to lie to you, it's going to be rough. Pack structure is pretty heavily ingrained in these guys, and you're going to be an outsider."

"Well, doesn't that just sound like a barrel of laughs?" I jerked my head away and stared at the ground. High school all over again. Just what I never wanted.

"But you're not going to go through this on your own," Shaun continued. "I'm going to schedule you some sessions with me, daily to start with. And you can come and find me any time you need to talk."

"What, you're a student counsellor now?"

"And advisor, all wrapped into one. And speaking of advice, I have some for you."

"Yeah? And what's that? Wait, let me guess. 'Embrace my true nature.'"

He laughed.

"Yeah, no." He wrinkled his nose. "Take a shower before you meet the other students."

I sniffed myself and frowned. Ah, crap, the compost heap.

"Yeah, that's good advice," I admitted. He smiled to himself and carried on down the corridor. I fell in behind him. He glanced back over his shoulder at me.

"Here's some more. Next time you try to run off – I'm not naïve, Jade, please don't do me the disrespect of lying to me–"

I snapped my mouth shut mid-way through said lie, and he nodded.

"Next time, don't roll in the compost heap."

"I was covering my scent!" I protested. I'd thought it was smart. I was quite pleased with myself for thinking of it.

"Sure. And how many trails that reek of compost do you think there are leading away from the academy?"

"Oh."

I mulled that over as we climbed a set of stone steps and left the basement.

"So, um, what would you recommend?" I asked.

"I'd recommend not trying to break out of the academy."

"Right. Obviously. But you know, just academically speaking…"

I trailed off as he turned round and fixed me with his gaze. A prickling started up at the back of my neck and my eyes itched to look away.

"Would you stop doing that?" I snapped, but my anger was undermined by the fact I was staring at his shoes. Again.

"I'm serious, Jade," he said. I couldn't see his face, but I got the feeling he was glaring at me. "You're wearing a training cuff now. That comes with responsibilities. And if I think for one moment you're a danger to the mundane population, then I will have to do what it takes to protect them."

"The cage?" I asked, my voice laced with uncertainty. He shook his head, once, short and sharp.

"No."

"Worse?"

"Depends on your definition. Do you understand what I'm saying?"

I nodded. I wasn't sure that I did, but I knew one thing. If I decided not to stick around, I was going to have to do better than compost. Shaun seemed to pick the thoughts right off my face.

"Just give it a try, okay? One semester. It's only a few months. You might even like it here. What've you got to lose by finding out?"

Damn him, being all logical like that.

"Come and see me in my office tomorrow after your lessons, and we'll contact UCL about deferring your place. Just so you're not burning any bridges."

He had me, and he knew it – I could see it all over his entirely-too-satisfied smile. I exhaled in a huff.

"Fine."

"Excellent. Dorm rooms are on the second floor, second corridor on your left. Yours is the eighth door on the right."

We parted company, and I mulled over his words as I traipsed up the staircase. It was true that I could defer my place at UCL for a while, and it was also true that it would make for a better university experience if I didn't accidentally kill anyone. And I might not like the rules, and my lack of a choice about being here, but it did seem like Fur 'n' Fang was my best chance of making that happen.

Dammit. I hated when other people were right.

"Watch where you're going!"

My shoulder bounced off something solid and I found myself facing a trio of girls, the blonde in front looking decidedly irked about my clumsiness.

"Oh, sorry, I–"

"Oh, my God," the pretty blonde cut me off, raking me up and down with her eyes. "What is that awful smell?"

Great. Of course I'd have to walk right into the gang of stereotypical bitches on my way back to my dorm. Wait. Was bitch a racial slur now?

"It smells like something died around here," she sneered, tossing her hair and looking back to her pair of friends, who smirked and tittered in amusement. Fuck's sake.

"Something's going to die around here," I told her, "if you don't get out of my way."

"Jade," a voice said loudly from behind the trio. "There you are."

I looked past them to Dean, who stepped out of our dorm.

"Madison," he said, nodding a cold greeting to the blonde. "Tiffany, Victoria."

"Please," Madison said. "Don't tell me you're friends with this… cur. I know your taste isn't what it used to be, but this is a new low, even for you."

"Cur?" I snapped. "Who are you calling a cur?"

"Oh, I'm sorry," she said, looking down her nose at me. "Do you belong to a pack? Because you smell like a mundane. One who rolled in something dead."

"Madison," Dean said. "Shouldn't you be checking in with Alpha Blake? And Jade, I've got your schedule. Come on."

I glared at the bimbo a moment longer, then pushed through the middle of the trio, slamming my shoulder into her as I passed. I could practically feel her boring holes into the back of my neck as I sauntered into my room.

"You shouldn't have done that," Dean said. "Madison has a lot of friends. If you get on the wrong side of her, she could make your life difficult round here."

"Like it isn't already," I said, rolling my eyes and tossing my hoodie on the end of my bed. "You know her, then?"

"I, uh, used to."

Something about the way he said it made me look at him, and then I got it.

"Oh. You dated."

"Last year. She's the daughter of her pack's alpha, I'm my alpha's only son… our families encouraged it. The whole thing was a massive mistake."

He dropped down on the end of his bed and tried not to look bothered, but he was fooling no-one – probably not even himself. But if he didn't want to talk about it, who was I to pry?

"Well," I said, grabbing a clean set of clothes, "if you think you can resist her allure for an hour, I'm going to take a shower. Call me if she tries to seduce you."

"Thanks," he said, with a short laugh. "I'll be sure to be on the lookout for that."

I hit the shower room and took my frustration out with a scrubbing brush, sawing at my skin until it was pink and glowing, and hopefully, didn't smell of dead shit anymore. Shame I couldn't fix smelling like an outsider so easily.

I pulled on the clean uniform and unwrapped my hair from a towel, leaving it tousled around my shoulders.

"Hey, Dean," I called as I barged back out into our room. "You better not be getting busy with any daughters of–"

I lifted my head, and my eyes caught on a pretty, dark-haired, Asian girl.

"…alphas," I finished belatedly. "Shit. I was joking. Want me to clear out for a bit?"

Dean laughed.

"I'm Mei-Ling," the girl said, with a slight accent. "Call me Mei."

"Mei is our roommate," Dean said.

"Oh. Hey. Good to meet you." I stretched out a hand and shook hers. I'd have hugged her, but I didn't want to risk covering her in outsider stink.

"Dean says you're a troublemaker," Mei said, only the way she said it, it didn't sound like a bad thing.

"I did not say that," Dean protested, holding his hands up. He gave me a look. "I just might have mentioned you have a bit of a tendency to climb out of bathroom windows."

"Same difference," Mei said, shrugging easily.

"And I know you had your reasons," Dean said.

"Yeah, well, only because no-one told me the wall was spelled." I shot him an accusing look.

"How was I supposed to know you were going to try to climb the damned thing? And we call it 'warded'."

"It's called, 'it would have been nice to have some warning.' Anyway, that's all in the past." *For now.*

Dean eyed me like he didn't believe me, then shrugged it off.

"Well, if you're sticking around, then you'd best dry your hair or whatever. Alpha Blake is giving his start of year speech soon."

Chapter Nine

Good afternoon, everyone, and welcome to the start of a new semester at the Sarrenauth Academy of Therianthropy."

Blake stood behind a small lectern, which was positioned on a stage at the front of the vast hall we now occupied. It was the same hall we'd been dining in since I got here, but the tables had been pulled aside, and rows of chairs laid out, which were now occupied by shifters. I glanced around. There had to be a couple of hundred of them – us – all wearing cuffs like mine. Exactly how many shifters were there roaming this green and pleasant land of ours?

"Each of you has your own loyalties and pack bonds, but I remind you that within these walls, those pack bonds no longer exist. Your loyalties are to this academy. To the student on your left, and the student on your right. Within these walls, you are all equal."

I snorted under my breath. Equal, my arse. Madison had already made it perfectly clear what they thought about outsiders round here. *Curs.*

Blake locked eyes with me across the hall, and it took me a moment to realise that he'd probably heard me snort. Shifter senses. Oops.

"This academy has much to offer you," he continued, allowing his eyes to rove amongst the others. I slumped back in my seat. "I urge each and every one of you to take full advantage of the time you spend here."

I rolled my eyes – because I figured not even he could hear that. Dean's elbow nudged me in the ribs, and I shrugged. I'd agreed to give the place a fair trial. That didn't mean I had to buy into all the BS Blake was spewing.

"Meditation will take place by the lake each morning before breakfast. I remind you that these sessions are compulsory for first and second years, and recommended for third years."

Meditation classes? He had to be kidding. I shot a glance at Dean, but he didn't look surprised by this revelation. Not kidding, then. Great. Just what I needed. I'd been cursed into a damned cur, and they wanted me to go all new age.

Blake droned on for a while longer about the academy's history, and the unity of the packs. I probably should have paid more attention, but honestly his voice had a dreary quality and I couldn't have cared less about why the founding fathers erected this neutral territory and decreed that each shifter would study here until they learned to control their inner beasts. It was all I could do to keep from drifting off, but I figured even Blake might lose his composure if I started snoring.

"Classes will begin tomorrow. You will each receive your schedules, and you may spend the rest of the day getting acclimated."

People had already started moving before I'd processed the fact that we were dismissed. Great. Another afternoon kicking around inside my gilded cage. Or not-so-gilded cage. I got up and traipsed in the general direction of the door.

"Hey, wait up!"

I turned around to see Dean hurrying after me. I rolled my eyes.

"There are hundreds of shifters around," I said to him. "And the walls are warded. I don't think I need a damned chaperone anymore."

A look of hurt flashed over his face, and I couldn't quite bring myself not to care. It wasn't his fault everything about this place chafed, and it wasn't his fault Blake had asked him to keep an eye on me when I got here.

"That wasn't…." he started, and then trailed off again. God, I was such a bitch. Like I was the only one with problems round here. I was going to have to work on getting over myself.

"Sorry," I said, exhaling in a heavy sigh. "I didn't mean that."

"Yeah, you did. I'll catch up with you later."

"Wait," I called, as he joined the masses and disappeared through the door, ignoring me. Bollocks.

There was no sign of Mei, either, so it looked like I was on my own. I decided to head for a walk outside, see if I could clear my head. If I could remember the way, that was, because I didn't fancy climbing down another drainpipe. It was painfully clear that I wasn't cut out of that sort of behaviour. And besides, if Blake thought I was trying to escape again, I'd be back in a cell in the dungeon faster than you could say, 'false imprisonment'. Nope, I was going to have to do it the old-fashioned way, through an actual door. Only, my tour hadn't been real big on highlighting ways out.

I emerged into the corridor with the last students, and weighed my options. I didn't much feel like roaming the hallways endlessly, and I got the feeling that if I got lost here, it might take a long time to get unlost.

"Hey, excuse me," I called to a uniformed guy and a girl leaning against the walls, chatting to each other. They broke off from their conversation to look at me.

"I'm looking for the door onto the grounds," I said. "Any idea which way?"

"Uh, sure. Keep heading down this corridor right to the end, take a right, then you want the third left, and the second right."

"Thanks." Right at the end, third left, second right. This bloody castle was a maze.

I headed off, following their directions through the stone corridors, lit with a jarring mix of wooden torches and electric strip lights. I guess running wiring through an entire castle took some time. So did cleaning it, if the state of the walls and the cobwebs hanging by the ceilings were anything to go by.

Then again, I'd come from Uncle Bob's farmhouse, and this was practically the Ritz by comparison. Except for the warded wall surrounding it.

I paused, looking around me. This corridor was even darker than the last. They had said third left, and second right, hadn't they? Or had it been second left, and third right? Crap.

No. No, it had definitely been third left, and second right. *I think.* Well, whatever. If it led me nowhere, I'd just turn back. It wasn't like I had any place to be in a hurry. Still, something about the deep, flickering shadows made me uneasy. I laughed at myself, and the uncertain sound echoed back at me from the dark, ancient walls.

Maybe it was time to turn back.

…But how stupid would I feel if the door was at the end of this corridor? I'd been bitten by a damned werewolf and survived. I wasn't about to go running from a few shadows and cobwebs.

And then I saw it – the heavy wooden door set into the wall at the very end of the corridor, with a large ring of iron for a handle. There was something familiar about it, about the whole eerie corridor, actually, now that I thought about it. Maybe Dean *had* shown me this as part of his grand tour. It wasn't like I'd been paying much attention back then, seeing as I hadn't been planning to stick around at the time.

I gave a shrug, took hold of the handle, and twisted. The door didn't budge. I rattled it again – the damned thing was locked. Surely there wasn't a rule about students not going outside? Blake hadn't said anything about that, at least, not while I'd been listening.

"Ms Hart, what are you doing? Get away from that door!"

I jumped and twisted round, and found a compact, muscular figure advancing on me, a small sack in one hand, and the mother of all scowls on his face. Something about the way he moved, and the way my heart squeezed painfully in reaction to his scent, told me exactly who this was. Of course, last time I'd seen him, he'd been in his shifted form, and he'd been threatening to yank me out of a tree with his over-sized teeth.

"Fletcher."

"That's Instructor Fletcher to you," he snarled, stalking closer until he was towering over me. "Answer the question."

"I was just going to go outside," I said, shrinking back against the door. "Just for a walk."

"Do you take me for a fool? Get away from the dungeon door, right now."

Dungeon door? I spun around and stared at it. Shit. That was why I'd recognised it. It was the door Shaun had let me out of when I'd agreed to give this whole dumb academy a try. I so did not want to go back down there.

"Sorry, Instructor Fletcher," I said, pressing myself against the wall and squeezing past him under his glare. I turned and hurried back along the corridor. I heard the door open and shut behind me, but didn't dare linger in case he decided to throw me right back in there. If I never saw that place again, it'd still be too soon.

I was halfway back to the first year common room when the realisation struck me. I'd followed the directions I'd been given to the letter. Third left, second right. I hadn't ended up at the dungeon by accident. I clenched my fists into balls by my sides. They'd sent me there on purpose. Shaun hadn't been wrong when he'd said I was going to have it tough as an outsider.

It was official: Fur 'n' Fang *sucked*.

Chapter Ten

My name is Instructor Davis, you can call me Brendon, and this is, without question, the most important lesson you will attend here at Fur 'n' Fang."

I straightened a little in my seat. It was Monday morning, first day of the semester, and this was our first lesson, if you didn't count the meditation session out by the lake before breakfast – which I didn't.

Shifting 101.

This was where they were going to teach us how to shift – or hopefully, how not to – and once I mastered this, I might actually have some hope of getting my life back. That alone was enough to make me take what Brendon was saying seriously. There were twenty of us in the old stone room, all dressed in our stupid uniforms – about a quarter of the first years.

I'd grabbed a table near the back, and Dean and Mei were sitting with me. Dean seemed to have forgiven me for being a self-centred bitch yesterday, and whatever the reason, Mei was sticking with us. Maybe because I was the only person in the room Madison was sneering at even more than her. I guess the blonde wasn't just a bigot; she was a racist, too. Figured.

Even now she was darting disgusted looks in our direction. Whatever. I had more important things to worry about.

"If you pay attention in my lessons, you will achieve ultimate control over your shifted form. If you choose not to pay attention, you'll find yourself repeating a lot of classes. No-one passes this year without passing my class."

"Without passing all the classes," Dean said from the corner of his mouth. I laughed, and quickly turned it into a cough. Brendon's head pivoted in my direction. Ah, shit. *Great start, Jade.*

"Some of you will learn control faster than others. Discipline, patience, and determination are the cornerstones of control. Those who exercise them will achieve their goals faster than those who do not."

He turned and wrote the three words on the board behind him. I scribbled them down in my notepad. *Discipline, patience, and determination.* If that's what it took, that's what I'd do. I was going to learn to stop myself shifting, even if it killed me. And hopefully in time to get my university plans back on track.

"You will have lessons with me every day," Brendon continued. "These lessons will be primarily practical in nature, and I expect nothing less than your absolute focus when you are working. Anyone acting irresponsibly will find themselves on report. Am I clear?"

His eyes roved the room, and everyone nodded.

"Excellent. Then let's get started. Pair up."

Madison leaned in close to her pair of cronies and eyed the three of us, her lips twisting into a nasty smile, and then she rose from her seat and sashayed over to us.

"I'll work with you, Dean," she said, twirling her hair around one finger and giving him a smile that was all teeth and bad intentions. "You shouldn't have to work with… lesser students, just because Blake saddled you with her."

"Uh, I'm fine, thanks," he said.

Anger flashed over the blonde's face, but she quickly recovered.

"Fine. I'll work with Jade then. Since you can't work in threes."

"On second thoughts," Dean said, "I'll partner with you. Since we already know each other."

I gave him a grateful smile. Not that I wasn't up for dealing with that bimbo, but it was my first lesson, and I really wanted to focus. The sooner I mastered this, the sooner I got my freedom.

"Today we will be focussing on transitioning from your human form to your shifted form. Cuffs will remain on, to assist those who struggle to return to their human forms."

"Brendon," Madison said, her voice saccharine sweet, "What about those of us who don't need cuffs to control themselves?"

"Everyone will keep their cuffs on," Brendon repeated. "Decide who will work first, please."

"I don't get it," I said to Mei. "You guys were all born shifters, right? You must be able to control it by now?"

She shook her head, her straight, blue-black hair cascading around her face.

"Many shifters do not manifest their powers until their mid to late teens. Those who receive them early are required to wear cuffs until they attend Fur 'n' Fang – to prevent accidental exposure to the mundane population. Though there are some who suspect that not all the local packs," she broke off and eyed Madison, "adhere to the law."

Madison laughed; a high-pitched tinkling sound that made me want to punch her in the throat.

"Some of us," she said, "are above the law."

"No-one is above the law," Dean said firmly. "Not even your family."

"We'll see," she said. "Do you want to go first, or shall I?"

"Be my guest," Dean said, rolling his eyes.

I looked to Mei.

"I don't mind going first, if you want," she said. I nodded my thanks. My stomach was churning. The memory of my agonising change in the dungeon was all too vivid in my mind. If the cornerstones of control were discipline, patience and determination, then I definitely needed a moment to compose myself.

"Right," Brendon said. "Everyone through the door at the back of the room, please."

I pivoted round in my seat. Set into the back wall was a solid-looking wooden door, with large metal hinges attaching it to the stonework, and a heavy ring for a handle. It reminded me a lot of the door to the dungeon, in all the wrong ways.

Get a grip, Jade. It's just a door.

The rest of the students were already on their feet, so I tagged along behind them as they filtered into the room. This room was much bigger than the one we'd come from – and far more menacing.

Set into the wall on my left and right were a dozen cages, each fronted with a row of bars that ran from floor to ceiling. I could smell the distinctive tang of silver, and as I got closer, I could see arcane symbols etched into the bars, not unlike the ones from the cell in the dungeon.

I suppose it had been naïve of me to think we might learn about controlling our shifted forms in a nice, calm way. They were expecting us to lose control, and judging from the claw marks gouged into the solid stone flooring, plenty of others had before us.

Heavy locks were set into each cage's door, and I suppressed a shudder, reminding myself that it was a *good* thing that none of us would be able to break out while we were in our shifted forms. No-one needed a pack of feral wolves rampaging through the castle.

The rest of the room was in stark contrast to the nefarious cages – clean, spacious and airy, with light streaming in through several large windows – though I could pick out the flecks of silver in the bars covering them from here. I was getting good at recognising even trace amounts of what was rapidly becoming my least favourite metal.

"Those who are working first, please find yourselves a cage. I will come round and lock your doors. No-one is to begin their shift until I say so. Those of you observing, collect a clipboard and stopwatch from the desk and sit opposite your partners."

There was a flurry of movement as half the students stepped into cages, and the rest of us headed to the front of the room to pick up stopwatches, clipboards, and pens.

I grabbed a chair and dragged it over to the cage Mei had chosen, while Brendon started working his way round, locking students inside. The cage was maybe eight foot wide and six deep, and in the middle of it the Chinese girl stood looking completely relaxed – except for the way she kept hooking and unhooking her hair from behind one ear.

"Hey, you okay?" I asked. She nodded.

"Fine. I… I've only shifted twice. Neither time on purpose."

I'd be lying if I said I wasn't at least a bit relieved to discover I wasn't the only one who was shitting themselves at the prospect of trying to change forms on demand. But of course I didn't tell her that.

"You can do it, Mei."

She nodded again, a curt, sharp motion.

"Yes. I must."

"Observers," Brendon said, as he passed in front of me and locked Mei's cage, then rattled it to double check, "your job is to record your partner's shift. You will complete the form you each have in front of you, detailing how long each part of their shift takes, any difficulties they run into, and any other observations you make."

He gave Mei's cage door one more rattle – he was thorough, I had to give him that – then moved on to the next cage.

Mei removed her trainers from her feet, then pulled her hoodie over her head, folded it neatly and set it in one corner of the cage. Then she grabbed the hem of her t-shirt.

"Mei, what are you doing?" I hissed.

"The same as everyone else," she said with a shrug. "If we don't remove our clothes, they'll be destroyed."

I blinked and swept my eyes round the room. She was right – everyone inside a cage was starting to get undressed. I twisted back round to her, trying to not get an eyeful of what anyone had been hiding under their clothes. Especially the fit Scottish guy in the end cage. I remained convinced that one look at him would ruin me for life. These people had weird standards when it came to nudity.

Mei was watching me, her eyes sparkling with amusement.

"What?" I said, my voice tinged with a hint of irritation. "It's not like I've had my whole life to get used to this. Anyway, it's a mixed sex class. This is crazy."

"Crazier than turning into an animal?"

Well, she had me there.

"Besides," she said, as she pulled off her t-shirt and folded it, "everyone's going to be too busy worrying about their own problems to be looking at each other."

If she'd gone to the same high school as I had, I didn't think she'd be quite so confident on that point. She set her t-shirt on top of her hoodie.

"Don't worry, look – there are privacy curtains."

I followed the direction of her eyes and realised she was right. Pushed up against one wall was a heavy curtain I hadn't noticed – on account of my attention being diverted by the dozen individual cells in what would otherwise have been a nice room – and its runner along the ceiling divided the room in two. As I watched, Brendon grabbed the curtain and pulled it the length of the room, so that I could no longer see any of the students behind us – and none of them could see Mei. I was the only one who could see her, and because of the depth of the cages, I couldn't see the people in the cages on either side of me. I still didn't like it, but at least no-one was going to be getting an eyeful.

She wriggled out of her trousers and I dropped my gaze to the floor. I'd never been a communal locker room sort of girl, and the fact that I had a tendency to sprout fangs and claws when I got angry wasn't about to change that.

The sound of Mei's laughter made me frown.

"If you don't look at me, how are you going to take notes on my shift?"

Oh, right. I blushed and lifted my eyes, trying to see her without *seeing* her. I was starting to understand why Madison had wanted to pair up with Dean – I bet she was flaunting herself at him. Poor bastard. Well, he couldn't say I hadn't warned him about the whole seduction thing. There's no way someone gets that bitchy about her ex's friends unless she's jealous.

"Okay everyone, prepare to shift."

Mei settled herself on the floor, sitting cross-legged with her eyes closed. I positioned my thumb over the button on the stopwatch, then looked down at my sheet. Under 'position' I ticked 'lotus', mildly amused to see the list also included mountain, bound ankle, plank, and corpse, all next to little diagrams of the positions. They did not seem likely positions to prepare yourself to shift. Seemed to me like Mei had picked the only logical one.

"Begin."

Nothing happened. There wasn't a sound throughout the entire room. I glanced over my shoulder to see if anyone was having any more luck than Mei, but of course the curtain blocked my view. It sure didn't sound like anyone was shifting, though.

Several minutes passed with no sign of any movement from Mei, and I doodled on the edge of the sheet. Who knew shifter training was going to be so boring?

I was on the verge of drifting off, pen dangling lazily from my hand, when a scream of pain ripped through the air from somewhere behind me. I spun round, but I could see nothing through the curtain. At least someone was having some success.

"Come on, you can do it." I recognised Dean's voice, and my hand twitched in irritation. It figured that Madison would be the first one to get anywhere. There would be no stopping her gloating after this. But at least for now I could listen to the sounds of her pain.

Nope. It didn't matter how much I hated her, I just couldn't quite convince myself I was enjoying that. Why the hell would anyone choose to put themselves through this? If any of them had an ounce of sense, they'd just get fitted with cuffs permanently, and be done with the whole painful business.

A gasp rent the air in front of me and my eyes snapped back to Mei. Her head was flung back and her back arched. Trembles ran through her entire body, and her face was twisted with pain. Her hands curled into fists, and as I watched, their edges blurred. Then the skin rippled, and the knuckles under it moved, cracking and reforming. Her fingers splayed wide, and each became wider, and curved, and fur broke through the skin on the back of her hands.

One of her shoulders twisted, like some unseen force had dislocated it, and she cried out in pain, then snapped her jaw shut again. The same unseen force rocked her forwards so that she was on all fours, and her tail bone elongated and flexed into a long, lean tail.

Belatedly, I remembered my clipboard and jotted down a half dozen notes, my pen scratching across the paper as I described the process, marking down what changed first, which parts seemed to take longer to reform in their new shapes, and which caused her to shake with pain.

And then I stopped, my pen freezing mid-word. Her legs were long and lean, her fur close cropped, and her snout short. I wasn't looking at the form of a wolf. Mei was a leopard.

She locked eyes with me through the bars and snarled, then paced the small space with an easy, feline grace, lashing her tail as she moved. I stared at her, my mouth hanging slightly agape. I mean, I know Dean had said there were one or two students who weren't wolves, but... And then Madison's comments made sense. She didn't hate Mei because she wasn't the same race. She hated her because she wasn't the same species.

The leopard snarled again and swiped at the air with one claw. The cuff glinted in the sunlight, now much wider than it had been, still sitting snug against the animal's leg.

"Mei... Mei?" I whispered, leaning forward in my seat. Her head whipped round, and she stared at me through amber eyes. She understood me. Or at least, I thought she did, but I didn't know how in control of herself she was right now.

"Excellent work," a voice said from beside me.

I yelped in surprise and almost fell right out of my seat. I hadn't heard Brandon approach.

"Let's get you changed back."

There was a baton of some sort hanging from his belt, and he unhooked it then flicked it out, doubling its length, and fed it through the bars. Mei lashed out at it, but the baton just flexed under the blow. With deft hands, Brandon pressed the end of the baton to the gleaming cuff, and a shudder ran the length of Mei's entire body.

Her outline blurred again, and the hair along her body became sparser. She snarled in pain, and her body shrank, getting closer to its former size. No wonder they made everyone wear these cuffs. It wasn't just about taking the edge off our feral power. One touch from that baton and we returned to our human form. I wondered if all the instructors carried them. And I wondered if I could get hold of one.

"Alright everyone," Brandon said, moving away. "Once your partners are back in their human forms, you can collect the cage keys from the front and switch places with them. Don't worry if you haven't managed to shift, there's plenty of time to get the hang of it."

I headed up to the front and grabbed the key marked 'cage nine', and by the time I got back to Mei, she was fully clothed.

"Nice work," I said, unlocking her cage. "You totally nailed it. Didn't scream like a little bitch either, like some people round here."

I cast a glance in the general direction of Madison, and Mei's lips curled into a tired smile.

"By the way, your shifted form is badass. Way cooler than a wolf."

The smile dropped from her lips and her face darkened.

"Uh… isn't it?" I asked, this time uncertain. Because if my shifted form looked half as cool as hers, I might not hate it quite so much. Mei cocked her head at me.

"What am I missing?" I asked, as I pulled the door open. Because, as always, it was evident that I was missing *something*.

"Most wolves despise other types of shifter," she said, slipping out. "Or at best, tolerate them. The packs do not welcome other species."

"Ah. Well, I don't have a pack," I said. "So there's that."

"You're stalling," she said, holding the door wide for me. Crap.

"Alright," I said, slinking inside. "Here goes nothing."

104

Chapter Eleven

Nothing, it turned out, was exactly what happened. The class finished for lunch, and I hadn't managed even a hint of a shift. My only consolation was that I wasn't the only one – about a quarter of the class hadn't managed it, either.

Of course, Madison and her two besties were firmly in the category of those who achieved a shift, as was Dean, and she still had her arm wrapped around his waist as we left the lecture room. He delicately disentangled himself, and she pouted as he joined me and Mei on our way to the main hall for lunch. It turned out even my non-shift had given me an appetite. Honestly, I was just amazed that being in the same room as Madison for three damned hours hadn't put me off food for life. The way she flaunted herself at Dean was enough to turn anyone's stomach. Which was weird, because when he spoke about her yesterday, I got the impression that she was the one who broke things off. Maybe she'd had a change of heart. Maybe she just couldn't handle the fact that he wasn't pining after her. Whatever the reason, if I ever went panting after a guy like that, I hoped someone would do the decent thing and put me down. Like, eugh, where was her self-respect?

And then we reached the main hall, and all thoughts of anything other than food left my head. Feeding several hundred hungry shifters was no mean feat, but from the way it smelled in here, Mickey had it in hand. The queue was about twenty deep, and no-one had started fighting – yet. With all the students back at the academy, it seemed like there'd be no more table service, and no more unlimited menu. There was a board on the wall, detailing the three lunch choices on offer, one of which, of course, was steak. Seemed like it was a staple round here – not that I was complaining. Mickey made the best damned steak I'd ever tasted. I edged further along the queue, eyeing the number of people between me and food. They better not run out of the good stuff before I got there.

The three of us finally made it to the front, grabbed our food – Mickey hadn't run short – and headed for one of the long wooden tables set out around the hall. I sunk into my seat with a groan, rolling out my shoulders and stretching my spine.

"That was brutal," I groaned. "I can't believe we have three hours of that every day."

"What did you think you were going to learn at a shifter academy?" Dean asked, his lips curving into a smirk.

"I don't know," I said, carving my steak with more vigour than strictly necessary. "I hadn't really thought about it, seeing as how I never planned to come here."

"Right," Mei said. "You were going to be a lawyer, right?"

"*Am* going to be a lawyer," I corrected her. "Just as soon as I get rid of this."

I waved my manacled wrist. A tingle on the back of my neck warned me that someone was standing behind me a split second before Madison's irritating whine hit my ears.

"Well, I think you should just go."

I eyed at her, waiting for the other shoe to drop, because in my admittedly limited experience, she wasn't the encouraging, pep-talk type. She pulled out a chair next to Dean without bothering to ask, and Tiffany and Victoria sat with her.

"I'm not even convinced you are a shifter," she said. Ah, there it was. I took a careful sip of my cola and said nothing.

"I mean, you don't smell like a shifter. And you don't move like a shifter. And you can't shift."

"Along with a quarter of the class," Mei said, levelling a cutting glare at the blonde.

"Who asked your opinion, feline?"

"Give it a rest, Madison," Dean said, about a half second before I could thump her.

"Sure, Dean," she said sweetly, and turned a dazzling smile on him. Damn, her mood swings were giving me whiplash. "Let's talk about something else. Did you hear my father was given a commendation by the Alpha of Alphas? That makes my pack the fifth most powerful in the country now."

"Alpha of Alphas?" I asked, pausing with a piece of steak halfway to my mouth. Madison wrinkled her nose at me, and I took a moment to enjoy the mental image of it smeared across her face.

"Well, of course a common cur wouldn't know anything about the Alpha of Alphas. It's not as if someone like you has any cause to move in such circles. I mean, you don't even have an alpha, do you?"

"I think we've established that I don't," I ground out, and then forced a smile. I'm not going to lie, holding that image of her nose went a long way to helping. "But I guess that just means I don't have to whore myself to try to further my pack."

Her jaw ground together so tightly I could hear it. She clenched her hand around the fork she was holding, and the metal crumpled in her grip.

"How dare you speak to me like that? Me?"

"Well, I guess being a lowly cur, I've got nothing to lose." I locked gazes with her over the table. "You should remember that."

She glared at me for a long moment, then snatched up her plate.

"Come on, girls. There's a bad smell around here."

The three of them sauntered off to another table, and I glared at their retreating backs.

"You're not going to let things lie with her, are you?" Dean said. I leaned back in my seat with a grin.

"Nope. Where's the fun in that? So, who's going to answer my question?" I looked between Dean and Mei. "The Alpha of Alphas?"

"Okay, so you know just about every wolf in the country is part of a pack, right?" Dean said. I rolled my eyes.

"I think I got that, yes."

"Well, every pack has an alpha – the wolf who's in charge of everyone in the pack."

"Hey, I'm new to being a shifter, not new to popular culture. I watched Twilight like everyone else."

Dean shook his head in mock disappointment.

"Of course you did. Right, so every alpha in the country gets a place in the alpha pack – kind of like a grand council of shifters. The Alpha of Alphas is the wolf in charge of the alpha pack. The most powerful shifter in the country."

"Wait," I said, setting my fork down – the steak was done and I'd lost interest in the salad. "You said every alpha wolf gets a place. What about other types of shifter?"

Mei gave a little bitter laugh.

"Our place is to obey – or be banished from the pack's territory."

"Their territory being...?"

"The whole of England, Scotland, Ireland and Wales."

"So you just have to fit in with whatever they decide, or you have to leave your home?"

"That's how we came to be in this country to begin with. My parents were driven out of China when I was a baby."

"That's..." I groped for the right word and decided that my anger wasn't what was needed here. "That's awful. I'm sorry."

Mei shrugged, feigning indifference and fooling no-one.

"It is ancient history. I was too young to remember home, and you can't miss what you don't know."

She picked up her glass, lifted it halfway to her mouth, then set it down again.

"My mother, though, she spoke about it often. She would have liked to have returned, I think."

"I'm sorry," I said again, but it didn't seem like enough. Not even close. This new world was a mess, as prejudiced and screwed up as the one I'd grown up in.

"Don't be. It's just the way things are."

I had the sense not to press it. I cast around for a change of subject and caught sight of my schedule sticking out of my bag, and plucked it out.

"I've got Law next," I said. "What about you two?"

"Same," Dean said.

"Ah." I put my schedule down. "I'm guessing we have every class together, courtesy of Blake? Not that it's a problem," I tacked on hastily, before he had a chance to get his feelings hurt again.

"We do," he said. "But not for the reasons you think. They just divide everyone up according to room assignments."

"Oh." *Way to go, Jade. Your paranoia's showing.* "So, I'm guessing this Law isn't the same law I was planning to study at UCL?"

"Not unless you were planning to study pack law. You finished with your food? We should get going."

I was, so we grabbed our bags and left the hall, cutting through the castle's winding corridors until we reached a plain door. I saw Madison stepping through the

111

door in front of us and rolled my eyes. I was going to be stuck with her in every single class. That was just bound to be a bundle of laughs.

Dean made for a seat near the front, and I grabbed his arm with a shake of my head, then led him to a table at the back of the room. No way was I sitting near the front in a class that I was – at best – a decade behind everyone else in. I mean, I didn't even know shifters existed a month ago. You could count the number of their laws I knew on one hand – and have three fingers and a thumb left over. Nope. I needed to be at the back of the class, where I could take as many notes as I needed, and no-one was going to ask me any questions.

"Good afternoon, everyone. I'm Instructor Lewis Taylor, and you'll be studying law with me this year. Now, I know no theory lesson is going to hold that much interest for you, so I'll try not to take it personally if this isn't your favourite class, so long as you try not to actually fall asleep during my lectures – it looks bad on my review."

My lips twitched into a smile. Maybe things weren't all bad at Fur 'n' Fang. I mean, sure, it wasn't exactly the law I'd been planning to study, but it was still law, and Lewis wasn't the dullest speaker I'd ever studied under.

"Some of you may have very little knowledge of pack law," he continued, his eyes sweeping the room – for me,

I was sure. "Rest assured, I intend to bring you all up to the standard required by the end of the year. Let's start with the basics."

He turned his back on us and walked over to the whiteboard hanging on the wall. I grabbed a notepad from my bag and flipped it open. They might be basics to him, but I was starting from zero here.

"The law exists to protect everyone, be they shifter, mundane, or one of the other magical communities."

"Magical communities?" I asked Dean from the corner of my mouth.

"Druids, and such," he said.

"As in, actual magic?"

He dipped his chin in a curt nod. I wasn't sure why it surprised me, I turned into a damned wolf for crying out loud – but magic? Come on, I was just getting my head around the idea of shifting. Magic and druids seemed like one ask too many, if you asked me. But no-one had, so I crammed the thought in a dark box at the back of my mind and focused on what Lewis was saying.

"Officially, we reside under druidic law, but the packs have always ruled their own, and it has been generations since druids interfered in the affairs of shifters. The enforcers act for the Alpha of Alphas, dispensing justice on his behalf. Name a law. Anyone."

There was a long moment of silence – maybe a few of the less academically inclined students had already drifted off to sleep. Then one of the guys – the hot Scottish one – spoke up.

"Dinnae hunt on pack lands without yer alpha's consent."

"Yes, good," Lewis said. "And the punishment? Someone else."

"Banishment," a voice answered from somewhere near the front. Lewis nodded, wrote it on the board, and I copied it down into my notepad. Good to know. Not that I'd been planning on going poaching any time soon, but still.

"Give me another."

Madison cast a look in my direction, her lips curving in amusement.

"Biting a," she sniffed, "mundane."

A few students twisted to look in my direction, and whispers whipped around the room. Lewis ignored them.

"And the punishment?"

It was Dean who answered.

"Death."

"What?" I twisted round to stare at him. "We don't have the death penalty in this country!"

Madison's answering cackle set my teeth on edge.

"This isn't the world you thought it was, little mundane. We have rules, and we're not afraid to enforce them."

"Right," I said. "Because that's worked out so well for you. I mean, bang up job of keeping everyone in line."

"You have no idea what you're talking about. No surprise, given your... breeding. Without pack law, there would be anarchy."

"There's a reason countries with the death penalty don't have a lower crime rate than ours, and that's because it's a shit deterrent." I gestured up and down my body with one hand. "Case in point."

"Well, no wonder you think the cur who bit you shouldn't be punished. After all, he plucked you from your mediocre little life and gave you something that was meant for your betters."

"That's enough," Lewis said firmly, and I bit down on my tongue and jerked my eyes away from Madison. Mediocre little life, my arse. I *liked* my life. None of this shifting bullshit, and magic, and banishments, and secret societies killing people.

Lewis levelled his eyes at Madison.

"Name?"

"Madison," she said with a pout. Then, with a hint of smugness, "Capell."

If she'd been expecting a reaction when she dropped her family name, she'd have been disappointed. Lewis didn't so much as blink.

"Well, Madison," he said, "in this lecture room you will hold a civil tongue in your mouth. Healthy debate is encouraged. Racial slurs are not. Do I make myself clear?"

"Yes, Instructor Taylor," she said, abruptly contrite. It lasted as long as it took him to nod and look away, then the sour look was back on her face. She clearly wasn't used to being slighted.

"Now, where were we? Someone give me another law."

Chapter Twelve

I left Law feeling like maybe Fur 'n' Fang wasn't the worst place in the world – a feeling which lasted until I spent an hour and a half looking completely incompetent in Combat class. I was the only person there who couldn't even throw a punch properly. It was only thanks to Dean and Mei getting in the way of Madison's attempts to partner with me that I wasn't completely humiliated. But we had Combat twice a week, so there was plenty of time for that.

As if that wasn't bad enough, it was followed by an hour of fitness training – because apparently getting thrown around for an hour and a half wasn't fitness training enough. Worse, alongside meditation and Shifting 101, fitness would be a daily staple of my routine. And, of course, they weren't the only things. By the time I'd taken a shower and grabbed a meal in the dining hall, it was half-past six, and I was knocking on the door to Shaun's study.

"Come in," he called. "Ah, Jade. Thanks for coming."

I shrugged. "I said I would."

We both knew what he really meant – thanks for not trying to break out again. Though the way my day had gone, it didn't seem like such a bad idea right now.

"Talk to me," Shaun said, scanning my face. He perched on the edge of his desk and gestured to a chair in front of it.

I slumped into the chair and wondered where to begin. Like any good interrogator, Shaun stayed silent, giving me enough rope to hang myself. No, wait, that wasn't fair. He really was trying to help. It was just, I wasn't sure there was anyone who could help with this. Not unless they knew how to take this shifting power back out of me. Even if they could, which I knew they couldn't, I'd never be able to unsee what I'd seen. I knew this entire secret world existed now, had existed the whole time, hidden in the shadowy corners of my own. Shaun couldn't change any of that. But neither was it his fault.

"It's, um… I'm adjusting."

"I heard you had a bit of a run in with Madison." I jerked my eyes up to meet his. "Yes, instructors do talk to each other."

"I can handle it." I had no idea how I was going to do that, but I'd dealt with worse than spoiled little princesses in my life. I'd handle it.

"Okay then," he said. "Why don't you tell me what's really bothering you?"

"You mean other than my whole life being irrevocably changed?"

"Yes, other than that."

He stared at me so long I started to fidget. I avoided his eye when I answered, looking instead down at my own hands twisting in my lap.

"She's right. I don't belong here."

"I disagree," he said. "You're a shifter. This is exactly where you belong."

"And after I leave here? My life will never go back to normal, will it?"

He grimaced. "Normal is going to mean something different for you from now on. But that doesn't have to mean worse. Speaking of which," he twisted round and picked up some sheets of paper. "Your deferment papers. You can fill them out now, if you want, or you can take them with you and drop them back when you're done."

I helped myself to a pen from his desk. Might as well get it over with. Plus, if I was doing this, he might give the psychoanalyst routine a rest. I was entitled to be a bit screwed up right now. I'd been turned into a freak, thrown into a world where I was an outcast, and I was being held against my will at a secret academy. Who the hell would be okay with that?

I was half-way through filling out the form when a realisation struck me. I stopped, my pen frozen mid-word. Shaun looked up from whatever he was doing on the other side of his desk.

"Problem?"

"Yes, there's a problem." I tossed my pen back on the desk. "You can only defer for a year. I'm stuck here for at least three."

He said nothing, just watched me across the desktop.

"You knew! You knew, and you had me doing this anyway. What, did you think it was a good way to keep me quiet, get me to play along without making a fuss?"

I glared at him, and he didn't even have the decency to look ashamed.

"Look, Jade…"

I shook my head sharply, pushing my chair back.

"Are we done here?"

"Yes, we're done."

"Good." I turned and stalked to the door.

"Your hands are shaking."

"So what?" I spun back round, ignoring the pounding in my ears. "Stop pretending you give a damn!"

"You're going to shift. The training cuff won't stop you." His words were calm and measured, and he made no move to get out of his chair.

Shit. He was right. My hands were already starting to blur.

"The way I see it, you've got two choices. You can walk out of that door and try to handle this by yourself. If you shift and Alpha Blake gets wind of it, the consequences could be severe. Or you can let me try to help you."

"I don't want to shift," I said through clenched teeth. I could feel movement under my skin, and the memory of my agonising shift in the dungeon flashed to the forefront of my mind. I never wanted to shift again. Damn them for putting me in this position!

"Good," Shaun said. "I'd also like you not to shift, because we don't have a cage in here and your shifted form seems particularly aggressive. Why don't you take a seat?"

"I…" My shoulders rippled, and I grunted in pain, staggering back and bracing myself against the wall.

"Okay, the wall's good," Shaun said, stepping from behind his desk and coming closer.

I bared my teeth at him, an inhuman snarl ripping from my throat.

"Easy," he said, stopping halfway across the room from me. I tracked his movements, waiting for him to come within range, snarling again as I warned him not to. Pain ripped along my spine and I doubled over with a gasp.

"Jade, listen to me." I snapped my head back up to glare at the instructor. "You can control this. You need to calm down."

Calm down? Why the hell should I?

"You did this to me! All of you!" My voice was hoarse and scratchy as I shouted, but Shaun didn't so much as blink.

"Control your anger, and you'll control the shift."

I didn't want to control my anger. I had every right to be pissed at them, and it would feel good to take it out on him. I could smell his blood pulsing beneath his skin, and soon I would taste it as I ripped and shredded–

I shuddered with revulsion and sucked in a deep breath. I didn't want to shift. I was the only one who could control that now. I wanted to stay human. I did not want to attack Shaun. I took another deep breath that juddered all the way into my lungs.

"That's it, Jade," he said. "Just keep breathing. You can do this."

A shiver ran through me, and I leaned back against the wall, panting. The pain eased, but my hands still trembled. They weren't blurred around the edges anymore.

"Come on," Shaun said, closing the gap between us. "Let's get you into a chair."

He steered me back to his desk and I went obediently, barely in control of my own limbs. I sank into the chair, every part of me shaky and cold.

"Drink this."

He gave me a glass of water and my hands shook so much that I slopped half of it over the rim. Fuck's sake.

"Don't worry, that's normal. Your body is just reacting to the aborted shift."

I tried again, and this time managed to get a mouthful of the cool liquid inside my mouth. Shaun watched me in silence from his own seat, and it wasn't until my shivers had all but given up that he spoke.

"I'm sorry. I shouldn't have given you false hope about deferring your studies. We– *I* thought it would help you adjust if you had something else to focus on."

I snorted, but I didn't trust my voice not to shake, so I kept my mouth clamped shut.

"For what it's worth, I know you've been dealt a rough hand, and I was trying to help you get through it."

"By lying to me?" Dammit, I was right. My voice *was* shaking. "You, and Blake, and everyone else, just telling me what I want to hear, until I agree to play along like a good dog?"

"Like it or not, Jade, you're stuck here–"

"I'd go with not."

"–and you're going to have to find a way to deal with that. You already know why you can't return to your old life right now. What would have happened if all of that–" he gestured to the wall I'd been braced against, just in case I hadn't been able to work out what he meant by all of that, "–had happened at UCL?"

I didn't answer because I knew he was right. That didn't mean I had to like it, though.

"I know you didn't ask for this, and what happened to you was deeply unfair–"

"Yeah, no shit."

"–but sooner or later you're going to have to decide if you want to keep being a victim."

"Excuse me? None of this was my fault!" I couldn't believe he was dumping this victim blaming crap on me. Of all the nerve.

"No, it wasn't. But you can't change what happened. You can only change how you handle it."

I slumped back in my seat, in no mood to sass his obvious logic. His face softened.

"Give yourself a break," he said. "This is still new to you. You're doing better than anyone could expect."

They must've had low expectations, then, because I was a mess, and I didn't have the first idea how not to be.

"How am I supposed to deal with this?"

"Let me ask you something."

I lifted my eyes from the desk, and he continued.

"Is this really the very worst thing you could imagine happening to you?"

"Yes." I sighed. "No."

"Well, that's something, right? Maybe start there."

Chapter Thirteen

I fell into a routine after that. A crappy routine that I despised and resented, but a routine none-the-less. Every day after fitness training, a shower and dinner, I'd drag myself up to Shaun's office, and he would talk to me about adjusting, and I would give him attitude in return. Neither of us brought up UCL again, but on the plus side, I also didn't try to change into an animal again, so that was something.

On the downside, I didn't manage to change into one when I wanted to, either. Three weeks in, I still hadn't managed a single shift on demand. My only consolation was that there were still two other students who hadn't managed it, either, so I wasn't alone in my failure. On the other hand, I was still a mundane who'd been bitten, so I was no less an outcast than I had been.

"Alright, everyone. An easy exercise to finish up with. In front of you are three cloths. You're going to look away and your partner will handle one heavily, one lightly, and the other not at all. Then you're going to use your sense of smell to determine which is which."

We were coming to the end of another painful Tracking lesson, and it was clear that Shaun's idea of easy and mine were very different. But that was nothing new. I turned my back on Dean with a sigh and heard the faint rustle of movement. When it stopped, I turned back to him.

"I don't suppose you want to tell me which one it is?" I asked hopefully. He crossed his arms over his chest with a smirk.

"I guess not. Fine." I snatched up the first cloth and pressed it to my nose. It smelled of cotton. But did it *just* smell of cotton, or was there a faint impression of something else on there – something not quite human? I was damned if I knew. I tossed the cloth down. That one was a maybe.

I tried the next cloth. Cotton. Just cotton. And, well, maybe something else. I wasn't sure. I slumped in my seat with a groan, balling the stupid cloth in my fist. Maybe my sense of smell would never catch up with everyone else. Maybe bitten mundanes didn't develop full shifter senses. Maybe this was all a giant waste of time – like pretty much everything else I'd done round here for the last three weeks. I shouldn't even be here. *Dammit!*

Dean coughed and arched a brow, and I shook out the cloth with poor grace. A sharp, acrid smell hit my nose and caught in the back of my throat. I pressed the cloth to my nose again. It smelled like... smoke. Burning. Then I saw it. The cloth had a tiny burn mark on it. Someone must have been over-enthusiastic taking an iron to it. I peered at the tiny black circle. Weird. It didn't *look* like an iron burn. And I should know, I ruined enough clothing getting to grips with my iron before I moved out and my whole life went to shit.

"Well?" Dean said.

I shrugged and picked up the third cloth. I held the square of fabric to my nose, and recoiled immediately.

"Dude, what the hell have you got on your hands? This stinks."

"You… you scented it." Dean stared at me, looking more surprised than was polite. A slow smile spread over my face.

"Yeah, I did, didn't I?" And there'd been no mistaking it. It couldn't have been more obvious if he'd painted a bright red 'X' on it. That was the heavily handled cloth. I picked up the first cloth again. The same scent, but fainter, layered over the crisp odour of cotton.

"This one," I said. "You handled this one lightly."

"Yeah," he said, his grin spreading. "I did."

I picked up the third one and held it to my nose again. Just cotton. And that odd burn patch. I tossed it aside.

"Nice work," Dean said. "Alright, my turn."

He turned his back, and I reached over and picked up two of the cloths in front of his seat. One I put right back down, and the other I rubbed in between my hands a couple of times. I put it back with the others, taking care not to let them touch.

"Okay."

"Ready to watch a master at work?"

I rolled my eyes.

"Yeah, yeah, just get on with it."

It was embarrassing. He didn't even have to pick the cloths up. He just lowered his face an inch or two towards them.

"Left one lightly handled, middle untouched, right heavily handled. And you borrowed Mei's hand cream again this morning."

"Flipping show off. And it's not my fault no-one will let me go back to the farm to get my own stuff."

"Okay, everyone, that's all we have time for today," Shaun called. "I'll see you again next week."

I scooped up my bag, then headed for the door with Dean and Mei.

"Jade, can I talk to you for a moment?" Shaun asked as I passed. I shrugged. It wasn't like I was in any hurry – we had fitness training next and I could live with being a little late for that. I hung back while the other students left, then Shaun crossed the room and shut the door.

"What did I do wrong this time?" I asked. Might as well cut straight to the chase. If he was pulling me back after class and shutting the door, then I was in trouble for something. May as well find out what it was right away so

I could decide whether I cared enough to make up an excuse.

"Nothing," he said, and perched on the edge of his desk. Oh. I recognised that face. That was his 'I've got something I need to tell you and you're not going to like it' face.

"I've got something I need to tell you," he began.

"And let me guess." I crossed my arms over my chest. "I'm not going to like it?"

He smiled, but it didn't reach his eyes. He looked… tired.

"No, you're not. I only found out this afternoon, and I wanted to give you some warning."

I swallowed. I didn't like where this was headed.

"About what?"

"The Alpha of Alphas arrived at the academy today. When you come for your session with me this evening, he'll be wanting to interview you."

"Me? About what?" He was right. I didn't like the sound of that at all. The Alpha of Alphas? The most powerful shifter in the country? A shiver ran through me and I wrapped my arms more tightly around myself. I didn't want to see him. Not ever.

"About your attack. He has some questions."

I shook my head. "I don't remember anything. Just tell him that. He doesn't need to talk to me."

"I'm sorry, Jade," Shaun said, and he looked it. "It doesn't work that way. If the Alpha of Alphas summons you for an interview, you go. Even if you don't remember anything."

I bit my lip. I didn't want to go. I didn't want to be in the same room as the man who could order my death with just a raised eyebrow.

"It wasn't my fault I was bitten!"

"No-one's saying it is, Jade. I promise you, you're not in any trouble."

"Not yet, anyway."

"You're going to be fine. Just remember what you've been taught about etiquette in Cultural Studies."

Oh, my God. What if I said something that offended him? What if I accidentally made eye contact? What if I sassed the most powerful man in the country? Oh, shit.

"Jade, take a breath. He just wants to make sure they're covering every angle of the investigation."

"Since when does the Alpha of Alphas get involved in that?"

The question hung unanswered in the air between us. I frowned, searching his face.

"What's going on? What aren't you telling me?"

"I can't say."

"Can't, or won't?"

"Both," he said firmly. "The reason he's involved doesn't affect you, and it's a distraction you don't need right now. You just need to focus on answering his questions as best you can."

He was right. I was going to be in the same room as the Alpha of Alphas. I didn't need anything else on my mind. It would be hard enough to avoid screwing this up as it was.

"It will be fine," Shaun said. "I'll be right with you the whole time."

"You will?"

He nodded. "I will. Now, go and run off some of your anxiety and get a decent meal. I'll see you at six thirty."

It wasn't as easy as he made it sound. No amount of running cleared the churning in my gut, and food wasn't an option, either. I gave up trying to eat after twenty minutes of pushing food around my plate, and slunk off to my dorm, glad to get away from my friends' well-meaning but grating attempts to distract me. It turned out that was a mistake, and I spent the next half an hour pacing and staring at the clock hands edging round its face. Eventually, I decided it was best to get it over with, and headed for Shaun's office.

I raised my hand and knocked on his door. *He's just a man,* I reminded myself and sucked in a deep breath. *Just a man.*

"Come," Shaun invited from within.

Yeah, a man with the power to have me killed or caged. I exhaled in a sigh and opened the door.

"Ah, Jade, you're early. Come on in."

I clicked the door shut. Shaun was standing behind his desk, at the shoulder of the heavily muscled, dark-skinned man sitting in his seat. Alpha Draeven.

A shiver ran through me. Even from here I could feel the power and dominance pouring off the man, like an aura of authority. He rose to his feet, and I shrank away, taking a step back before I managed to steel myself. Everything about him screamed danger, and every instinct in me screamed to start running and not stop until I was as far away from him as possible. I didn't do anything that stupid.

Shaun coughed quietly, and I remembered myself. Shit. I was supposed to show respect as soon as he stood. I dropped into a crouch and ducked my head, glad for the excuse to hide my face. *Dammit, Jade, get it together. He's just a man.*

"I see you," the Alpha of Alphas said, his voice deep and rumbling. "You may rise."

I rose to my feet, but kept my eyes averted. The last thing I wanted to do was land myself in an accidental staring-contest with the most powerful shifter in the country.

"Please, be seated," Draeven said, and I sank into the chair positioned in front of Shaun's desk, fighting the urge to move it back. Draeven sat again, and Shaun stayed standing at his shoulder. He gave me what I was sure was supposed to be an encouraging nod, but it was still taking all my self-control to keep from running screaming from the room.

"You need not be afraid," Draeven said.

I didn't snort, proving how seriously I was taking this. Nothing to fear from the Alpha of Alphas? Right, and I wasn't a shifter.

"Tell me, what do you remember of the night you were bitten?"

I shook my head.

"Nothing. I mean, not much." I'd been turning it over in my head ever since I'd spoken to Shaun earlier, but much of the attack was still a blur. "I was at the farm, taking my stuff to the barn. It was…"

I'd been going to say 'creepy', but knowing what I knew now, that just didn't cut it. I shivered, and rubbed my hands over my arms, now covered in goose pimples.

"Go on."

"The wolf attacked me when I was heading back to the car. I tried to get away, but it was too fast. Too strong. Nothing I did made a difference. I tried. I did."

"No-one expects you to have been able to fight off a shifter, Jade," Shaun said. I nodded and drew a shuddering breath.

"It bit me. On the leg. It bit me and wouldn't let go."

"Just bit you?" Draeven asked.

"Isn't that enough?" I snapped.

There was utter silence for a moment, and my brain caught up with my mouth. Oh, shit. I opened my mouth to stutter an apology, but Draeven cut me off with a sharp shake of his head.

"You misunderstand me. Did the wolf try to kill you?"

"I don't know. I don't remember! I think…" I rubbed my hands over my face, trying desperately to recall something – anything – else about that cursed night. "I think it dragged me. My nails were all torn up from the gravel."

"And you have only one bite?"

I nodded, glancing down at my leg without meaning to. Only one horrific scar to remember that night by – oh, and a newfound tendency to erupt in fur whenever I got mad.

"Wait. What does it mean that the wolf only bit me once, that it didn't try to kill me?"

Draeven ignored the question.

"Do you recall–"

"What does it mean?" I was on my feet and shouting over him before I even knew what I was doing. He looked up and me, his face somewhere between shocked and pissed. Really, really pissed. He rose to his full height, towering over me and glaring at me like he wanted to do me serious harm. I stumbled, colliding with the chair, and a pressure burned into the back of my neck, so strong I couldn't even raise my eyes from the floor.

"Sit. Down." His voice was quiet, each word slow and precise, and more terrifying than if he'd yelled them. I shrank back into the seat, still keeping my eyes low, and after a moment, the pressure eased and I heard Draeven sit back down.

"Do you recall the wolf's colour, or any distinguishing features it may have had?"

"No. I'm sorry. Please, Alpha Draeven, just tell me what it means."

It was Shaun who answered, earning himself a look of disapproval from Draeven.

"It means whoever attacked you intended to turn you into a shifter."

"But… why?"

"Why is not important," Draeven said with a cold finality. I disagreed, because I sure as heck wanted to know why someone had set out to inflict this on someone else – and if targeting me had been deliberate. But I'd come close enough to landing myself in trouble already. I let it drop.

"Can't you just–" I shot a look at Draeven, then ducked my head again, biting my lip. I wasn't about to tell the Alpha of Alphas how to do his job. It was just... well, it was kind of obvious, wasn't it?

"Speak."

I swallowed and tried to phrase it more diplomatically than I'd been going to.

"Couldn't the enforcers have just followed the trail from the farm? They chased it off, right?"

"Perceptive." He inclined his head a fraction, and I thought I saw a flicker of approval on his face before it reverted to its impassive mask. "The scent was muddied, most likely by magic. But no matter. The wolf was injured by my men, and those wounds will not heal lightly. It is only a matter of time until he is caught."

"I thought shifters healed quickly from any wound."

"Not those inflicted with silver."

I flinched at its mention, my eyes flicking to the cuff around my wrist, with its tiny silver flecks, nearly too small to see, but still enough to allow the instructors' batons to force me back out of my shifted form. I didn't want to think about what would happen if silver got into my bloodstream. Instead, I turned his words over in my head again. A chill spread over me.

"You said he," I said quietly. "You know who did this to me?"

"I am not here to answer your questions."

No. Of course not. Because that might be the decent thing to do, and heaven forbid the mighty Alpha of Alphas treated me like a human being.

You're not human anymore.

The thought cut me like a silver blade, and I wrapped my arms around myself again. When would this nightmare end? Suddenly, I wanted this whole thing to be over, and I wanted to be as far from this claustrophobic room as physically possible. I ground my teeth together.

"Are we done?"

"We're done when I say we're done." He looked across to Shaun at his shoulder. "She has quite the temper on her."

"Don't blame me," I said, my voice loaded with all the bitterness of this entire bullshit situation. "I was just a normal person until that psycho bit me. So what if I have anger issues?"

"Jade has made a significant effort to overcome her difficulties," Shaun said, before Draeven could respond to me. "She has a way to go, but she is trying."

He locked eyes with me as he said the last three words, and I couldn't miss their double meaning. Trying, indeed. Trying his patience? I'd give him bloody trying… Or I would, if he wasn't doing his best to keep me from getting caged or killed. I hung my head and tried to paste a look of contrition on my face. Picturing my bloody guts all over the room made it easier.

"I apologise, Alpha Draeven. I spoke out of turn."

Draeven stared at me for a long moment, and I watched his stern face through my lashes. It didn't soften, even for a moment. Great. I'd pissed off the Alpha of Alphas. Could my life get any worse?

"I will require measurements of the scar," he said to Shaun. "It may be useful in proving the feral's culpability, once he is captured. We will continue when the Bitten has a better grasp on her place."

That would be a yes, then. Just great.

Chapter Fourteen

lpha Draeven did not summon me again the next day, or the one following it. On Friday evening, I decided I would broach the subject with Shaun, but before I could, he took the measurements of my scar, along with dozens of photos from every angle. I wasn't sure why Draeven hadn't done it himself, or even sent an enforcer – maybe he had more urgent alpha duties to attend to, or maybe Shaun had interceded on my behalf. Maybe Draeven was just sick of my attitude. Whatever. I wasn't about to look a gift horse in the mouth. That man was dangerous, and I wanted nothing to do with him.

I didn't hear anything back about the wolf they were hunting in the following weeks – but then, I hadn't really expected to. Draeven seemed like a need-to-know kind of guy, and he clearly thought that I didn't. It didn't matter. He'd face justice eventually. Not that it would change what I was or give me back my future.

The fist thudded into my stomach. Air exploded out of me and I doubled over, gasping. My eyes flicked up to Madison's smug face, and I forced myself upright.

"Keep your guard up, Ms Hart," Fletcher said, "or don't be surprised when a strike lands."

I rolled my eyes round to him and I could have sworn there was a look of amusement in his eyes. Like Combat wasn't bad enough without the instructor having it in for me. But that was nothing new. He'd taken a dislike to me the night I'd tried to escape, and nothing I'd done since had changed his opinion – although, to be fair, it wasn't like I'd put myself out trying.

Something whipped through the air towards my face and I ducked back, narrowly avoiding taking Madison's fist to my nose. Right. Don't get distracted. Every bit the pack princess, Madison had probably been fighting since she was a pup. She wouldn't miss an opportunity to punish my weaknesses. And there was no shortage of them. If I gave her long enough, she was going to take me apart.

I got my hands up in time to block her next attack, then surged forwards in a flurry of aggression and bad intentions, throwing fists and elbows with ferocity and no particular skill. I landed a glancing blow with my first, she blocked my second, and the third went wide. She moved in a blur of motion before I could readjust, locking her leg behind mine. She did something I couldn't see with her hip and I thudded into the ground, knocking the air from my lungs. I gasped, but before I could recover, she landed on top of me, straddling my torso and pinning my arms to my sides, and landed three fast and hard blows to my face.

Pain exploded through my head and I felt the strength go out of me. My vision blurred so that I could barely make out the triumphant smirk plastered all over her face.

"Excellent throw, Madison," Fletcher said. "Right everyone, that's it for today. I'll see you all next week." He tossed a glance my way, still lying in the dirt. "Do try to get some practice by then. Some of you need it."

I sat up with a groan, and then paused, waiting for the grounds to stop spinning. Most of the class were already on their way back to the castle – few people lingered after Fletcher's lessons. I wouldn't have, either, if I thought I was capable of walking in a straight line right now.

"Ouch, that looks painful."

I squinted up to see Dean towering over me, a sympathetic wince on his face.

"Sorry," he said, stretching a hand down to me. "I tried to partner with her, but Fletcher stopped me."

I accepted his hand, letting him pull me to my feet. I waited a second, checking my balance – I didn't want to land back on my butt, I was pretty sure Madison was still around here someplace, gloating.

"Had to happen eventually," I said with a grunt. "Fletcher's right. I really do need to practice."

I probed my eye with a finger and hissed in pain. I could already feel the bruise forming under the skin.

"For fuck's sake," I griped, as we headed back to the castle. "That had better heal up before the party tonight."

Dean and Mei shared a look, and my shoulders slumped.

"It's not going to, is it?"

"I think the swelling may go down by then," Mei said, peering at my eye more closely.

"And the bruising?"

"There's a guy in my pack who completely heals from bruises in eight hours," Dean said, in what I assumed was supposed to be encouragement.

"Great. I've got six. Bloody Madison, she did that on purpose. I'm going to look a right mess tonight."

*

My mood did not improve during our last lesson of the day. The opposite, in fact. By the time I'd dragged myself up to Shaun's office for my daily waste of time, I was in a worse mood than ever. Alright, so it was just a stupid Halloween party. But I'd been looking forward to it, dammit. And now it was ruined because of Madison. Mei had even been going to lend me something decent to wear so I didn't look like an idiot wearing my uniform. Now it didn't matter what I wore, everyone was going to be staring at my stupid face.

I rapped on Shaun's door and opened it without bothering to wait for him to invite me in. He looked up from behind his desk.

"Alright," he said. "Let's have it. What's wrong?"

I shut the door with maybe more force than necessary. What a dumb question. Like he couldn't see the bruise covering half my damned eye from where he was sitting. You could probably see the stupid thing from the other side of a darkened corridor. I gestured to it and said nothing.

His brows knitted, and his lips pressed together in a confused half-smile, like he wasn't sure if he was missing out on a joke.

"You're not upset about that little bruise?" he said. "You've had worse injuries than that."

"Yeah, but it's the party tonight," I said, slumping into my usual seat opposite his desk.

"So?"

I huffed in frustration.

"You wouldn't understand."

"That's never stopped you before."

Well, he had a point there. Saving up all my frustration and letting it out inside this room was what had gotten me through my first month here, and Shaun had never complained about being my verbal punching bag – for some reason. He was pretty good at this whole student counsellor gig. I sagged.

"I was looking forward to it. Getting dressed up, doing my hair. I know it sounds stupid." I picked at my nails and avoided his eye. "I just wanted one night to pretend everything was normal."

"And now you can't?" He sounded confused, in the way that only guys can when you start talking about this stuff.

"Look at it! It's a mess. I don't even have any makeup to cover it up with because it's not like Caleb stopped to pack a bag when he dragged me out here." I shook my head and exhaled slowly. "But who cares, right? I'd have looked stupid in Mei's clothes. They don't even fit me properly."

Shaun raised a hand, opened his mouth, paused, and closed it again. Guys. They just don't get it.

"Let me get this straight," he said after a long moment. "You're weeks behind in Cultural Studies, you clearly came off worse in combat class, and there's a full moon in three days, but the worst thing going on in your life right now is that you can't get dressed up to go to a party?"

"Yes," I said, folding my arms across my chest, and trying not to think about the full moon coming up. The last one hadn't been pretty. Hell, that was half the reason I needed a distraction.

"And the reason you can't do that is because you need your makeup, which is at your uncle's farm?"

I nodded, trying not to pout.

"Well, that's easy."

If he said one word about focusing on my other priorities, I was going to vault this desk and give him the twin to my eye.

"We'll just head out there and get it."

I stared at him for a long moment. I blinked. I ran his words through my head again.

"Leave… the academy?"

He nodded, and I felt a grin spreading over my face.

"We can go get my stuff? You're serious?"

He nodded again. "But you have to give me your word, Jade. I need to know that you won't resist coming back here."

"Are you kidding? I've got a party to get to." I glanced up at the clock behind him, and my grin died a premature death. "We can't."

"Why not?"

"Look at the time. We'll never make it there and back." I didn't know exactly where the academy was, but I knew it was isolated, probably in the heart of the countryside.

"The party starts at eight?" he said. I nodded. "Then fear not, Cinderella – you shall go to the ball. Come with me."

Huh. Maybe we were closer to the farm than I thought. I followed Shaun through the castle and out of the front doors. He paused long enough to do something I couldn't quite see, disabling the wards on the front gates, and then we were through them, too.

"Uh, I don't see your car."

"We're not going by car. We're going by portal."

"Excuse me?" I stared at him, one eyebrow arched, because I'd thought I was beyond being shocked by now – but a portal? He had to be kidding.

He stretched one hand out in front of him, and the hairs on the back of my neck stood on end.

"*Eachlais!*"

Right. He wasn't kidding. I was staring at – well, at a portal. A large, oval surface hanging vertically in the air a few feet in front of us. And in it, I could see the farm. I shook my head, open-mouthed. A freaking portal. Seriously.

"With training," Shaun said, "you'll be able to tap into the primal power buried deep inside you. The power expresses itself through therianthropy, but that's not the only form it can take."

"How much training?" I asked, my eyes skimming the portal's rippling surface.

"A lot. Some shifters never manage it. It takes a great deal of discipline."

Well, that was me out, then. But that was some Harry Potter shit right there, and I was going to at least try whenever I next had some alone time.

"Eachlais, right?" I asked. Shaun shook his head with a smile.

"The word is just a focus for the power. You have to access it first."

Obviously. Access the power I knew nothing about.

"And the castle is warded against portals, that's why we're out here. Speaking of which, we can either continue this impromptu lesson – which I'm more than happy to do – or we can actually go through it."

I eyed the solid-looking portal, glanced at Shaun, then turned back to it.

"I better not bruise my other eye," I said, and stepped through.

Chapter Fifteen

My foot touched down seamlessly on the farm's gravel track, and I quickly stepped away from the portal – I didn't want Shaun crashing into me. I took a deep breath of the crisp country air, drinking in the autumn scene. The old oak by the farmhouse had shed the first of its leaves, and the rest of them had turned a shade of burnt orange. All around, nature was continuing its patterns, undisrupted by everything that had happened to one almost-human girl. Last time I was here–

I buried that thought with a shudder. I wasn't here for a trip down memory lane. But I couldn't quite tear my eyes from the gravel track, that spot right there where the wolf had grabbed me, sunk his teeth into my flesh while I screamed and flailed, and dragged me unwilling towards the treeline. I scanned it, searching the deepening shadows.

"You okay?"

I jumped and spun around, my heart racing. I hadn't heard Shaun coming up behind me.

"I'm fine," I said, shoving my hands into my pocket so he wouldn't see them shaking. "Hey, where's my car gone?"

I'd just been looking for something to take his attention off me, but seriously, where the hell was my car? I left it right here... with a door open, and a whole load of blood around it.

"The enforcers would have cleaned up after they brought you to Fur 'n' Fang, in case anyone came looking for you. The car would have aroused suspicion."

I shivered. That was creepy as all hell. It seemed like the enforcers knew what they were doing when it came to making people disappear. I didn't want to get on the wrong side of them.

"Try the barn," Shaun said, nodding to the dilapidated building. I took a couple of steps towards it, then stopped and shook my head.

"The house," I said. "Caleb brought my bags in after I was... after it happened."

I wasn't quite sure why the word 'bitten' stuck in my throat, and I didn't feel like working it out right now. I pivoted on my heel, heading for the old farmhouse. When I got there, the sight pulled me up short. There was a brand new lock on the door. Crap.

"How am I supposed to get in?"

Shaun glanced at the lock, then ran his fingers under the window frame. I shook my head.

"There's no way either of us is going to fit through that window, and besides–"

I broke off, staring at the key in his hand. Right. Because of course my DIY-loving abductor who could make people disappear without a trace would leave a key for if I came back. This whole world was screwed up.

I unlocked the door and swung it inwards, then stopped, staring over the threshold.

"I don't... I don't think I can go in there," I said at last. It felt like a strange thing to admit. The farm had always been a home to me, but so much had happened last time I was here, none of it good.

Shaun placed his hands on my shoulders and turned me around to face him.

"If you want me to, I'll go in for you and get your stuff. But I think you need to go inside, if you can. A decision based on fear is never a good one. You are stronger than what happened to you."

I stared into his eyes for a long moment, then swallowed and ducked my head in a nod.

"Come with me?" I asked in a tiny voice.

"Of course," he said.

We crossed the threshold together. The kitchen was almost exactly as I'd left it, except Caleb had cleaned up any sign that we'd eaten a meal there. It looked as deserted as it had when I first arrived. I didn't dwell on it, instead hurrying through to the bedroom I'd woken up in.

My bags were right where he'd left them, piled up against the wall.

But that wasn't what caught my attention.

I pressed my hand to the wall, tracing the deep gouges carved into it. Gouges that I knew could only have come from a set of claws. *My* claws.

"This is where I shifted for the first time," I said. "I didn't know what… I was so scared. I thought I was losing my mind."

I thought I'd forgotten that first shift, but I guess I'd just buried it. I couldn't have done a more thorough job of uncovering it if I'd brought a shovel.

"It can't have been easy." Shaun perched on the edge of the bed, watching me. I barked a bitter laugh. That didn't even begin to cover it.

"Why couldn't he have just told me?"

"Would you have believed him if he had?"

We both knew the answer to that. I hadn't even believed them when they'd taken me to Fur 'n' Fang. Not until I'd seen him shift. Even then, I'd tried to convince myself I'd imagined it.

"Why are you doing this? Why did you bring me here? Why now?"

"That's a lot of questions."

I narrowed my eyes. "A lot of questions that you're not answering."

Shaun nodded, drew in a breath, and exhaled it slowly.

"I've got some news," he said.

"News I'm not going to like?" I hazarded.

"Leo, the wolf who attacked you, has been caught."

"So why doesn't that sound like a good thing?"

"It wasn't the enforcers who caught him. At least, not our enforcers."

"I... don't understand."

Shaun grimaced. "He turned up at a druid academy. Dragondale. The druid enforcers have him. And they don't want to give him up."

I sagged back against the wall, nausea churning in my stomach. Then abruptly it was gone, replaced by a fire that was all bitterness and anger.

"So, what, he just gets away with it? Is that what you're saying? He can do this to me, ruin my whole life, and he gets to walk away?"

"No. Jade, that's not going to happen."

"You don't know that." I paced the tiny room, wall to wall. "What claim have they got on him? He did this to *me*."

"The alpha pack are going there to negotiate, tonight."

I stopped pacing.

"Draeven is going?" I couldn't imagine anyone defying the intimidating shifter.

"*Alpha* Draeven," Shaun corrected me. "And yes. He's taking a party to meet with the Druid Grand Council. Leo broke their laws, too – he trespassed in their academy, and…"

Indecision flickered across his eyes.

"Just tell me."

"He bit one of their students this morning. We won't know if he turned her until the full moon."

"And if she turns?"

"She'll be a halfbreed – part druid, part shifter. A crime against nature. The druids will stake a claim on Leo's life if that happens. They'll want to imprison him. The alpha pack will argue that he's one of ours, and we should be the ones to punish – and kill – him."

"Instructor Martin says the druids and the shifters used to be at war. That we have a truce. A tentative one."

"He's right. And there's no telling if it will be strong enough to survive this."

"The druids and shifters could go to war? Because of me?"

"Hey, no." Shaun shook his head sharply. "Don't think that. Whatever happens, it's not because of you. It's because of Leo, because of his crimes."

"What if I say I don't want him punished – that I don't care what he did to me?"

"It doesn't work like that. He broke the law, and he has to face the consequences."

"Whose?"

"Hopefully we'll know by tomorrow. Neither side has anything to gain from a war right now. Alpha Draeven knows that, and so do the druids. They'll do what they can to avoid it."

"Except giving up their claim on Leo."

"Except that. Some crimes are unforgivable."

I swallowed bile. I couldn't handle this. It was just too much. This was supposed to be my night of pretending this whole sorry mess wasn't happening, not finding out we were on the brink of war.

I stalked over to my bag and snatched one up, fumbling with the zip until it burst open and spilled its contents all over the floor.

"Fuck's sake." I stooped next to the mess and sifted through it with trembling hands.

"I'm sorry I had to tell you. But I thought you deserved to know."

I closed my eyes for a moment. I was behaving like a victim. Like prey. I wasn't that person anymore. Leo would face justice for what he'd done, one way or another. And Draeven wouldn't let it come to war – but if the druids did come for us, I'd be ready to fight. I might not have liked how it happened, but I was a shifter, and I would fight for my world.

But not tonight. Tonight, I had a party to get to.

I hunted through the rest of my stuff, fishing out my makeup bag, hairdryer, and a dress that would have all the guys in Fur 'n' Fang staring at me for the right reasons for a change. I threw them into a bag along with a few more essentials, not least the book I'd started reading two days before I came here, and then nodded to Shaun.

"Okay, I'm ready. Let's get out of here."

*

"Jade, you look amazing!"

I rolled my eyes and hoped the low lighting would hide the flush on my cheeks.

"That would be more of a compliment if you didn't sound quite so surprised."

The heavy thrum of bass covered most of Dean's spluttered response. He wasn't the first guy who'd tracked my movements across the small dancefloor when I made my fashionably late entrance. The dress hugged my figure in all the right places, and the heels did the rest of the work. With my makeup carefully applied, and my dark hair falling around my face in sculpted waves, the shadow of bruising around my eye was all but invisible. In the hall's soft lighting, no-one would notice it. I owed whoever had done the decorating a massive thank you. I owed Madison something, too, but I wasn't going to ruin my night worrying about her. I was going to make every guy here see what he was missing out on, and then I was going to get very, very drunk.

"Uh, Jade, lass?"

I turned around and almost crashed right into Cam – the hot Scottish guy who was in most of my classes. He looked a little flushed and his eyes were wide as they drank me in. He must've hit the bar early. I mean, I looked good, but I didn't look *that* good.

"Would yer, I mean, d'ya want tae dance? Wit' me, I mean?"

He ran a hand through his thick dark hair, looking all kinds of anxious. That was kind of flattering. A girl could definitely get used to this sort of attention. I flashed a smile at Dean over my shoulder and ignored him rolling his eyes.

"I'll see you later."

I wrapped my hand in Cam's. "Lead the way."

We made our way onto the dancefloor, more than one pair of eyes following us. I was more than just the mundane who'd been bitten right now. I was the new girl: exotic, desirable, the one none of them had ever met growing up. And it felt good.

I leaned into Cam as we moved to the music, inhaling his scent. Across the room, I caught a flash of blonde hair and glaring eyes. Madison clenched her jaw, staring at my hand on Cam's hip. I wasn't exactly clear if she had a problem with me being with him specifically, or just the concept of someone noticing me as anything other than an outcast, and I didn't much care. If I was upsetting the little pack princess, that was the icing on an already perfect cake. I blew her a kiss over my partner's shoulder and then put her from my mind.

"You look stunning," Cam said, leaning close to me.

"Thank you," I purred up into his ear, swaying my hips to the heavy bass. The music picked up and words became a thing of the past. *This* was what I'd been craving. The lights, the music, the closeness to another person. The feeling of being so absorbed in the moment that nothing else existed, not my bite, not the academy, just me and the guy I was dancing with.

Time fell away. We danced, we laughed, we acted like normal people doing normal things.

"Do yer want a drink?" he asked as another song wound down.

"Sure." Alcohol was the only thing my night was missing right now.

He wound his hand in mine – shifters were all about tactile – and led me from the floor, locking eyes with anyone who dared to look at me too long. I hadn't figured Cam for a caveman, but I liked it. I liked a lot of things about him, not least the way his body moved as we wound through the packed bodies, carving a path through the other shifters. Cam may not have been the blood of an alpha, but dominance rolled off him in waves.

He claimed a couple of drinks and handed one to me. I chugged half of it back, then Cam caught my eyes and held them, but there was nothing confrontational in our gaze. It was all challenge and compulsion, mine and his. He lowered his lips to mine, and I stretched up to him, head tilted back.

As he bent lower, I caught a flash of movement behind him. I frowned, ducking out of the way of his lips.

Oh. My. God.

I couldn't believe it. Madison and Dean.

Kissing.

Chapter Sixteen

She's using you!"

Dean glared at me across the dorm room. I glared right back. After the amount I drank last night, I should have felt like my head was exploding – I'd earned the mother of all hangovers. But it wasn't my head that was troubling me.

Dean twisted his head away, breaking eye contact and staring at the wall behind me.

"Maybe she is, maybe she isn't. It doesn't matter."

"What the hell is that supposed to mean?"

"I don't expect you to understand."

"Why, because I was bitten, not born like this?"

"Yes!" He turned his eyes on me again, and they were burning with frustration. "Jade, you didn't grow up in our world. You don't understand the pressure I'm under. My parents expect me to form a bond with the daughter of another alpha – to strengthen our pack."

"That's bullshit."

"That's the way things are. The way they've always been. One day I could be alpha of my pack, and I have to have a strong mate. And I know you don't like Madison, but she's strong. And she's clever. Beautiful."

"And a bitch. Dean, can you even hear yourself right now? She's shallow, and the only reason she wants anything to do with you is because of me."

Dean snorted a bitter laugh and shook his head.

"How full of yourself are you, Jade? This is nothing to do with you. Our parents matched us, and our bond will strengthen my claim for alpha."

I ground my teeth together. Dean was infuriating.

"Why can't you see how fucked up this all is?" I demanded.

"And why can't you just accept that this is the way it is?"

"Because it's wrong! You don't even like her."

"Enough, Jade!" He rose to his feet and towered over me. "I'm with Madison. Get used to it."

I glared at him, getting up in his face, my hands curling into fists at my sides.

"So you'd still be with her, even if she wasn't the daughter of an alpha?"

"Why do you care so much, anyway? I saw you sloping off with Cam last night."

How could he even ask– Wait… he was right. Why did I care so much? It didn't matter to me who he hooked up with, and he'd made it perfectly clear he wasn't interested in my opinion.

"I don't," I said, pivoting on my heel and snatching my hoodie from the end of my bed. "I hope you're both very happy together and have lots of fat little puppies."

I stalked out of the room, slamming the door behind me.

"Whoa, easy there."

A pair of powerful arms wrapped around me, and I tensed to fight until the scent penetrated my senses. I blinked up into the dark eyes watching me.

"Cam."

He frowned.

"What's wrong, lass? If yer dinnae want t' see me…"

Hurt flashed across his face, making him look vulnerable as a lost kid. I shook my head.

"It's not that. I need some air. Come on."

I led him through the castle with no particular idea where I was headed. I needed to put some space between me and that idiotic, pig-headed moron. I mean, Madison, of all people. What was he thinking? Sure, she might have a good pedigree, but… Madison!

Eventually we emerged outside in the stark morning light. It was as good a place as any. I slowed my march to an amble, and Cam slowed beside me. For a moment I'd forgotten he was even there, I was so wrapped up in my anger at Dean's stupidity. I sucked in a breath of the crisp air and exhaled it slowly. I wasn't going to let him ruin my morning, any more than I'd let him ruin last night.

Cam was watching me cautiously.

"Sorry," I said, steering us towards the treeline in the distance. "I guess I'm a little caught up in my thoughts this morning."

"Do yer… do you regret last night?" he asked. "I wasnae tryin' to take advantage."

I shook my head fiercely, and my lips curled into a dreamy smile. I had my share of regrets, but last night was incredible. Well, what I remembered of it.

"No. Last night was amazing. You were amazing."

"Are yer sure? When I woke up this morning and you were gone…"

He trailed off, and I peered up at him. I'd never seen him so unsure of himself before. He seemed so confident in class.

"You're a worrywart, anyone ever tell you that? It's kinda sweet."

"T' tell yer the truth, I dinnae have all that much experience with girls."

"Really?" I looked him up and down – seriously, his body was ripped, and the only thing hotter than his face and the shadow of stubble was his accent. "I find that hard to believe."

He laughed. We were far enough from the castle now that there was no-one around, and we started drifting through the treeline, into the shade of the woods.

"It's true," he said. "I, uh, I first shifted when I was just a lad, fifteen."

I frowned, not really getting the connection between the two.

"Ah, I forget, yer didnae grow up in a pack. When a wolf has his – or her – first shift, they get pulled out of school and fitted with cuffs."

"Wait, you never finished school?"

He shook his head.

"I finished up my schooling in the pack. It's a small pack. Hard tae get much… uh… experience when yer related to half the girls yer own age."

"I'm sorry. That must've been rough – getting taken out of school, away from all your friends."

He shrugged. "That's just the way it is, lass."

"Yeah, I've been hearing a lot of that recently. I thought I had it bad."

"It's for the best. The pack dinnae like us fraternising with mundanes. Better ter keep ter our own kind."

"Why?" I stopped walking and turned to him.

"For one, there's the whole lifespan thing. For another, if a shifter loses control around a mundane – you've seen what can happen."

164

I nodded. Yeah, I was uniquely familiar with how dangerous shifters could be to mundanes.

"Wait, what lifespan thing?"

"Shifters live a lot longer than mundanes – surely yer knew that, lass?"

He cocked his head at me, and I leaned into him. Every time I thought I had a handle on what the hell was happening to me, the rules changed. It wasn't right. How many changes was I going to have to deal with? How long were the surprises going to keep on coming?

"Jade, lass… are ye crying?"

"No," I lied, dragging a hand over my eyes. He wrapped his arms around me, holding me against his chest. I stayed there in his embrace, the closest thing to safe I'd felt since this whole damned mess started, until the tears stopped flowing. It took longer than I was proud to admit. I pried my head from his chest.

"I'm sorry."

"You don't have to apologise tae me, lass."

"Still, hardly what you signed up for, right?" I gestured myself up and down. "I don't normally turn into an emotional wreck the morning after. If you want to forget last night happened, I won't hold it against you."

"Not likely," he said, brushing a lock of hair from my cheek.

"Why?" I hated the way my voice sounded. Small, vulnerable. Weak.

"Yer not like the other lasses."

I laughed and leaned back, looking up at him.

"I'm not entirely sure that's a compliment."

"It is," he said, leaning down and catching my lips with his. I drank in the kiss, the physical closeness, the intimacy, melting against him until nothing existed but me and him, and the kiss. After a moment he broke away, leaving me wanting more.

"Someone's coming," he said.

"Oh, ashamed to be seen with me?" I cocked an eyebrow and grinned.

"I thought you might value yer modesty," he said. His voice dropped an octave. "And if you keep kissing me like that, I'm gonna take you right here."

"Then let's go find someplace more private."

*

I spent the rest of the weekend forgetting all about Leo, and Dean, and Madison, and long lifespans and being bitten, and every other screwed up rule of my screwed up new world. Cam was a very good distraction.

But I couldn't hide from the world forever, and after meditation and breakfast – which I couldn't help but notice Dean spent at Madison's table – Monday morning found me back in my own personal hell: Shifting 101.

It wouldn't be so bad if there was anyone left in the class who hadn't managed to shift on command yet, other than me, of course.

"You'll get it today," Mei said, as I shut myself in the cage, and smiled at Cam over her shoulder.

"Don't hold your breath," I grumbled. It wasn't that I objected to being paired with Mei for the entire semester, but she shifted every single lesson. Without fail. Sometimes she even shifted back without any help from Brendon. It was enough to make a gal feel inadequate. Luckily, the cure for that was hot, muscular, and eyeing me from across the room. Hard to feel inadequate for too long when there was a Scottish hunk wanting to spend every spare minute by your side. That sort of thing was definitely good for my ego. Who even cared if I could turn into some dumb wolf?

Next to Cam's cage was Dean, and my eyes hardened. Madison was shutting him in, and as always, she was all over him, her hands lingering on his arm. I curled my lip. I couldn't believe he'd fallen for her act. She was using him. It was so blatant that the only thing she cared about was his chance of becoming alpha. But he was just as bad. He only hooked up with her because of who her father was. The whole thing made me sick. Stupid, twisted shifters.

Brendon slid the privacy screen across the room, cutting off my view of them, and of Cam. Probably for the best. If I was going to give this my best shot, then it was better that I wasn't distracted.

I kicked off my shoes and the rest of my clothes, and sat cross-legged, as I'd watched Mei do every time.

Just focus, Jade. Picture your body becoming the wolf.

I gave it a good sixty seconds before frustration got the better of me. This was useless. I was never going to get the hang of it. I'd been trying every day since I got here, and the only time I'd ever managed to shift was when I didn't want to.

"Dammit!"

Mei looked startled, and I just shook my head. From the other side of the room, I heard the tinkle of laughter: Madison's. No doubt she'd heard my frustration. No doubt they all had, but of course she couldn't pass up a single opportunity to mock me. I bet Dean was laughing at me, too, now that he was all cosied up with her.

I bit down on my lip, clamping my jaw shut and swallowing the stream of curses I wanted to let out. I paced the tiny cell, growling my irritation. I couldn't deal with this. Not today. I needed to be outside. I needed to be free of this stupid cell in this stupid room, inside this entire stupid academy. I didn't do a damned thing to deserve this. I had a life, and Leo had no right to take it from me. None!

My legs trembled and my entire body shook with the injustice of it. Why me? What did I ever do to deserve to be cursed? There was no justice in this whole screwed up world, and I deserved justice for what had been done to me. I had damned well earned it!

I collapsed onto my hands and knees with a shout of anger, but it came out as a feral snarl. Hair erupted along my arms and my shoulders burst from their sockets. I let out another cry, half human, half animal, as pain screamed through my body. Bones broke and reformed, joints dislocated, too big for their sockets, and fire burned through my spine as it buckled, twisted, and straightened into a new shape. A more powerful shape.

And then the pain was gone.

I spun around, pacing the confines of the cell on four legs. All the hurt and the pain of the last three months was less than a memory, replaced with white hot anger. My yellow eyes locked onto the pretty Chinese girl watching me from beyond the bars. My lips peeled back from my teeth and a snarl boiled up from the depths of my being. I sunk on my haunches, and threw myself at her.

169

Chapter Seventeen

I don't understand why my shifted form is so aggressive."

A whole month had passed since I first shifted intentionally, and I'd done it a dozen times since then. And every single time, without fail, my shifted form attacked Mei. *I* attacked Mei. And Brendon. And anyone else who got close enough. I tried to maim, and to kill, and only the warded bars stopped me from doing it.

Shaun leaned back in his chair with a heavy sigh.

"I wish I had answers for you. No-one knows much about Bittens. The last case was hundreds of years ago."

"So you think it's because of how I was turned?" I groaned and rolled my head back to look at the ceiling. "Am I ever going to learn control?"

"For someone who's recently gained shifter hearing," Shaun said, and I could hear the amusement in his voice, "you're not so good at listening. I just said we didn't have answers. It could be because of how you were turned, it could be that you're still adjusting. Or it could be that you don't want to control it."

"Excuse me?" I jerked my head down and glared at him. "Mei is my friend. How could you possibly think I would ever want to hurt her?"

"I'm not saying you consciously want to hurt her. But you can't deny you have a lot of anger issues." He held his hands up in a placating gesture, and continued, "And you have every right. No-one blames you for that. But your shifted form gives you an excuse not to have full control, and maybe part of you wants a way to vent your anger."

"Maybe I wouldn't have so much anger if Leo was punished."

But since he was still at Dragondale, and since the damned druids were still refusing to hand him over, that was looking less and less likely by the day. They'd been negotiating for a month – a whole month – and still they were at a stalemate. Draeven should just take him.

"That's not the only thing you're angry about. You're still not talking to Dean?"

"He's not talking to me," I said, crossing my arms over my chest. "Anyway, what do you care? I don't need a chaperone anymore. I still come to these stupid sessions, don't I?"

"When are you going to stop lashing out at people who are trying to help you?"

"When are you going to stop acting like my damned shrink?" I shoved my chair back. "We're done here, right?"

"Actually, Jade, we're not. Sit down."

Shaun glared at me, and for a moment I considered just walking out of the room. I didn't owe him anything.

…Except I did. I slumped back into the chair and gave him my most unimpressed look.

"Well?" I said, rolling my eyes. "Go on, then."

The muscles in Shaun's jaw clenched and then smoothed out again.

"Firstly, you will remember who you are talking to. I am your instructor. You don't have to like that, but you do have to treat me with a certain amount of respect."

Respect. Etiquette. Dominance and submission. I had all that crap drilled into me twice a week in Cultural Studies, and it still seemed like a bunch of self-serving bullshit.

"This stroppy teenager routine isn't going to cut it. If you're not mature enough to get yourself under control and act like an adult, there are alternatives to completing this year."

My blood ran cold, draining from my face. He was talking about the dungeon. He was talking about keeping me locked up there until the next intake. Eight months in a cell. I wouldn't survive eight days.

"I'm sorry," I said.

"I know."

"It's not like I try to escape anymore. I could have run on Halloween, and I didn't."

"I know."

"I'm doing my best! It's not my fault that–"

That what? That I was acting like a spoilt brat? That I was taking my temper out on everyone around me? That I refused to accept the hand fate had dealt me, even if it was a shitty one? No. All of that was my fault.

"I'll do better," I said.

"Okay. Good. I'm only asking you to try. I'm going to schedule you some extra sessions with Brendon."

I groaned.

"Aw, come on. I already see him every day. And I'm miles behind on the stuff for my other lessons."

"If you don't get some sort of control before your exams, you're going to have to resit this entire year."

"Exams?" This was the first I'd heard about any exams.

"Did you think you could just coast through lessons for three years, and then leave here without any sort of control, or understanding of how the shifter world works?"

Well, yeah, I kinda had. Attend Fur 'n' Fang for three years, and then I got my freedom back. No-one had said anything about exams.

"When you leave here, you're going to need to find your place in our world. You're a part of it now, and you need to start thinking about how big of a part you want that to be."

"I'm going to UCL to study law," I said without hesitating. "I'll go as a mature student. That hasn't changed. When I'm done at Fur 'n' Fang, I'm done with this whole world."

"Well, that's your choice, but first you're going to need to demonstrate that you're not a danger to the mundane population, and that you can follow our laws. You'll have exams every year, and you'll either graduate – or not."

Shit. I really should have seen that one coming. I slumped over his desk and groaned into the wood.

"I am so screwed."

Shaun laughed.

"Well, if it's any consolation, you're not failing Tracking. And Lewis tells me you're doing well in Law, too."

Law being the only subject here that held any interest whatsoever for me, even if shifter law was completely FUBAR'd.

"So, you're going to have private sessions with Brendon every Saturday and Sunday. You've got a few months yet. You can do this, Jade. We all believe in you. And if we didn't, we'd be having a very different sort of conversation right now."

I'm sure he meant that to be reassuring, but it really wasn't.

"There's one more thing we need to talk about."

I straightened in time to catch the uneasy look on his face that matched the tone of his voice.

"Christmas break is in two weeks. Most of the other students will return to their packs. But you don't have a pack to return to."

"I'm going to get stuck here, aren't I?"

"You should be, yes. But I'm inclined to give you the benefit of the doubt, and Alpha Blake agrees. You can stay here, if you want. Or you can return to the farm."

I weighed that for a moment. I had no family at the farm, and I didn't think going back to the city to catch up with old friends was going to be an option. And all my new friends were here. Cam was here. But they were probably all going home for Christmas.

Shaun kept quiet, giving me the space to work through my decision. But it wasn't much of a decision, not really. Alright, I was never going to be Fur 'n' Fang's biggest fan, but this place had become my home over the last few months. And I didn't think it was the smartest move for me to spend four weeks by myself.

"I'd like to stay here, if that's okay."

Shaun didn't quite manage to keep the look of surprise from his face, but I'd give him ten out of ten for effort.

"Of course. If you change your mind…"

"Yeah. And thanks."

*

I didn't change my mind. When the day came, the instructors opened up a dozen portals, sending the students back to their packs – but not before fitting each of the first and second years with a set of suppressor cuffs. At least staying here meant I wasn't subjected to those.

I wasn't the only one who stayed. Most of the wolves left – family and pack being as important as it was to them. A few stayed, though. Cam offered, when he found out I was going to be here. He didn't want me to be alone, he said, but it would have been selfish of me to deny him his only chance to see his kid brother before the end of the academic year, so I told him I'd be fine. I wasn't completely sure it was true – four weeks rattling around here by myself didn't sound like much fun. Luckily, Mei was staying, too. Dean wasn't, but at least that meant I didn't have to watch him and Madison fawning all over each other.

My time wasn't entirely my own – some of the instructors were staying, amongst them Brendon and

Shaun, which meant my daily dose of torturous shifting sessions would continue. But at least Shaun agreed that I didn't need to see him every day for our chats – presumably since I didn't have any proper lessons to show up my numerous inadequacies. For now, he agreed to cut our sessions to twice weekly.

Which meant I suddenly had a lot of free time on my hands.

It turns out I wasn't great with free time. I hadn't had a whole lot of it up until now – what with school, and college, and trying to get accepted at UCL. And then coming here, being miles behind, and of course Cam keeping me busy...

My mouth stretched into a lazy smile that faded as I looked down at the book in front of me. It turned out Fur 'n' Fang had a library, which probably wasn't that surprising given that this was an academy. It was just that I hadn't had much cause to find it before now. But I'd meant what I said to Shaun – I fully intended to convince UCL to accept me as a mature student when I was done here, and since I wouldn't be able to tell them what I'd been doing for the last three years, I figured I'd have to wow them with my legal genius instead. Unfortunately, it turned out Fur 'n' Fang didn't keep that sort of book in their library. But since I was apparently going to have to sit a load of exams, and since apparently I was failing most of my subjects, I'd decided now that I'd found the library, I might as well use it to get caught up in some of them. The trouble was, there was nothing about the role of therianthropy in the first Roman invasion of Britain that particularly held my attention, and I'd read the same paragraph half a dozen times before my mind had gone to more interesting subjects. Like Cam.

…But, pleasant though those daydreams were, they weren't going to get this paper written. I scanned the book again and jotted some names down. Anarevitos was the guy in charge of the British defence, and by all accounts, he was a bit of a bastard. His druids had cast rage spells on a bunch of shifters he'd conscripted onto the front lines, turning them into mindless killers – right up until the Romans slaughtered them with silver-tipped spears. Even back then, druids had been controlling shifters and forcing us to do their bidding, the self-righteous, sanctimonious–

I heard a cracking noise, and glanced down at the splintered pen crushed in my hand. Great. Now they'd made me ruin a perfectly good pen. Bastards.

"I know the assignment is dull, but don't you think that's a bit of an overreaction?"

I twisted round with a grin.

"Mei! What are you doing down here?"

"I think that is my line. Brendon asked me to find you."

"What? What time is it?" I threw a glance over my shoulder at the clock on the wall. "Shit. My lesson. Gotta go!"

I slammed the book shut and crammed my notepad in my bag, and almost fell over the chair in my haste to make it to Brendon's lecture room before I gave him another excuse to chew me out.

"Here," Mei said, untangling my bag strap from the chair leg. I nodded her my thanks. "I'll walk with you."

"How did you even know I'd be here?"

"Oh." She shrugged. "I followed your scent."

I groaned, hefting my bag onto my back, and wondering how quickly I could heal from a broken spine.

"I am so far behind everyone it's ridiculous."

"I can help you… if you want?"

I shot a glance at her to see her chewing her lower lip. I got the sense that offering to help me was a big deal, and I thought I knew why. I mean, I was an outcast because of what had happened to me at the farm. But before that, I'd fit in my entire life – more or less. Mei hadn't. She'd always been an outcast. Therianthropy was genetic. Both her mother and her father had been leopards. There had never been any doubt that she would be, too. And in this world, if you weren't a wolf, you were an outcast. People didn't often turn to outcasts for help.

I, on the other hand, had no such reservations. A grin spread across my face.

"Mei, if you can get me caught up, I will love you forever."

Chapter Eighteen

Of course, when I'd said that, I'd thought it would involve a little less… work. It turned out Mei was doing well in all our classes because she actually worked her arse off, which was a shame, because I'd really been hoping for some sort of magic shortcut. But beggars can't be choosers, and it wasn't like I had a whole lot else to spend my days doing, so we spent a couple of hours a day outside, with Mei laying scent trails and me attempting to follow them.

The days whiled away. I studied in the library, tracked with Mei, practiced shifting with Brendon, and questioned my sanity with Shaun.

"I'm impressed with how much effort you're putting into your studies," Shaun said, on the afternoon of New Years' Eve – because apparently the fact the dozen of us who'd stayed at Fur 'n' Fang had plans to get very drunk tonight wasn't enough to get me out of my counselling sessions.

I didn't mind, not really – sometimes I even found them quite helpful. And honestly, I hadn't expected Shaun to let it drop. It was the full moon last night – the one time a month when I couldn't prevent myself from shifting. At least, not yet. Most of the wolves in my year had already learned to control it, and Mei's leopard had never been subject to the call of the full moon, but I still had to be locked up in the shifting room from moon rise to moon set, and as usual when I'd come to this morning, I'd had no memory of anything that had happened between those two moments.

"Jade, did you hear a word I said?"

I blinked Shaun back into focus and tried to recall the last thing I'd heard him say.

"Uh… I'm putting effort into my studies?"

Shaun shook his head slowly from side to side. I think he moved passed exasperation to acceptance a long time ago. Guess I'd zoned out for a while there.

"Never mind, it wasn't important. Rough night?"

"The same as always – I woke up feeling like I'd been hit by a truck." I groaned and leaned back in my chair. "Why can't I ever remember what happens?"

"The full moon has a powerful influence over your shifted form, like a drug. Until you learn to resist its call, it will control your inner-beast."

"I know, I know… When the beast controls me, the memories are hers, not mine. But I can't control that side of me."

"It will take time. You just have to be patient."

"No-one else is taking this long."

"They all grew up in this world. Eighteen years. And we both know there are still students in your year who can't control the change. You've been a shifter for four months. So cut yourself some slack. It wasn't that long ago you were trying to dig under the walls. Yes, I was aware."

He watched me with amused eyes, so I figured I probably wasn't in that much trouble. It had been months ago, not long after I'd discovered the walls were unclimbable. And I'd figured if I couldn't go over the wall, I'd go under it. Back when I still thought I could outrun this. But it turned out wards didn't work that way. Neither did running.

"I was an idiot."

"No. You needed time to accept what happened to you. Believe me, Jade, you handled it much better than anyone could have hoped." He leaned back and regarded me for a long moment. "And you're not going to like what I have to tell you."

I barked a bitter laugh.

"How many conversations are we going to have where you tell me things I don't like?"

"Well, to be honest, Jade, I thought we'd reached the end of them, but it turns out I was wrong. It's about Leo."

My right hand twitched, and I made a conscious effort to still it. Just his name was enough to burn my insides with white hot fury. But if Shaun was bringing him up…

"The druids aren't handing him over, are they?"

"No. But not for the reasons you think. There's no easy way to tell you this, so I'm just going to come out and say it. Leo is innocent. The wolf who attacked you is still out there."

"What? No, he can't be. He… He bit me. You said so. Draeven said so."

"We were wrong. I'm sorry."

"Then… who?"

Shaun shook his head.

"We don't know. But we will find them, and they will pay for what they did to you. I promise."

Leo was innocent. This whole time, these last two months, I'd had a name to pin on my attacker. I'd known that someone would face justice, one way or another, for the shit show my life had become. Someone would be held accountable. It made getting out of bed more bearable. And now Shaun was telling me they'd had the wrong guy? After all this time, they had nothing. I was no closer to getting closure than the day I'd been bitten.

"Wait." An icy feeling was clawing its way up my spine. "How do they know it wasn't him?" Because I doubted they'd have taken his word for it.

"Someone else was attacked. They turned last night."

My stomach churned, and I doubled over. Someone else. The shifter who bit me had gone after someone else. Their life had been ruined, because Draeven and the druids had been fighting over the wrong guy. A guy who'd been locked up because *I* hadn't been able to tell Draeven anything about the night I'd been attacked. Because I hadn't been able to identify the wolf that had done it. I was as guilty as the wolf who'd bitten me. That wasn't acceptable.

I gritted my teeth and forced myself back upright.

"What can I do to help?"

"You need to focus on yourself."

"That's not going to cut it, Shaun," I said, and caught the rising volume of my voice. I lowered it and made myself carry on. "This is my fault. I need to make it right."

"No. This was the action of a criminal. You aren't to blame, Jade. Look at me. This is not your fault."

His eyes burned into mine and I broke away, not because of any compulsion to submit, but because I couldn't stand to see the faith there. The sincerity. Because I could have stopped this, and we both knew it.

"Look at me," he said again. "This is not your fault. You didn't bite that man."

"No, I just didn't give Draeven what he needed to know he had the wrong person. Two months, Shaun.

Two months they could have been looking for the shifter responsible. That's on me."

I wrapped my arms around myself, like I could disappear into them and hide from this whole sorry mess. This sorry mess I could have prevented.

"No, it's not. What happened is not your fault."

"Please," I said, and my voice came out as little more than a whisper. "Please, stop saying that."

"You need to hear this. It was not your fault."

"I should have found a way to remember. I should have fought back harder when he attacked me. I should never have gone to the farm alone. I should–"

The words dissolved into sobs, and then Shaun's arm was around me, comforting me when I didn't deserve any comfort, and I gave in to the tears and just let them flow.

I don't know how long I cried – truly cried for the first time since this had all started, but Shaun just let me get it all out, making soothing noises until I ran out of tears.

I drew in a shuddering breath and dragged my hand across my eyes. Shaun squatted in front of me at arm's length.

"I'm going to say it one more time," he said. "And then you're going to say it. Okay? It was not your fault. There was nothing you could have done."

"It... it wasn't my fault," I mumbled, my voice uncertain. Shaun nodded his encouragement. "There was nothing I could have done."

"Exactly." His eyes searched my face, and I wasn't sure what they found there. "You're not responsible for the actions of another person. Nothing you did caused any of this. None of it, you understand?"

I nodded and he got up and moved away, then returned with a glass of water. We both sat in silence until I finished it.

"I still want to help," I said. Shaun opened his mouth to speak, but I shook my head and carried on. "Not for the reasons you think. I know what he's going through. Probably better than anyone else alive. I remember how awful those first weeks were."

Shaun watched me silently, and I could see him weighing my words. Eventually, he nodded.

"I think you're right. But I don't want you jeopardising your own progress. You've worked so hard to get where you are. We'll go and see him, but only as long as it doesn't set you back. The minute it gets too much, I want you to tell me."

"Oh, please," I said, forcing false bravado into my voice, and a cocky smile onto my face. "I'm Jade Hart. I can handle anything."

"Yeah, that's what I was afraid of. Come on."

.le led me from his office down to the once-familiar angeon door. I hadn't been back here for a while, and I hadn't planned to come back any time soon – but fate seemed to take a certain amount of pleasure in pissing on my plans.

He paused, one hand on the door.

"Ryan, he… Well, I want you to prepare yourself. He's not adjusting well."

"Pfft. I survived your psychoanalysis attempt. This is nothing."

"I'm serious, Jade."

I held his eye.

"So am I. I'm ready for this."

He searched my face for a long, uncomfortable moment before he dipped his chin, and pushed open the door. We descended the stone staircase in silence, into the corridor lit with an odd combination of flickering lights and flaming torches. A shudder ran through me, and I stifled it before Shaun could notice and insist I go back out again. Truth was, I had no idea if I was ready for this. But that had never stopped me before.

A figure loomed at the bottom of the stairwell, and it took a moment for my eyes to pick him out in the dim light. When I did, my bravado failed and I blanched, falling a few steps behind Shaun. Fletcher fixed his eyes on us – on me – and I could see the tension in his jaw.

"What is she doing here?"

"Jade thought she could help, and I agree," Shaun said, as we reached the bottom of the steps. Fletcher stood in the middle of the corridor, blocking our path.

"She shouldn't even know."

"She had a right to know."

"A right?" Fletcher laughed; an angry, mocking sound. "She's not even one of us. Four months ago, she was trying to scale the walls and endanger the local mundane population."

"Uh, I never wanted that," I put in, raising a hand. Both the instructors ignored me.

"And that is exactly why she's uniquely qualified to help with this situation."

"And what else have you told her?"

My interest sharpened, though I stayed half-hidden behind Shaun. Fletcher scared the crap out of me when he wasn't pissed off.

"She knows about Ryan, and she knows about Leo."

The two men shared an unspoken conversation in the dimly lit hallway, and eventually some of the stiffness eased from Fletcher's shoulders.

"Fine. But I don't like it, and I want that on record with Alpha Blake."

"Noted."

Fletcher glared past Shaun to me, and the skin between my shoulder blades prickled with cold anxiety.

"You will not utter a word to anyone about Ryan until we deem that he is ready to join the academy's population. And you will *never* come down here without an escort, or you will find yourself back in a cell. Permanently. Is that clear?"

I swallowed and ducked my head.

"Yes, Instructor Fletcher."

He turned and placed his hand on the first door on the left.

"Why don't you leave this to us?" Shaun suggested. "I'm sure Alpha Blake would like to be appraised of recent developments."

Fletcher brushed past us up the stairs, and the tingling sensation went with him.

"Still want to do this?" Shaun asked. I nodded. "Alright."

He opened the door and swung it inwards, then stepped aside for me to enter. I took a deep breath and crossed the threshold.

Chapter Nineteen

He was a little older than me, perhaps by a year or two, and he was sitting at the back of his cell, glowering out at us like his personal trip to hell was our fault.

It wasn't an entirely unfair accusation – Shaun had let him get locked in a cage, and I was standing right here with him. Guilty by association. When I'd been on the other side of those bars, I probably looked at them all like that, too.

"Hey, Ryan," I said, stepping closer to the bars so he could see me properly. "I'm Jade."

Ryan looked from me to Shaun and snorted.

"What, the intimidation act didn't work, so you decided to try the honey trap instead?"

"I'll take that as a compliment," I said, and his eyes snapped back to me. "But no. That's not why I'm here."

"Then why?"

"I know what you're going through."

He curled his lip, running his eyes over me, sizing me up. I could guess what he saw: an eighteen-year-old uni student, naïve looking and innocent, with maybe a little trace of red around her eyes. Someone who hadn't lived a whole hell of a lot. Someone who'd had a sheltered upbringing.

"I doubt that." He gave his head a sharp shake.

"Really?" I yanked my trouser leg up, showing the circle of scar tissue from the shifter's teeth. "Then explain this."

He leaned forward an inch, narrowing his eyes at my scar.

"That's... a bite. Like mine."

I nodded and let my trouser leg drop.

"You okay?" Shaun asked in my ear. I nodded. I hated showing my scar, but it was the fastest way to get through to this guy. Maybe the only way. And he needed to know I was on his side.

Ryan took hold of the hem of his t-shirt, and hesitated. It was a Fur 'n' Fang t-shirt, I couldn't help but notice. He must have already shredded his own. That meant he'd shifted at least once – probably last night, under the full moon. He pulled the fabric up.

I gasped before I got a hold of myself. His bite wasn't like mine. He hadn't been bitten just once. He'd been bitten again, and again. At least five bites, all over his torso. How the hell had he survived that?

Ryan let the material fall again, covering his mutilated flesh.

"Did you get bit by the same bastard that got me?"

I nodded, and took a moment to find my voice.

"Yes. I'm sorry that happened to you. It's a lot to take in, huh?" I glanced around the room, underscoring my meaning.

"They say there's no cure for this," he said. He jerked his chin at Shaun, who stayed unobtrusively at my shoulder. "Him, and the others. Is it true?"

"It is. Everything they've told you is the truth. But it's not that bad." I wrapped my arms around myself. "Once you get used to it."

He got to his feet and moved to the bars, wrapping his hands around them and looking them up and down through bitter eyes.

"And these?"

"Temporary," I said, taking a step closer to him. I searched his face and took a step closer still, closing the gap between us. "I've been where you are now. And believe me, nothing you can do is going to change what happened, or what you've become."

"So, what," he said, clenching his trembling hands tighter around the bars until his knuckles turned white. "Just accept that my life is over?" I could hear his teeth grinding as he clenched his jaw.

"Not over," I said. "Changed."

"Not over? How can you say that? Look at me!"

He thrust an arm through the bars and grabbed hold of my wrist, yanking me closer to him until we were almost nose to nose through the cage. I pulled back, but his grip was too strong, his fingers cutting into my skin.

"Ow, you're hurting me, get off!"

"Get off her!" Shaun shouted, surging forward.

I grabbed hold of Ryan's wrist with my other hand, trying to prise him off me, but he was too strong. This was what I got for trying to help people. Fuck's sake!

My hand flashed red and Ryan staggered back, clutching his wrist to his chest. The acrid stench of seared flesh stung my nostrils, and a series of red burns marked his skin. Burns in the shape of my fingers.

"I'm sorry," Ryan said, trembling as he backed up to the far wall. "I'm so sorry. I don't know why I did that."

Shaun ignored him, turning to stare at me. His face looked pale in the flickering light, a mirror of my own.

"What did you do to him?"

"I don't know, it just happened." My voice shook as I stared down at my hands. I jerked my eyes up to Shaun, pleading with him. "It's a shifter thing, right? It's got to be."

"No, Jade, that's not a shifter thing."

I reached out to the bars for support. I'd burned Ryan. With my hands.

"What the hell's going on?" Ryan said, shooting looks between me and Shaun, as if he thought one of us might have the answer to this craziness. Shaun shook his head.

"I don't know. And until I do, this never happened. Understand?"

Ryan nodded. I nodded. We both stared at each other in horror. I took a shaky breath.

"Are you okay?" I asked him. "Sorry, dumb question. Of course you're not."

"No, I'm fine. It's okay." He held his wrist up. "Barely stings."

He lowered his wrist, frowning at it, and I knew what he was thinking. Same thing I'd have been thinking in his position. *Why* did it barely sting? Why were the burn marks fading already?

"Shifter healing," I said, lowering myself onto the floor, just out of arm's reach of the cage. "See, told you it wasn't all bad."

"I think we should take a break," Shaun said. "Jade?"

I glanced up at him and shook my head.

"I'm fine. Honestly."

I was pretty sure I'd never been less fine, but if Ryan saw me freaking out right now, how was he ever going to come to terms with what was happening to him? We could worry about what was happening to *me* later.

"Do you..." He broke off, and then started again. "Is the rage a part of it?"

I threw a look over my shoulder at Shaun, because that was a good question.

"Is it?" I asked. "Is the rage because we were bitten?"

Shaun grimaced.

"We don't know. There's nothing documented about Bittens being more aggressive, but it does seem to be a… common factor."

"Sucks to be us," I said. Ryan grunted his agreement.

"I think that's enough of a pity party for one day," Shaun said. "We should go."

What he meant was he thought *I* should go, before I had another breakdown. But I wasn't the important one right now. I got up and took a few steps back from the cage, lowering my voice.

"I can help him. Please, Shaun."

"You are my priority. You've had a stressful day, and I don't think being here is helping you."

"And I don't think," I echoed his words with an edge, "I'll be able to sleep tonight if I don't at least try."

"This isn't–"

"–My fault. I know. But if I walk away and leave him, when I could be of some comfort, then that would be my fault. And it would be unforgiveable. I've been there, remember? In that cage. Confused. Scared I was losing it. He needs to talk to someone who knows what he's going through."

"Alright. We'll stay a while longer."

I shook my head.

"I need to talk to him alone. He's not going to open up while you're here. I'm guessing he didn't exactly find his way into that cage willingly."

"No, he didn't." He drummed his fingers against his thigh and darted a look at the Bitten. "I don't know Jade, I don't like this. His temper seems worse than yours ever was."

"But hey, at least he's not crying, right?" My attempt at levity fell flat. "I'll be fine. Just ten minutes. Just so he knows he's not alone."

"Fine. I'll get him some food. Ten minutes. And you stay away from those bars. I mean it."

He locked eyes with me in case I didn't realise he meant it, and I nodded.

"I've got it. It'll be fine."

Shaun turned and left, making a point of leaving the door open behind him. I rolled my eyes – behind his back – and then turned to Ryan.

"How much have they told you?" I asked, strolling back to his cage, but making sure I was out of arm's reach. Though, apparently, I now had a pretty effective way to defend myself. I lowered myself onto the floor again and watched him.

"That I'm a…" he swallowed, then twisted his lips around the word, "werewolf. That I'm dangerous to people now."

"Just until you learn to control yourself."

"I guess I'm stuck in here until I can?" He gestured to the cage, then pounded his fist against the wall. "What the hell gives them the right to lock me up?"

"No, you're right," I said. "Much better they let you out to maul someone."

He turned his head away.

"Look, you've got two choices," I told him. "You accept what you are now, and make an effort to control yourself, and join the rest of the academy, or you stay down here until you do."

"Well, those both sound like a barrel of laughs."

"Yeah, not gonna lie. The dungeon sucks, but up top they make you do term papers. It's kinda hard to say which is worse."

He made a sound that was almost a laugh and traced his fingers over the brickwork at the back of the cage.

"What about the other option?"

"Other option?"

He twisted round and locked eyes with me.

"You know the one I'm talking about."

"You can't break out of here. The bars are inlaid with silver, and the academy's surrounded by a warded wall."

"Warded?"

"Enchanted. Trust me, you can't get out. And why would you want to – have you been listening to me?

You're a shifter, and if you lose control, you're going to hurt someone."

"Right. The, uh, the mundanes? They care about protecting them, yeah? Well, what about protecting me? Where were they then? Where were they when that... wolf... was ripping me to shreds? Why was no-one there for *me*?"

I had no answer for that. No good one, anyway.

"You survived," I said. "That's something. And this life? It's not as bad as you think, if you give it a chance."

I got up and dusted myself off.

"Or you can carry on feeling sorry for yourself. What happened to you – to us – is shit. No-one's denying that. But what happens next? That's in your hands." I headed for the door. "I'll see you soon."

I paused and threw a glance back over my shoulder.

"Or I won't. Your choice."

Chapter Twenty

I'm sorry. I was out of line. I didn't mean what I said. Madison really isn't that bad."

I rolled my eyes at Mei and stretched out on my bed.

"Yeah, I'm not going to say any of that."

"Well, you have to say something. Dean is coming back today."

"I know, I know." I groaned and pulled my pillow over my head. The rest of Christmas break had flown past with dizzying speed, and now here we were, a week into January and getting ready for the semester to start up again soon. Tomorrow, in fact. Which meant, as Mei had so helpfully pointed out, that everyone was coming back to the academy – and I was going to have to face Dean.

"Good. Because if you two don't stop squabbling, I'm moving out."

I rolled my head and squinted at Mei from under my pillow. She was sitting cross-legged on her bed, making notes from a textbook.

"The only spare bed is in this room."

"I'll sleep in the hall."

"Alright, I get it," I said, sitting up and tossing the pillow back down. "But I'm not going to take back what I said about Madison. She's a bitch, and she'd maul both of us if she thought she could get away with it."

Mei shrugged. Not even she could argue with that. But she was right about one thing: it was time I got over myself and made it up with Dean. I'd never have got through my first weeks here without him. And visiting Ryan in the dungeon was giving me a very stark look at what my life could have been like. But I couldn't say any of that to Mei, since Shaun was holding me to my promise not to say anything about him being locked up. As far as my friend was concerned, I was just having an extra couple of sessions with Shaun a week. Apparently, I was screwed up enough that she didn't question my cover story, which wasn't the most flattering thing in the world, but it wasn't the worst thing going on in my life right now, either.

A knock sounded at the door.

"You decent?" Dean called from outside.

"Yes, come in," Mei said.

The door swung inwards and Dean greeted Mei with a smile.

"Hey, Mei, good to see you."

He seemed to notice me for the first time, and his smile faltered.

"Oh, hi, Jade. I thought you'd be with Cam."

"He's not back yet," I said. Mei coughed and arched an eyebrow at me.

"It's, uh, it's good to see you again," I said.

"You, too."

I sucked in a breath and swung my legs off the bed. Best to just get it over with, right? Then he could tell me he still hated me, and we could get back to ignoring each other.

"Look, I'm sorry. I was out of order before." I stared down at my hands, entwining my fingers with each other, and ignored the way he was looking at me. "I don't like Madison, but I understand why you're with her, and I'll try to be happy for you. I promise. Can we just… can we go back to being friends? Please?"

"Come here, Just Jade," he said. He crossed the floor and wrapped me in a bear hug, then lifted one hand.

"I swear to God, if you even think about messing up my hair, I'm going to bite you."

He laughed but dropped his hand back down.

"It's good to have you back, you bitey midget," he said, as I wiggled out of his bear hug.

"I'm not the one who went anywhere," I said with a pout, which I quickly banished. I squinted up at him. "So, we're okay? Friends again?"

"Friends again," he agreed. "Look, I know you're never going to see eye to eye with Madison – not least because she's several inches taller than you–"

I aimed a swipe at his head, but he dodged and continued,

"–but can you at least try? She's not all bad."

"I'll believe that when I see it," I grumbled, but if pretending to be nice to Madison was what it would take for things to go back to normal between me and Dean, then I was willing to put on my best acting face. Or at least, try.

"Crap, is that the time?" I asked, throwing a glance up at the clock on the wall. "I gotta go."

"Where?" Dean asked, frowning as he pulled off his shoes and tossed them to one side of the room. Mei followed their trajectory with a scowl but said nothing. I guessed she was too happy that there was finally some sort of peace to moan about Dean's sloppy habits. For now.

"I've, uh, got a session with Shaun."

"On a Sunday? Brutal."

"Don't I know it." I yanked open the door. "Catch you later."

I hurried off down the hallway before any of them could question it further. The academy was getting busier now, with half of the students already back from their break, and more arriving by the minute. I threw a few glances over my shoulder as I went, making sure that no-one was paying attention to me as I made my way to the dungeon.

I grabbed the door handle and rattled it, but it was locked. Crap. I obviously wasn't the only one who was running late today. Shaun usually brought Ryan his evening meal around this time. I was going to be a bit conspicuous loitering around outside the dungeon if anyone happened past. But I promised Ryan I'd be back this evening, and I really did think my visits were helping. He seemed less angry, at least.

I'd just decided to head over to the main hall and see if I could find Shaun when there was a loud creak, and the door opened. Blake stepped through, then stopped, furrowing his brow when he caught sight of me.

"Ms Hart. What are you doing here?"

"I've, um, I've come to see Ryan."

He glanced up and down the hallway, but we were alone. He beckoned me through the door, and shut it behind us.

"I'll thank you not to loiter outside the dungeon door. You do understand the concept of discretion?"

"Yes, Alpha Blake. Sorry. I was just – well, I was supposed to meet Shaun."

"I'm sure he'll be along shortly. He had some… other duties to attend to. For my part, I'm not sure how much benefit either of you will get from this visit."

He slotted his key into the first door on the left.

"But Alpha Blake, I thought he was making good progress. He's wearing a training cuff, not a pair of suppressors now, right?"

"It is not his progress that hinders him, but his attitude."

He fixed me with a look. Oh, I got it, now. Blake had thought I had a bad attitude, too, when I first arrived here. He didn't think all that much of my attitude now, come to that. And he obviously didn't think I was a good influence. What else was new?

"I have offered him a place within the academy's programs this coming semester, but he continues to resist. And if he refuses to learn, then eventually Alpha Draeven will be forced to pass judgement."

I swallowed. I didn't think that would end well – nor did I want to find myself in the same building as him again, if I could help it. He might decide to pass judgement on me, too. He was another one who'd had an issue with my attitude. Seemed like it was a common theme with alphas.

Blake unlocked the door, and I slipped inside. The key scraped in the lock behind me, sealing me inside, and

I tried to ignore the panic clawing its way up my throat. Unlike Ryan, my incarceration was temporary – just until Shaun got here.

"You're back."

I picked out the figure sitting in the gloom, with his back pressed to the wall at the back of his cell and inclined my head to him.

"I'm back," I agreed.

"Where's your chaperone?"

"Yeah, good question." I grabbed the stool from the corner of the room and dragged it over to the cell. "Looks like it's just us for now."

"Don't suppose you've got a key hidden in that hoodie?"

"Nope," I said, parking myself on the stool. "But I don't need one. I just saw Blake. He literally offered to let you out of here."

Ryan snorted and folded his arms.

"Sure, to go upstairs and play student with the rest of the pack puppies. I need to get out of here. Right out."

"And that's how you do it," I said, rolling my eyes. Ryan dropped his arms and leaned forward.

"You've got a way over the wall?"

"What? No, you idiot. I meant, you go upstairs and learn how to control yourself, and then they let you out of the front gate."

"I'm not an idiot."

He glared at me, then stared down at the pitted floor between his feet. One of his hands was curled into a fist, and its outline was blurred. He took a few deep breaths, glaring down at the floor, and then the tension dropped from his shoulders, and the outline of his hand became sharper again.

"No, you're not," I agreed, once he had himself fully under control. "So stop acting like one. Three years, and you get to walk away and go back to your own life."

"Three years for a crime I didn't commit."

"Better that than a death sentence."

He jerked his eyes up to meet mine.

"Death sentence?"

"What do you think is going to happen if you keep fighting them? Best case scenario, they'll keep you down here until you're not a threat anymore – however many years that takes. Sooner or later, Blake will summon the Alpha of Alphas, and if he thinks you can't be integrated, if he thinks they can't stop you being a threat to mundanes, he'll have you killed. They don't mess around with this stuff."

"Yeah, I'm getting that."

He leaned back against the wall, staring up at the ceiling. I gave him a moment alone with his thoughts. It was a lot to process, I knew that. But I also knew that given the choice of death, a cage, and three years of schooling, it should have been an easy decision. Even if he was pissed off. Even with the same bad attitude I had. I had come around, eventually. He had to, too.

"Look, it's not as bad as you think. They teach you how to control your shift. And they teach you the rules. We have meditation classes to help us control our emotions. And sure, there's some crap, too, and some of the other shifters are dicks. But it's your only way out of here. Alive, at least."

"I always sucked at school," he said, still looking up at the ceiling. "I flunked high school, never bothered with college. I hated it. I built myself a life away from all that."

"Funny how life works, huh?" I figured it was best not to mention that there was no flunking Fur 'n' Fang, because they'd just keep holding you back until eventually you got it. "I can help you. Shaun can help you. It's not like high school here. And really, how can it be any worse than this?"

I gestured to his cell.

The sound of the key turning in the lock made us both jump, and I spun round in time to see Shaun coming in with a tray of food. Ryan got to his feet and dusted his hands down on his dark cargo trousers.

"Hey, Shaun," he said, nodding at the tray. "Can I get that to go?"

Chapter Twenty-One

I can't believe you didn't tell us," Dean said, and Mei nodded her head in agreement. I shot a glance over at Fletcher, but he was busy correcting Madison's attempts to reverse Tyler's grip.

"Hey, I'm shacked up with her, and she didnae tell me," Cam said. I slapped him on the shoulder.

"We are not shacked up – and you weren't even here! Anyway, Shaun swore me to secrecy. It wasn't like I had a choice."

"Right. Because y' always do what the instructors say."

Well, he had me there.

"Fletcher," Mei said from the corner of her mouth.

"Saved by the instructor," Cam said, and grabbed hold of my throat. I tensed my neck to protect my windpipe, but relaxed the rest of my body. One hand shot up to trap his hand against me, pinning him in place, and I twisted sideways, opening up a tiny gap between his palm and my throat. It was all I needed. I forced my thumb into the gap and squeezed down between his thumb and index finger. His hand spasmed, and I wrenched it away and bent it back, keeping the pressure on his wrist. One small step put me behind him, with his arm outstretched between us him. A few more pounds of pressure would be enough to break his shoulder, but I was quite attached to those hulking shoulders, so instead I just stood over him, smirking.

"I'm not the one who needs saving," I told him sweetly.

"Damn," he said, rubbing his shoulder as I released him. "Yer've been practicing."

"Good to see my lessons haven't been entirely wasted on you, Ms Hart," Fletcher said, and we all put on crap pretences of having not seen him lurking behind us.

"Switch partners," he said. "Jade, with Madison. Dean, with Ryan."

He gestured them over from opposite ends of the clearing, and Mei and Cam headed off to take their places. Just my luck. Madison. She didn't look any happier about it than I was as she headed over, her lips pressed tightly together – but then I realised her glare was directed at Ryan, not me.

"Carry on," Fletcher said, then moved off to terrorise someone else for a while.

"Bad enough that there's one outsider here," Madison said to Dean, and eyeing Ryan. "We shouldn't be subjected to two."

I didn't punch her because it was only yesterday I promised Dean I'd make an effort with her. I had to stop making dumb promises.

"Mads," Dean said, raising an eyebrow at her. She flicked her blonde ponytail aside.

"Well, it's true. Fur 'n' Fang used to stand for something."

"Trust me, Princess," Ryan said, glaring at the blonde, "this is the last place I want to be. And if it hadn't been for one of your kind, I wouldn't be here."

"How dare you speak to me like that! Get away from me, you dirty cur."

Tension shot through Ryan's jaw, and he squared his shoulders. His hands curled into fists.

"Back off, tough guy," Dean said, putting himself between the pair.

"All of you, knock it off," I snapped, grabbing hold of Ryan's arm and towing him a step backwards. I left Dean to deal with his bitch of a girlfriend, because frankly I was all in favour of letting Ryan deck her. I stopped short of letting Ryan know that, though.

"Are you really going to make it that easy for her?" I asked him. "Get a grip on yourself. This is exactly what she wants."

"She shouldn't have called me a cur," he said, his voice sullen.

"What are you, twelve?" I glossed over the fact I'd nearly lumped her on my first day for much the same thing. "You think I haven't been called that, and worse?"

"We shouldn't have to put up with that."

I took a breath and let it out slowly.

"You're right. We shouldn't. But in case no-one's told you, the world isn't a fair place. People like that, born with privilege and status? They are everywhere, and like it or not, they're going to flaunt it. And if you go round hitting them all, the only thing you're going to prove is that everything they ever said about you was right."

"So, what, let it go – that's what you're saying?" He didn't sound convinced. "Just turn the other cheek?"

"Hell, no," I said with a grin, and turned back to the she-wolf. "Hey, Madison, are you done stalling? I mean, if you're too scared to train with me, you could always just say."

Her hands clenched into fists – way too easy – and her lips twisted into a snarl.

"I'm not afraid of you, *cur*."

"Sticks and stones," I said, rolling my shoulders as I advanced on her.

"Jade…" Dean said in my ear as I reached him. I felt a stab of remorse – just a tiny one, though. It couldn't be easy for him to be stuck between us. I lowered my voice.

"Relax, I won't hurt her." Because she was probably going to kick my arse any second, like she had every other time we'd 'trained' together. "Take it easy on Ryan, okay?

He's all kinds of messed up right now. It's a lot to deal with. I know."

Some of the tension eased out of Dean's shoulders.

"Yeah, okay. You're right."

I left them to it, hoping Ryan wouldn't blow it by trying to rip Dean's head off. Tensions had a habit of spilling over in Combat class, but even shifters had limits. I'd just have to trust he was capable of not acting like a child – while I went off to do exactly that with Madison.

"Come on, then," I said, raising a hand and beckoning her forward. She rushed me, covering the ground easily, and clamped one hand around my throat – then squeezed. Yup. This was going to end about as well as taking a cruise on the Titanic. Fletcher really had it in for me. Just once it would be nice if he didn't partner me with someone who'd been fighting since before they could walk. I could already feel my skin bruising under her grip.

I held her eye and clamped my hand over hers, pinning it to me, and twisted sideways. A sharp sting buried itself into my skin, too sharp to be human fingernails. Shit, had she partially shifted? One look at the malice in her eyes, and the cocky smile on her face, told me the answer. When the hell had she learned to do that? She clenched her fingers, and I felt her claws burrowing deeper into me. I hissed in pain, then clenched my jaw and jammed my thumb between her hand and my neck. I squeezed the pressure point and twisted, putting my shoulder into it. Her claws ripped from around my throat, coated in a dark layer of wetness. My blood.

I ignored the pain and forced her arm up behind her, snarling as I put all my weight into it. She twisted round sideways, righting herself and throwing me off balance. I caught sight of her face for long enough to see the smirk as she tossed me into the dirt. *Oh no, you don't. Not this time.* I gripped her wrist harder, yanking her towards me as I fell, and ignored the sharp rap of pain as I thudded into the ground. The impact rattled her balance, and I lashed out with a leg, hooking it behind her knee and tossing her onto the ground next to me. Shock pasted itself all over her face – it was a lucky blow, and neither of us had been expecting it – but I recovered first and leapt on top of her, straddling her chest and pinning her arms to the ground with my knees. Huh. So, this was what it felt like to be the one doing the arse-kicking.

A few stray drops of blood dripped down from my neck and Madison stared up at me in horror. Not at the wound she'd inflicted – that'd heal soon enough – but at the knowledge that in this second, she was at my mercy.

And then I remembered my promise to Dean. Crap.

I stepped off her and offered her my hand. She stared at it and peeled her lips back in a snarl. I shrugged and let my hand drop back to my side. Couldn't say I hadn't tried.

She flexed her hips and leapt straight up onto her feet, then threw herself at me.

"Madison Capell." Fletcher's voice cracked through the air, and Madison froze. I clearly wasn't the only one who hadn't heard him approaching. "Enough. Go and take a walk. Come back when you're capable of behaving like a Fur 'n' Fang student."

"Sorry, Instructor Fletcher," she said, hanging her head – but not before sending one last hate-filled glare in my direction. She turned and walked past him.

"Not bad, Jade," Fletcher said, looking me up and down. "It seems like I'm not completely wasting my time with you, after all."

I had the sense not to point out that it was Mei's training that had given me my newfound edge – proving that my self-restraint had come a helluva long way in four and a half months.

With Madison cooling off, the rest of the session passed peacefully. Even Dean and Ryan seemed to overcome their animosity. Dean was a decent guy, despite his upbringing, and he knew when to cut someone some slack. Too bad his decency hadn't rubbed off on Madison, but I supposed not even Fur 'n' Fang could work miracles.

We hit the showers before lunch, and by the time I made it to the dining hall and grabbed my meal, the wounds in my neck had already scabbed over and started to shrink. They'd be gone by morning. Too bad the same couldn't be said for the person who'd put them there.

I spotted Cam at a table at the back of the hall and headed over. Dean and Mei were with him – but they weren't the only ones. I exhaled slowly and reminded myself I was supposed to be playing nice with Madison and her little bitch pack. I set my tray down next to Cam and smiled at her.

"Nice moves in training today," I said. That flip onto her feet was cool. I had to get Mei to teach me that.

"Whatever. You got lucky. Don't think it's going to happen again."

I shot Dean an apologetic 'I tried' shrug and tucked into my food. It was no skin off my nose if she wanted to hold a grudge.

"So," Cam said, taking a break from devouring his steak long enough to raise an eyebrow at me. "How long have y' known about Ryan?"

The whole table went silent, and when I looked up, everyone had stopped eating to stare at me.

"Um, since New Years' Eve," I said. "But I told you, I wasn't allowed to talk about it."

"Figures," Madison said, with a delicate snort. "Your kind sticking together. Once an outsider, always an outsider."

"Come on, Mads," Dean said, looking pained. "That's not fair."

Madison held her hands up with a smirk.

"Just telling it as it is. It's not my fault if she can't handle the truth."

"It's fine," I said. "She can't help it if she feels threatened by us."

"You are not a threat to me," she said through clenched teeth.

"I mean," I carried on as if she hadn't spoken, earning myself a warning look from Dean, "it's natural to be afraid when you discover you're not as tough as you thought."

She glared at me, looked at Dean, and then turned her back on us.

"Ignore her," Tiffany said. "She only beat you by cheating, anyway."

Victoria murmured something unintelligible, presumably in agreement, and I hid my satisfied smile behind my burger. Madison's pride must really be hurting if that's what she was telling everyone.

"I can see you smiling," Dean said.

"No, you can't," I said, through a mouthful of food. Madison shot me a disgusted look and then went back to ignoring me. Honestly, too easy.

A flash of movement at the front of the hall caught my eye, and I gulped the rest of my mouthful down and waved a hand in the air.

"Ryan, over here!"

He spotted me and weaved his way through the crowds of seated students. I couldn't help but notice there weren't a whole lot of other students inviting him to sit with them.

"Oh, you must be joking," Madison said, as Ryan set his tray down at our table. "A leopard and one cur I can just about overlook. But two of you? Not happening. What next, are you going to invite the reptile to eat with us?"

Ryan made to pick up his tray again, and I grabbed his sleeve, stilling him.

"Well, like you said, Madison, us outcasts have to stick together. And for the record, if Kai wants to eat with us, he's more than welcome. If you don't want to be seen with us, you know what you can do."

"Yes, I do. Come on, girls. There's a bad smell around here and it's putting me off my food."

The three of them picked up their plates and left the table. Dean watched them go with a sigh.

"Really, Jade?"

"What?" I shrugged. "Nothing I said wasn't true. She's the bigoted one. And bearing in mind that you're friends with the leopard and the cur, you might want to consider pulling her up on that occasionally."

"I don't want to cause any trouble," Ryan said. "I'll sit somewhere else."

"No, you don't," I said, tugging down on his sleeve until he sat. "I'd rather your company than hers, trust me."

Dean cast a look over to where Madison was laughing loudly and shooting pointed looks at our table, and let out a long breath.

"My life was so simple before I met you lot."

"I think the word you're looking for is boring," I said. "And you're welcome."

He laughed and nodded.

"Yeah, you might be right. Who wants a peaceful life?"

"Exactly." I decided to ignore his sarcasm, and Dean decided to change the subject.

"So, Ryan, how are you finding it here?"

Ryan looked up from his food like it was a trick question. After a moment, he shrugged.

"I'm still waiting for someone to teach me how to shift so I can get rid of this thing."

He tossed a meaningful glance at the training cuff around his wrist. I ignored the bitterness in his voice – because apparently that was today's theme – and smiled brightly.

"Well, you're in luck, then." And here were two sentences I never thought I'd be stringing together. "We got Shifting 101 next."

Chapter Twenty-Two

Right," Brendon said, as we traipsed through into the shifting lab. "I've taken it easy on you so far. This semester, I'll be expecting more."

I gulped. If last semester was his idea of taking it easy on us, I was in all kinds of trouble. Even after all our practice, I *still* couldn't shift back, and I *still* tried to attack people every time I shifted. The best I'd managed was the odd moment of feeling like I might not want to completely saturate someone in blood – just gnaw on them a little.

"Now, I know we're all learning at different rates, and that's normal. But some of you are ready for a new challenge. Those of you who are ready will begin to work on their self-control. So, today, we will start working outside of cages."

He must have seen the blood draining from my face so quickly it left me light-headed, because he continued.

"Don't panic, we won't all be doing this right away. Get into your pairs, please. Ah, Ryan, yes, I was told you'd be joining us. I will be observing your change myself today. Please find yourself an empty cage, and I'll be along shortly."

"More cages?" he said to me, giving the iron bars a hard look. I shrugged, forcing as much nonchalance into my voice as I could.

"Unless you want to maul Brendon – and then who's going to be left to help you shift?"

He grunted and stepped inside one of the cages. Mei took the cage next to him, as usual volunteering to go first. I had no objections – we both knew that once I changed, I was going to be spending the rest of the lesson trying to change back, and there was no point in tying our cage up for longer than necessary.

Brendon worked his way round, locking and double-checking each of the cages.

"Once you have shifted, those of you who have absolute control will sit at the front of their cages, with one paw, or claw–" he glanced over at Kai, "–on the bars. Your training partner will alert me, and those who I think have sufficient control will be released from their cages. You will walk once – once – around the room, then return to your cage and shift back to your human form. Nothing more. Is that clear?"

A few murmurs of agreement sounded from around the room, and he nodded.

"Then when you're ready, you may begin."

I picked up my clipboard, and waited for Brendon to pull the privacy shield across, but it quickly became apparent that he had no intentions of doing so.

"What are you all waiting for?" he asked. "We're beyond first semester inhibitions – there's no-one here who can't shift almost right away now, and we'll need absolute visibility when you're moving around the room in your shifted forms."

I supposed he had a point – but I couldn't help feeling bad for Ryan, who probably couldn't shift right away. We'd had months of practice. He'd had a couple of weeks locked in a cage, resisting what he was. It didn't really compare.

Mei wasted no time turning her back on the room and setting her clothes aside. She sat in her usual manner, and I could hear her take a few deep breaths. I hit the button on the stopwatch, but barely a moment later, the skin on her back rippled, and her spine moved under the surface, cracking and elongating. That phase lasted only a few seconds, and then her skin changed, becoming thicker and darker, and then yellow-gold fur burst through her pores, covering her entire body from head to tail. I glanced down at the stopwatch. Less than thirty seconds. She was getting good at this.

"Nice work," I told her, jotting down the time on my clipboard. She stretched out and shook herself off, then came and sat in front of the bars. She lifted one paw, licked it in a distinctly feline fashion, then placed it on the metal. I shook my head in amazement. She was so far ahead of me. Seriously. And, unless I was mistaken, the first in the class to have managed it.

Brendon was right next to us, watching Ryan intently. I tried not to look, because I hadn't heard any screams of pain, so he was probably still human.

"Uh, Brendon," I said, and he turned to look at me. "Mei is ready."

He watched the leopard closely for a moment, and Mei swished her tail lazily, holding his eye, and still keeping her paw in place. After a moment, Brendon nodded.

"Excellent control. Now, you have some practice at moving in your shifted form inside the cage, but now I want you to practice a fast walk – do not break into a trot or a run – around the room."

He inserted his key in the lock and I stepped aside as he pulled the door open. Mei stepped out, pausing on the threshold to stretch out the full length of her spine. She wasn't as tall as the wolves, but her body was longer, and she moved with a casual grace that told me she was faster, and more flexible. Brendon watched her closely, one hand resting on the baton at his hip, but she just finished her stretch, and prowled around the room on silent pads. She kept the same pace the entire time, never once seeming to struggle to control the movement of all four legs in her shifted form, nor have to fight to maintain her steady walk. A stab of envy bit at me – there was no way I'd be getting out of my cage today, never mind be able to move with so much control. Everything came easier to the rest of them than to me.

I shook my head, and my bitterness with it. Mei was doing so well because she worked relentlessly. She deserved to succeed.

She finished her lap and came back to us.

"Excellent work, Mei," Brendon said. She paused for a moment, level with Ryan's cage, and it took me a moment to realise she was waiting for me to step aside. I guess she didn't trust her control as much as I did. I moved out of the way so she'd be able to pass me without making contact, but before she had chance to step through the gap, a cry erupted from Ryan's cage – half human, half beast; half pain, half rage.

Mei skittered sideways, and I twisted to look inside the cage, where Ryan was on all fours, caught in the violent spasms of his change. But his eyes didn't leave Mei, and his lips were drawn back in a snarl. She darted back inside her cage, and the instructor turned his attention to Ryan.

"Try not to panic, Ryan," he said. "That's a perfectly normal reaction to seeing another in their beast form. Don't resist your change, let it come over you."

He flung his head back and cried out in pain again. His shoulders burst from their sockets and re-set themselves, broader and heavier. I heard his spine crack and his lips, still human, cried out in pain again.

I jerked my eyes away. It didn't matter how many times I'd seen it, when we first started learning to shift, the slow, drawn-out process was horrific to watch, and I was glad it didn't take me that long anymore. I might not be as fast as Mei, but at least my shift only took a few short minutes now. I turned my attention back to the leopard, grabbed my stopwatch, and nodded to her.

She shifted back in less than three minutes, which I suspected was a personal best for her. She was going to ace our exams at the end of the year. I, on the other hand, was probably going to try to eat the examiner.

"Excellent work, Ryan," Brendon said from beside us. I glanced inside the cage. Ryan had finished his change. At the sound of Brendon's voice, he spun round clumsily on his four legs, and loosed a long, drawn-out snarl before lunging himself at the bars, snapping his jaws at the instructor. I took a step back away from him, unable to pull my eyes from the spectacle. That must be what I looked like when I lost control. His hackles raised a ridge the length of his spine, and he peeled his lips back to reveal foam was forming between his yellowed fangs. He leapt again, snapping at Brendon's face behind the bars, so loud I could hear his powerful jaws slamming on empty air. A shiver ran down my spine. It was horrific. Terrifying. I took another step away, no more in control of myself than Ryan was.

His eyes snapped to me. Another snarl worked its way up his throat, but it came out as a quiet rumble. He cocked his head at me, and his lips covered his fangs. I took a step towards him, my eyes fixed on his jet-black face, no longer contorted in fury, that seemed to draw me towards him. An arm shot out, barring my path, and snapping me out of my stupor. I twisted round to its owner – Brendon – who looked from me to the wolf and back again.

"Fascinating," he said. The sound of his voice – or maybe the sight of his arm blocking my way – raised the hackles on Ryan's spine again, and he took another snap at the instructor. "Very fascinating. In your cage, please Jade. Let's continue with the lesson."

I wasn't entirely sure having two raging wolves in cages side by side was going to be particularly helpful for the lesson, but he was the instructor. I stepped inside as he thrust his baton through Ryan's bars, and waited for him to lock me in, and let another of the students out to stroll around the room.

Three of them had completed their laps – some with more elegance and control than others – before I felt my change start to come over me. I'd shifted enough times by now that I knew better than to fight the pain. Instead, I embraced it, welcoming it and the transition it brought with it. A cry slipped from between my lips before I managed to clamp my jaws shut again. *Just breathe.* The faster the pain came, the faster it would leave again. The faster I would be rid of this weak, human body. The faster I would be in my true form, powerful enough to rend flesh from bone, to destroy all those who tried to cage and control me.

A snarl ripped from my throat, and my limbs moved under me, carrying me in short, deadly strides to the front of the cage. I bared my fangs at Mei as she stared in at me, silently judging me, silently trying to control what I was. I just needed to get out of this cage, and then I could end her. End the tyranny that kept me prisoner.

"Take control of the anger, Jade," a voice ordered me. Brendon. My eyes narrowed as I caught sight of him, and I peeled my lips back, showing him my lethal fangs, showing him what would happen if he didn't let me out right now. Blood pounded in my ears, drowning out his words. I didn't want to take control of the anger. I *liked* feeling this way. I liked the power that pumped through my veins, and I yearned to taste the hot blood spurting from his neck. I could see the artery throbbing beneath the skin. One snap of my jaws, that was all it would take.

I snapped at him, fighting to jam my jaws through the bars, but the gap was too narrow, and I could taste the silver tainting the bars. I recoiled from its bitter tang and slunk back, snarling and pacing, then lunged for him again.

"Focus, Jade," he commanded me – but I didn't take commands. Not from him. Not from anyone. Soon, I would be free of this cage, and I would punish each and every one of them for everything that had gone wrong in my life, every pain and indignity I been forced to endure. I would bathe in their blood, and I would leave a pile of corpses in my wake, testament to my supreme power.

"What's wrong with her?"

A new voice. My eyes flicked to its source. Ryan. He took a step towards me and I watched him through unblinking eyes. The pounding in my ears quieted, so that I could hear his sharp intake of breath as he stared at me. I stood rooted to the spot, listening to the sounds, and inhaling the scents around me. My senses were far sharper in this form, and I could smell the adrenaline fading from my system, leaving a faint, acrid flavour in the air.

Tension eased from my limbs, and the rumble died away in my throat. My lips covered my fangs, and I took a step forward, cocking my head.

"Well," Brendon said. "Isn't that just something?"

Chapter Twenty-Three

After that, my private shifting lessons with Brendon became semi-private. I didn't mind. It was the strangest thing. Every time I shifted, my aggression and rage were completely unchecked – until I laid eyes on Ryan, and then I'd get some degree of control over myself again.

It was the same for him, he said. And no-one knew why. Not Brendon, not Shaun, not even Blake. And sure as hell not me or Ryan. But every time I shifted around him, I seemed to be able to hold on to my control for longer. I was starting to wonder if there was some way I could sneak him into my exam. I'd managed a full two minutes without trying to murder anyone today. A personal best. I was feeling pretty damned good about myself as we ducked out of the shifting lab. I'd gained that much control in three weeks – more than I'd gained the whole of the last semester. It was Sunday afternoon, and I had no work due in for tomorrow. It was a good day.

I was so caught up in my self-satisfaction that we were deep into the castle's hallways before I realised the route we were following didn't lead outside. Or to the common room. Or the dorms. I looked around with a frown.

"Hey, where are we going? We told the others we'd meet them out by the woods."

"We will," Ryan said. "I just wanted to—" He looked around, then opened a door and beckoned me inside. I followed him into the deserted lecture room warily. "I just want to talk."

He shut the door.

"You know I'm with Cam, right?" I said, eyeing him nervously.

"Relax, it's nothing like that. Anyway, you're not my type."

"Uh, rude." I crossed my arms over my chest and arched an eyebrow at him.

"Dean's more my type."

"Oh." I dropped my arms again.

"So, if your fragile ego is back under control…"

"My ego is not—" He fixed me with a raised brow, and I cut off the lie halfway through. "What are we doing sneaking around a lecture room – on a Sunday?"

He shrugged and leaned against the wall.

"It's the only way to get any privacy round here. Like I said, I need to talk to you."

"About what?"

"About them."

"Uh, them who?"

"The others."

"Are you planning to make sense any time today?" I frowned, and he pushed himself off the wall.

"You must know about them."

I rolled my eyes.

"Let's say I don't."

"Wait, you don't know about the other Bittens?"

I put my hand on the back of a chair for support and blinked rapidly, trying to clear the fog that had descended over my mind.

"What… what other Bittens?"

"You never heard them in the dungeon?"

I gritted my teeth and clenched my hands around the back of the chair, feeling my fingers digging grooves into the soft wood.

"I think it's pretty damned obvious I didn't, or we wouldn't be having this conversation," I snapped.

"Alright, alright." He held his hands up, then ran one through his hair. "I'm sure that's what they are. I mean, what else could they be, right?"

I didn't answer that, because I had no idea what the hell he was talking about.

"What did you hear?" I asked him.

"Nothing, not at first. Not until they took the suppressor cuffs off me. Then I heard screams – like the sound of someone shifting. And I heard Blake talking to them."

"Them? As in, more than one?"

He nodded.

"Jade, there are others like us, locked up in the dungeon."

"No, there can't be," I said, slumping over the chair. I didn't seem quite able to support my own weight. "That doesn't make sense. Why would they keep them there? And why wouldn't they tell me? They told me about you."

"Maybe they don't want to integrate them."

"They integrated us."

"I don't know, Jade," he said. "But I know what I heard."

"Alright then." I pushed myself up from the chair. "Let's go and ask Shaun."

He caught my arm and spun me around.

"Are you crazy? You heard what I said, right? He's in on it, he has to be. There's no way he knew about us and not the others."

"Shit." I exhaled a trembling breath. "You're right. What do we do?"

"We need to get into that dungeon."

"Are you kidding? You haven't long been out of it."

"Right. And they've been there this whole time."

My shoulders sagged, and a memory pounded into the front of my mind, knocking the fight from me.

"Longer," I said. "I saw Fletcher heading down there with a bundle not long after I was let out. It must've been clothes or food or something. Shit. No wonder he wasn't happy about me hanging around while you were down there. He thought I'd stumble across them. That's why Blake insisted I had a chaperone. That's why he locked me in with you the last day you were there. They're trying to keep us away from the others."

"So, how do we get to them?"

I chewed my lip for a moment, then shook my head.

"I don't know. Maybe we shouldn't. I mean, this doesn't change anything, right? If they let us out, but not them, then there has to be a reason. There has to be."

"Maybe they just didn't want to conform," Ryan said bitterly, plucking at his Fur 'n' Fang hoodie. "Don't you think we should at least find out?"

I thought about it for a long moment, then nodded slowly.

"Shaun and Fletcher have keys. Blake, too."

"I don't like our chances of getting anything past Blake," Ryan said, and I had to agree, barely suppressing a shudder just at the thought of trying to pick the alpha's pocket.

"Fletcher, either," I said. "Pretty sure that's the fastest way to get thrown back in the dungeon, permanently."

"If they ever found your body," Ryan agreed. "Shaun it is, then."

I didn't like it. Shaun had done a lot for me since I got here, and even thinking about helping myself to his key felt like a betrayal. But if he was involved in this, and he was keeping it from me, then he'd betrayed us first.

"Alright. He probably keeps it in his desk."

The corridors were deserted – it was rare we got a clear and sunny day in February, and most of the students were probably outside making the most of it. I had no idea where Shaun was, but I couldn't hear him inside, and there was no recent scent by the door.

"You search his office," Ryan said. "I'll keep watch."

"No chance. This is your dumb idea. You search, and I'll keep watch."

"Fine. If Shaun comes back, distract him long enough for me to get out."

Clearly, Ryan had far more faith in my ability to keep anyone distracted than it deserved, but I wasn't about to argue.

"Just be quick."

He tested the handle and let himself inside, clicking the door shut behind him. I leaned back against the wall, scanning the corridor up and down every few seconds. A minute passed before I started to get restless. What the hell was taking him so long? Just open the drawer and find the key. It was a whopping great brass key, for crying out loud. It couldn't be that hard to spot.

I heard footsteps echoing along the stone walkway and jerked my head up.

"Hurry up," I hissed through the door. "He's coming!"

Shaun caught sight of me and frowned.

"Jade, what are you doing here? Is everything alright? I don't think we have a session scheduled today…"

Crap. The distracting part. Here went nothing.

"Um, no, we don't. I just, um, I was hoping we could have a chat."

"Of course. Let's step inside my office."

"No!" I took a breath and tried to wipe the panic from my face. "I mean, I can't sit still right now. Can we walk?"

If Shaun thought I was acting weirdly, he made no comment on it. Maybe he always thought I was acting weirdly.

"Sure. This way. What's on your mind?"

"It's, um, it's this whole thing with Ryan." It wasn't a complete lie. I didn't understand why I acted so differently around him when I was shifted, and honestly it scared the hell out of me. "We had another session with Brendon today, and I was the same again. It's the only thing my shifted form seems to respond to, and I don't understand why."

Shaun shook his head as we rounded a corner.

"I wish I had answers for you, Jade, truly. I've spoken to the alpha pack, and none of the alphas have any record of anything similar occurring. It could be that it's normal for Bittens to react more calmly around each other. Or it could be that you've shared a common trauma. There's no way to know for sure."

"But do you think…" I hesitated, and then pressed on, letting the words tumble out of me before I could think better of it. "Do you think I'll ever be able to control my wolf without him being there? Maybe I'm flawed. Maybe we both are. What if I can never control myself on my own?"

"We have no reason to think that. You've made great progress in your control over the last months. But if you think it would help for your extra sessions to be private again, I can arrange that."

I shook my head. I didn't think that would help, at all. And I didn't want to give up the only control I had over my beast, even if it was only for two minutes at a time.

"No. Um, thanks. I've gotta go. Thanks, Shaun."

I made to spin on my heel, and Shaun reached for me, then pulled his hand back when I stiffened.

"You can talk to me, Jade. About anything."

Something about the way he said it made me think that I'd been a whole lot less convincing than I thought. I nodded.

"Thanks, Shaun."

I hurried down the next corridor before he could ask any more questions, and as soon as I was out of sight, I made for the dungeon. Fresh scent told me Ryan had been this way only a minute or two before. It was laid over older scents, too. I guess he'd been this way before.

I caught up with him outside the dungeon.

"Well, did you get it?"

He reached a hand into his pocket and fished out the brass key.

"Ready?"

I nodded, and he let us inside. I slipped through, and he shut and locked the door behind us. It was eerie here without the instructors, and I hurried down the stone steps as quietly as I could. We went past the first door on the left, where we'd both been held during our time here, and on to the next door along.

We shared a long look, then he slotted the key in the lock, and opened it.

"Back again, Blake?" a voice snapped from off to one side. "I already told you—"

She cut off as we stepped inside, and I stared in horror at the woman locked in the cell that shared a common wall with the cell I'd occupied at the start of the year. No wonder Ryan had been able to hear her once his suppressor cuffs were off.

"Who the hell are you?" she demanded, pushing herself to her feet. She glared at us with undisguised hostility from behind a wave of mousey-brown hair that sat around her shoulders in a scruffy mane. How long had she been down here?

Ryan clicked the door shut behind us, and the sound snapped me out of my stupor.

"We're like you," I said.

"Like them, you mean." Her lips curled back in a snarl, but I cut her off with a shake of my head. I could see the ring of scar tissue on her arm – a single bite, probably.

"Like you," I repeated, and rolled up my trouser leg, so that the circle of pink scar tissue glistened in the light. "Both of us."

"If you're like me, then why aren't you in cages?"

"The better question is, why are you in one? They let us out ages ago."

"Bully for you. You've got a key, right? Let me out."

Ryan took a step forward, but I barred his path with my arm.

"We can't do that."

"Why not?" Ryan asked. I dragged him back out of earshot.

"We don't know anything about her."

"We know she's like us!"

"Great. So we let her out, then what? Don't you think someone's going to notice?"

"We'll help her escape," he said. "And us, too. We can get out of here. All of us."

I rubbed my temples.

"There is no escape," I said. And even if there was, I wasn't sure I'd want to go. I needed to be here. I had friends here, and I was learning to control my shifting power. Sure, it might not have been how I envisioned this year playing out, but I was determined to make the most of it. And that meant sticking around.

"What's your name?" I asked the woman.

"Laura," she said.

"I'm Jade. This is Ryan. We want to help you, but this isn't the way. I'm sorry."

"Bitch!" she screamed, and threw herself against the cage bars, rattling them and snarling. Her hands trembled and blurred around the bars, then she burst out of her skin and clothes, hitting the floor on four legs, snarling and snapping her jaws.

I took a step back. Bloody hell, that was a quick shift. And her aggression made both me and Ryan look tame. I turned to him.

"We need to get out of here. Now."

Chapter Twenty-Four

We put the key back in Shaun's office, and I tried to put the whole thing from my mind. Laura was locked in the dungeon? Well, maybe she needed to be. She sure as hell couldn't be let loose to roam the academy and its grounds.

It was days before Ryan broached the subject again, but of course he was never going to let it lie.

…And neither could I, not really. Like it or not, deserved or not, there was someone locked in a cell beneath our feet. I was on my way back from one of my now twice-weekly sessions with Shaun one evening when he ambushed me.

"Let's just… let's just talk to her again," he said.

"I already told you. We need to leave well enough alone. What's going on down there is none of our business."

He stepped in front of me, blocking my path. I stopped, exhaling heavily and staring at a spot on the wall behind him.

"We both know you don't mean that," he said. "If you did, you'd be able to look me in the eye right now."

"Look, just because I feel sorry for her doesn't mean we can let her put people at risk. You saw her, she tried to kill us."

"No worse than what we've both done in our shifted forms. And she's been down there for *months*. What do you think that does to a person's mental state?"

"Exactly. She's dangerous."

"Right." Ryan nodded and shot me a sarcastic smile. "And sitting in a cage is how she's going to get better."

I dodged his eye again. I knew *I* wouldn't get better if I stayed in a cage, and I couldn't imagine it would be different for anyone else. Hell, if they locked me up, and the first people I saw who wasn't one of my captors refused to let me out, maybe I'd have acted aggressively, too.

"I'm not suggesting we bust her out," he said, holding his hands up. "Just... let's talk to her, okay? Her and Brad."

I frowned.

"Who's Brad?"

"The other one. You knew that."

"No, I didn't. Wait, how did *you* know that?"

"She told us."

"No," I shook my head emphatically. "She didn't."

Ryan's face creased impatiently.

"I must've heard someone speaking about him, then. When they took my cuffs off. I don't know." His shoulders dropped. "To tell you the truth, the whole time

I was down there is a bit of a blur. I just… I get flashes. Of that, and of the attack. Do you get them?"

I swallowed the painful lump sitting in my throat and nodded.

"Yeah," I said hoarsely. "I get them. Not as bad as I used to. You should talk to Shaun. It helps, I promise."

"Maybe," he said. "Right now, he's not the first person I want to talk to, what with the people he's keeping caged."

It was hard to disagree with that, desperate as I was to try.

"Look, we won't let them out," he said. "You can have the key, if you don't trust me. I just want to hear their side of the story. Because we're not going to hear it from anyone else round here."

"I don't know. I'll think about it."

For a moment, I thought he was going to keep pushing, but instead he nodded.

"Do that. But don't take too long. I'm worried about what being down there is doing to them."

And I was worried about what letting them out would do to *us*.

*

I did think about it. I thought about little else. February became March, and the guilt gnawed at me a little more with each day that passed.

"Jade."

I jerked my head up to look at Lewis. He was standing at the front of the lecture room, looking at me expectantly.

"Sorry?"

Laughter sounded from somewhere behind me: Madison, I was sure. I ignored the urge to flip her off while Lewis went through the charade of pretending to be disappointed I hadn't been paying attention.

"Someone else, then. Madison."

"Execution of a pack member without the explicit order of the Alpha of Alphas was outlawed by the druids in 1831, but the Pack Hierarchy Accords of 1833 allows for an exception by the pack's own alpha acting against a pack traitor," she said at once, flicking her hair.

"Yes, good. Jade, it wouldn't hurt you to try paying as much attention as Madison."

I was pretty sure doing anything the same as Madison would be the death of me, but I decided to keep that to myself, and sunk a little further into my seat until Lewis continued with his lecture. Honestly, I usually enjoyed these lessons – the way the druid and shifter laws intersected and interacted with each other fascinated me – but I was having a hard time getting Laura's face out of my mind. I dreamed about being stuck in the cell again last night. And it wasn't like I could even talk to Shaun about it, because he'd want to know why I was suddenly so obsessed with the dungeon.

"Alright, that's all we've got time for today. I'll see you next week. Finish reading up on the Pack Hierarchy Accords before then. Remember, you have your end of year exams in two months."

Two months? How the hell were exams only two months away?

"Jade, are you coming?"

Dean, Mei, Cam and Ryan were already on their feet, books shoved back in their bags.

"Did he just say two months? Tell me I misheard him," I said, cramming my own notepad back in my bag.

"Yer'll be fine, lass," Cam said, wrapping an arm around my shoulders. I wished I had his confidence. Two months. I was still behind on half my subjects, and honestly the whole Laura thing hadn't exactly helped with my focus – and I *still* couldn't control my shifted form.

"Yeah," Dean said with a smirk. "You'll be fine. As long as they don't ask you any actual questions."

"Gee, thanks."

"Don't worry," Mei said, as we headed down the corridor a little behind the rest of the students – on account of the fact they hadn't been stunned into a stupor by the announcement of exams, presumably because they'd actually been paying attention to the date. "We'll help you get caught up."

"I'm not sure you can. I mean, I can put in more study hours for the theory stuff, sure, but how am I supposed to pass a shifting exam?"

Mei didn't have an answer, and nor did anyone else – including me. I knew one thing, though. I was never going to get caught up with Laura's face haunting me every time I closed my eyes.

"You know what? No time like the present. I'm going to find Brendon and see if he'll schedule me a couple of extra lessons. Ryan, you should come, too."

"Maybe later. We've got a lesson with him tomorrow, anyway. It's not like one day is going to make any difference."

I didn't roll my eyes only through a Herculean exertion of will.

"No, really," I said, trying to catch his eye. "I think it's better we talk to him now."

"Do yer want me to wait for you?" Cam asked, as I slipped out from under his arm. I shook my head.

"Go ahead and grab some lunch. We won't be long."

"This better be good," Ryan grumbled, crossing his arms over his chest as the others headed off for the main hall.

"I thought it might be a good idea to visit Laura and Brad while the rest of the academy is busy. But hey, if you'd rather be off stuffing your face, be my guest."

He dropped his arms immediately and stared at me.

"You changed your mind?"

"I'm still only going to talk to them. We're not going to do anything reckless."

Any more reckless than sneaking into the castle's dungeon and visiting people we weren't supposed to know about, that was. Ryan nodded quickly and grinned.

"Let's go, then."

He set off, and I grabbed his arm.

"Uh, where are you going?"

"The dungeon."

"Don't you think it might be a good idea to go and borrow the key first?"

He reached inside his bag and pulled something out.

"What, this key?"

I tossed a glance round the corridor, but we were completely alone. The key he was holding was the same size and shape as the one we'd taken from Shaun's office, but the brass looked new, and glinted under the hallway's lighting. A copy.

"How did you... never mind." There were some things I didn't want to know. And some things I did. "How long have you had that?"

"Not long," he said, tucking it in his pocket, and setting off towards the dungeon again. "I figured it might come in handy. You know, for when you were ready to hear their side of the story."

And when he said it like that, I felt like a total bitch. I should have gone back weeks ago. No wonder Laura's face was haunting me. I deserved to be haunted. But I didn't have time to beat myself up. The others would notice if we weren't back before the end of lunch.

As predicted, we made it to the dungeon without seeing another living soul. The whole shifter stereotype about food was true. Shifting burned through calories like a hot knife through butter. My stomach rumbled at the mental image, and I shoved it aside. Food later. Innocent people locked in dungeons now.

Ryan's illicit key opened the lock without problem, although he didn't look nearly as relieved as I felt. Apparently not everyone round here was as much as a wimp as I was.

"Come on," he said, locking the door and ducking down the corridor ahead of me. Maybe he was nervous, after all. "Brad first."

"Why?"

He paused, then slotted the key in the lock.

"Well, we haven't met him yet. And we should, right?"

I couldn't – and didn't – argue with that. Ryan let us in, then locked the door behind us.

"Ryan. You're back."

My head whipped round, and I stared at the wiry guy in the cell across the room. He was a few years older than us, in mid-twenties maybe, but it was hard to tell in the dim dungeon's lighting and under the dark shadow of his stubble, and honestly I had other things on my mind.

"How do you know his name?" I twisted back to Ryan. "How does he know your name?"

"Tell her," the guy in the cell said.

"Tell me what?" Uneasiness welled in my stomach and crept up my spine. Something was very wrong here. "And what does he mean, you're back?"

"Don't freak out, okay?" Ryan said. "I've been coming down here. On my own."

"You lied to me?"

"No, I didn't, I–" He paced two steps, turned around, paced back. "I couldn't leave them down here thinking no-one gave a damn. You see that, right?"

"What I see," I ground out, "is someone who looked me in the eye and lied for– How long have you been coming down here?"

And then I remembered his scent tracks, that day we first came down into the dungeon and met Laura.

"You were lying the whole time, weren't you? You've been coming down here since the day you got out. It was a setup. All of it."

"It wasn't like that. Please, Jade…"

"Then what was it like, huh?"

"They were locked down here, just like me – just like you. I could hear them screaming every time they changed. What did you expect me to do, just leave them here?"

"I expected you to be honest with me." I threw up my hands. "You know what? I'm done. Give me the key."

"No, listen to me."

"Give me the damned key!" I lunged at him, trying to wrestle it from his hands, and the pair of us thudded against the wall, and then into the cage bars. I gasped as my back thudded into the metal bars, knocking the wind from me. Before I could get my breath, a hand shot out from behind me, and wrapped itself around my neck. Brad's hand.

"Now, listen here, darling," he growled in my ear.

That seemed like a shit idea to me. I lifted my hands and clawed at the arm jammed against my throat, gouging with my nails and fighting to get him off me. He pressed tighter and shook me, rattling my head against the bars. Pain exploded behind my eyes. I couldn't reach his face behind me, and I couldn't get a foot through the bars to kick him. Pulled tight to the bars, I couldn't twist to get any leverage against him. All I could do was keep clawing at his arm, and I clawed with a vengeance, until my nails were slick with blood.

Brad hissed in pain, and jammed his arm tighter to my neck, until I couldn't breathe.

"Knock it off. Stop fighting and listen."

"Okay," I gasped, with what little air I had left. I dropped my hands, resisting every instinct that screamed at me to keep fighting while there was breath left in my body – which wouldn't be for long, if I did that. "Okay."

He loosened his arm enough for me to suck in a decent breath. I stayed still, other than to roll my head an inch to the side to get a look at him. The air stank of fear and adrenaline, and I couldn't tell which belonged to who.

"Brad," Ryan said, finally finding his voice. "Stop."

"It's fine," Brad said. "We're just going to chat. Aren't we, darling?"

"It's Jade," I spat. "And you'd best talk quickly before I find a way to rip your arm off."

"And I thought I was supposed to be the one with the logic-suppressing rage. I could already have broken your neck, if I wanted to."

His words gave me pause. He was right. If he was dangerous enough to justify being locked away down here, then why hadn't he killed me?

Brad moved his arm from my neck and took a step back, holding his hands out to his sides.

"Sorry I had to do that," he said.

I stepped quickly, putting some distance between me and his cage, then eyed him while I rubbed my throat. "I'm listening."

"I did nothing worse than you." He wrapped his hands around the bars and leaned against them. "I was attacked. Some feral wolf bit me, but I was the one who got punished."

His hands clenched until his knuckles turned white, and then he loosened his grip again.

"But unlike you, I didn't buy the company line. I didn't feel like going upstairs and pretending everything was shiny. So they left me here. They feed me, they bring me water – and then they leave me to fucking rot!"

He drew in a sharp breath, his shoulders heaving and knuckles turning white again, then shoved himself off the bars, and stalked to the back of the cell. He leaned against the wall, then thumped his fist against it. I shot a glance over at Ryan. This guy was a loose cannon. Anyone could see it.

"I'm sorry," Brad said. He turned around to face us again, clenching and unclenching his hands. "It's hard, being down here. How would you feel if they locked you up? What would you do to get out?"

"You know how to get out. You just have to tell them you're willing to train, to take control of your shifted form."

He shook his head sharply.

"I don't mean out of this cage. I mean out of this academy. Out of this whole damned world. I had a life, and I want to go back to it."

"Don't you want to go back to your old life?" Ryan asked me.

"We could do it, you know," Brad said. "If we worked together. Why should we have to pay the price for someone else's crime?"

"You're crazy. Both of you. Give me the damned key."

I held my hand out to Ryan. He didn't move.

"Give it to me, or I'll take it." I rolled out my shoulders.

"Wait!" Ryan drew in a slow breath, and let it out again. "Wait. You can have it. Just promise me you won't tell anyone we've been here."

"Are you kidding? That's the first thing I'm going to do."

"You can't." He took a step toward me, then stopped. "Look, we can't get out of here without your help, okay? You're the only one with any chance of busting through those wards. If you say we're not going, then we're not. But you have to forget everything that happened today."

"Why the hell would I do that?"

Ryan stretched a hand through the bars and took hold of Brad's.

"Because I love him."

Chapter Twenty-Five

Maybe I was going soft. Maybe some part of me wanted what they wanted. Or maybe I was just too anxious about the upcoming exams to want to cause any more trouble for myself. Whatever the reason, somehow I didn't march myself right up to Shaun's office. Not that day, not the next day, not even a week later.

I should have. Of course, I should have. But by the time a fortnight had passed – well, I'd have had a helluva time explaining to Shaun why I'd kept it from him that long. And it wasn't like there was any harm in Ryan just visiting Brad. And maybe, just maybe, he was right. He didn't deserve to be locked up for someone else's crime. Maybe he would get better – him and Laura – if they could get away from here.

I watched Ryan like, well, like a woman who was worried he'd unleash an uncontrollable shifter into the academy and kill us all. I barely let him out of my sight. It was easy enough – he shared a room with us, he was in all my lessons. If he tried to get into Blake's office to get the cuff key, I'd know. And if he did that, then I'd go to Shaun and tell him everything, consequences be damned. I would.

But Ryan didn't so much as look in that direction. He kept his head down, showed up for our extra sessions with Brendon – in which he was annoyingly doing much better than me – and visited Brad twice a week. I didn't try to stop him. Maybe he could help Brad come to terms with what he was. And even if he couldn't, they both deserved whatever happiness they could find, wherever they could find it. None of us had asked for this.

Maybe it was time to have another talk with Ryan about what was going on. Maybe even try to persuade Laura and Brad to give the academy a chance. I was pretty sure that would be a doomed attempt, but maybe if I could explain what it had done for me, they'd see it was for the best. I'd talk to Ryan in a minute. He was around here some place.

"Jade?"

"Huh?" I blinked Cam back into focus. Crap. I had to make an effort to be less distracted. "Hey, have you seen Ryan?"

"Ryan?" His face went from hopeful to hurt to angry in seconds. "Yer asking me about Ryan, now?"

He pushed himself up from the floor and glared at me.

"Yer unbelievable. I ask you that, and all you care about is him? You know what, if you care so damned much about Ryan, why don't yer just date him?"

"What? No, it's not like that, he's not even—"

I clamped my mouth shut. I had no idea who Ryan had told he was gay, and even I wasn't enough of a bitch to out him to save my own skin. Cam scowled at me.

"Tell it tae someone who cares. I'm done."

"But…"

I watched his retreating back with my mouth hanging open, and then I dropped my head into my hands. I'd really screwed up this time. Christ knows what Cam had been saying when I'd zoned out. How could I have been so stupid to ask about Ryan? I mean, was it any surprise he thought there was something going on? I was practically stalking the guy. Dammit. But he couldn't mean it. We couldn't really be over. He'd calm down. He had to.

I got up from the stubby grass, dusting myself off. There was no point in going after him. He obviously didn't want to speak to me right now, and I could hardly blame him. And it wasn't even like I could explain why I was following Ryan. It was all such a mess!

One that I wasn't going to fix standing around out here feeling sorry for myself. If I couldn't talk to Cam, then I could at least talk to Ryan and Brad. I grimaced. That was not going to convince Cam there was nothing going on between us. I trudged back to the castle in silence, trying to decide if there was a way I could have screwed myself any more thoroughly.

"Hey, Jade, we were looking for you. We are heading for dinner, are you– What's wrong?"

Mei broke off, searching my face. Dean was with her and he had the super-bitch and her cronies in tow – proving that, in fact, my day was always capable of getting worse.

"We'll catch you up," Mei said, catching hold of me and pulling me aside. Dean looked concerned for a moment, but then hurried after Madison and the bitch pack.

"Well?" she said, once they were out of earshot.

"I… uh, I think Cam just broke up with me."

"What? Why would he do that?"

I groaned.

"Because I'm an idiot, that's why. He was asking something and I wasn't really listening, then I asked him if he'd seen Ryan, and… I don't know. He got pissed off about it."

"Really, Jade?" She arched a brow at me and put one hand on her hip. "Cam's talking to you, you're thinking about Ryan, and you wonder why he's upset? Could you be any more obvious?"

"No, it's not like that. Seriously, why does everyone think I'm obsessed with Ryan?"

"Um, I don't know. Maybe because you've been following him around like a puppy-dog for the last month?"

Well, yeah, when she put it like that, it didn't sound great. But what was I supposed to do? It wasn't like I could tell everyone why I was paying so much attention to him. I'd kinda taken for granted that they'd assume it was a Bitten thing. And now look what it had cost me.

"I've lost my appetite. Go ahead without me. I think I'm going to head up to our room and hit the books for a bit."

"Oh no, you don't," Mei said, linking her arm through mine before I could protest. "Skipping meals is not going to help you. And an extra half hour of studying will make no difference to your exam results."

"It will if I learn something that comes up in the exam."

"Look, there's no point trying to avoid Cam."

"I wasn't– Okay, fine, I *was* going to avoid him. But just until he calms down enough that I can explain."

Exactly what explanation I could give him that wouldn't land me in a world of trouble remained a mystery, which was the other reason I wanted to avoid him. But Mei wasn't taking no for an answer. And to be fair, I was hungry.

I went with her without any more objections, and when we reached the dining hall, I was more relieved than I should have been that there was no sign of Cam. There was no sign of Ryan, either, but I figured this wasn't a good time to bring it up.

"Where's lover-boy?" Madison said with unmistakable glee as I set my tray down at our table. It was a bad sign that I wasn't sure exactly whose absence she was gloating about. Tiffany snickered, and Dean shot the pair of them a warning look.

"I was just being nice," Madison said, holding her hands up. Right. And I was the pope. How the hell had everyone found out so quickly?

Mei shot a nervous look at someone three tables away, and my heart squeezed painfully. Cam. I guess I didn't have to worry about avoiding him. He was avoiding me.

"It will be fine," Mei said. "He just needs to sleep on it."

"So," Dean said loudly. "Three weeks until exams. Who's ready?"

It said a lot about how shitty I was feeling that impending catastrophic failure bothered me less than Cam sitting at another table.

"Instructor Fletcher says I'm predicted a high pass," Madison said, flicking her hair over one shoulder. "And, of course, I've always been a natural at shifting."

The food I was chewing turned to clay in my mouth. Shifting. My weakest subject. Fail anything, and I'd get held back a year. I was scraping through on the theory stuff, but I still couldn't control my shifted form.

"What do we have to do for the shifting exam?" I asked.

"Well, I don't imagine it's trying to kill the instructor, so you're going to be in trouble."

"Madison, give it a rest," Dean said. Madison pouted, then slipped her hand into Dean's, practically purring with satisfaction.

"Whatever you say." She smiled up at him and pressed her lips to his.

"Really? I'm trying to eat. You two are putting me off my food."

"Sorry, Jade," Madison said, resting her chin on Dean's shoulder and sounding anything but. "I didn't mean to rub it in."

I put my knife and fork down.

"I'm done. I'll catch you guys later."

"Jade, wait," Dean said, but I grabbed my bag and made for the exit. I heard him chastising Madison behind me, for all the difference it would make. Once a bitch, always a bitch. And she wasn't about to pass up an opportunity to make me feel bad. She still hadn't forgiven me for bringing Ryan into our little group. I hadn't forgiven her for coming back, so I guessed we were even.

I wasn't in the mood for hitting the books, but I wasn't in the mood for dealing with anyone either, and the library seemed like the safest bet to avoid any sort of conversation. Plus, no-one would look for me there.

At least, that was the plan. But when I stepped into the usually deserted room and inhaled the scent of books that were older than me, I caught the scent of someone else, too. Fresh scent. Ryan was in here. For a moment I thought about just ducking back out – I really wasn't in the mood to have this discussion now, not when Cam thought I was sneaking around with him. But, like it or not, Brad and Laura were more important than my ailing love life. Or as important, at least.

"Found any Stephen King?" I asked, heading over to the lone figure. He shook his head and flashed the heavy tome at me. I frowned as I made out the worn lettering on the front. *Arcane Warding Spells.*

"Wards? Are you kidding?"

"Keep it down," he hissed, glancing around the room. He needn't have bothered. I already knew we were alone. "I just wanted to be prepared. In case you changed your mind about helping us."

"What did you find?" I mean, it didn't hurt to know, right?

"Nothing good. You need an alpha to deactivate one. Or a druid, but I can't see Blake letting any of them in here."

"Yeah, druids and shifters really don't play nice, do they?"

I was pretty sure it was only because Leo turned out to be innocent that things never came to a head between the two factions. The idea of a druid walking through Blake's precious academy? Laughable. Which was a good thing. Because there was no way smuggling Brad and Laura over the wall was going to end well.

"Forget the wards," I said. "No-one's getting out that way. But we can still help them. We have to convince them to join Fur 'n' Fang. Even if they break out, they still need to learn how to control their shifting powers. This is the best place for them to do that."

"I know that," Ryan said, glancing round again and shoving the book in his bag. "But they don't want to. Not after everything. And can you blame them?"

"They can get help here."

"Yeah, bang up job they've been doing of helping them. The cages really scream rehabilitation."

Well, he had me there.

"Blake has given up on them," he said. "But I haven't."

"Me, either. Let's go and see them. We've got a while until everyone's back from dinner."

One last chance to integrate, that was all I owed them. What they did after that was on them.

Chapter Twenty-Six

I could smell their scent leading through the woods. The trouble was, the entire damned woods were saturated with scent, and the trails layered over trails made it almost impossible to tell which way my target had gone. I glanced at Shaun beside me, but he gave me no encouragement.

And why would he? After all, he was here to assess my tracking skills. It wouldn't be much of an exam if he told me which way to go. But I sure wished *someone* would, because of all the things I'd envisioned failing this year on, tracking wasn't one of them.

"Fifteen minutes remaining," Shaun said.

Crap. I had to get a move on. The shifter I was tracking was out here somewhere, but if I wanted to find them, I needed to decipher the fresh scent from the old, and I needed to do it now.

I held the scent cloth to my nose and inhaled again. There was a faint leathery scent to it, almost like an old biker jacket, or a well-used purse. I disregarded everything else and focused on that as I took in a deep breath of air. Scenting was easier in our shifted forms – not that I'd progressed beyond wanting to kill everyone for long enough to find out – but for the exam we had to stay in our human forms. Level playing field and all that. This way, we could all suck equally.

I canned the pity party for *after* I failed and crouched down, plucking a crumbled leaf from the floor. Old leather. I nodded to myself. The scent was smeared all over this – they'd stepped on it, and recently. More recently than they'd touched that tree leading down the right-hand track. That was the decoy. I stayed left and picked up a slow jog. I had to find the target before I ran out of time, but if I was moving too fast then I might miss any twists in the trail. And if the way I'd already come was anything to go by, there'd be plenty.

Shaun followed silently at my back, keeping enough space between us that if I stopped suddenly, he wouldn't crash into me. Which was just as well. The trail stopped dead, and I skidded to a halt just past its end.

"What the…?"

I looked at Shaun, but he studiously avoided my eye. It was part of the test, then. I backtracked a little, circling around the end of the trail. There was definitely only one scent trail. My target hadn't doubled back on themselves, which meant they had to have kept going. A gust of wind shook the late-spring leaves in the branches above me, disrupting their scent. I caught the slightest trace of old leather and tilted my head back, squinting up at the trees. Yeah, that figured. Sneaky bastards.

I pinpointed the tree the scent had come from and jumped, grabbing hold of the branch and hauling myself up. The scent cloud was all around me, thick and fresh. They'd tried to cover their scent by staying off the ground. Which, when I thought about it, seemed kind of a dick move for a first-year exam.

I dropped back down to the track and carried on a few steps. My progress was much slower after that, having to stop and check every few trees to make sure I was still going the right way, and the trail grew harder to follow as we moved off the game trail, and into the heart of the woods themselves. Every step I took threw up a cloud of scent of damp earth and foliage, but it couldn't quite mask the leathery odour falling through the air above me. I was gaining on them, the scent growing stronger with each step.

"Five minutes remaining," Shaun said.

"Five minutes? Are you kidding?"

He wasn't kidding. Shit. I should have found the target by now. This was taking too long. The wind gusted again, bringing me a fresh lungful of scent – from three different directions. What the hell?

I frowned and twisted round to look at Shaun over my shoulder, but he looked just as confused as me.

"Um, that's weird, right?" I asked. "Wind coming from three different ways?"

"Continue with the exam," he said, his voice devoid of any inflection. Right. Good idea. I couldn't afford to waste a second of my five minutes. And if helpful gusts of wind wanted to keep blowing the target's scent in my direction, I wasn't going to be complaining. Confused, yes. Complaining, no.

I took off at a jog again – all or nothing, at this stage – turning my nose into the undulating breezes every few seconds. The scent grew stronger, and then stronger still, until I wasn't even having to make a conscious effort to detect it.

Ahead, the trees were thinning, and I pushed on. I burst through the undergrowth and into a small circular clearing, surrounded by trees. And in the centre stood two figures. The student I'd been tracking, and beside him, Fletcher.

"Very good, Jade," Shaun said.

"Did I make it?" I asked, trying not to sound out of breath. "Was I in time?"

Shaun gave me an apologetic smile.

"Sorry, I can't tell you that. You'll have to wait until you get your results."

Oh well, nothing ventured, nothing gained and all that.

"Get your breath back," Fletcher said. "Your next exam starts in thirty seconds."

"My next exam? No-one said anything about another exam."

"Combat often arrives unexpectedly. You must always be prepared to defend yourself. You will fight in your human form. You must last for five minutes against Jax. Tap out, or succumb to a battle-ending injury, and you will be deemed to have failed. Ten seconds."

I yanked off my light-weight hoodie – I was already hot from my jog through the woods – and tossed it aside.

"Begin!"

Jax launched himself forward almost before I'd straightened. I threw my arms up and backed up two paces. His punches thudded into my forearms – that was going to leave a bruise or two. I needed to rotate my blocks more before he snapped one of my arms.

He swept a leg at my ankles and I jumped, narrowly avoiding having my legs taken out from under me. I landed slightly off balance and caught a glimpse of his other foot flying at my face. I ducked low, but not fast enough. His foot scored a glancing blow and I swayed back, my head spinning. I needed to get in the fight before he took it clean off my shoulders.

I didn't straighten. Instead, I kept low and surged forwards, thrusting an uppercut beneath his rib cage. My fist connected with a wall of solid muscle that jolted the impact right up to my shoulder. Shit. This guy worked out. A lot. I should have known that Fletcher would make sure I was matched with someone who could kick my arse.

An elbow swiped at my head, discouraging me from getting distracted. I could worry about whether I was being stitched up later. Right now, I had to focus on not getting turned into a heap of Jade-mush.

I retreated, falling back a few quick steps, but that wasn't going to cut it. This guy was stronger than me, and he was taller than me, and he had longer arms – which meant a longer reach. If I wanted to get the better of him, I was going to have to get in close and remove his advantage. And there was absolutely no part of me that wanted to get close to Jax. That guy was like, all muscle.

He stalked towards me across the clearing and I pushed my arms up into a classic guard position. Jax chuckled quietly, the sound vibrating through his chest. I narrowed my eyes. He was enjoying this a little too much.

I stood my ground, letting him advance on me. He wanted to believe I was a weak little girl who wished she could run away? Fine. It just meant he wouldn't expect my attack. He swept a leg at my knees and I rushed forward, raising a leg in front of me to block his strike with my calf. That was going to hurt like a bitch in the morning. I pushed through and slammed my hip against his, then swept my forearm up into his neck, and used my momentum to disrupt his balance before he could get his leg back down. The force of my strike threw him to the ground, and I landed on top of him, straddling his chest and pinning his arms to the ground like I had that day with Madison.

He wasn't Madison.

He met my eye for a quarter second, and in that quarter second, I knew I'd made a grave miscalculation. Then his lips twisted into a grin, and he flexed his hips, and rolled.

His sheer strength tossed me aside like I was made of paper, but I didn't feel like paper when my back thudded into the earth – I felt like shit. The impact pounded the air from my lungs, and while I was fighting to draw in breath, he dropped on top of me, and wrapped a hand about my neck.

I gasped, wrapping my hands around his wrist and bucking under him like a fish out of water, but I was no match for his strength. The bastard was going to choke me out before the five minutes were up.

I squeezed his wrist, digging in my nails, but he just gritted his teeth and increased the pressure on my neck. Anger surged through me and suddenly he gasped in pain and drew back, clutching his wrist to his chest.

"Time, Ms Hart," Fletcher said, sounding distinctly disappointed. "You may return to the castle."

I got to my feet, staring down at the red glow fading from my palms. What the actual fuck was going on?

*

I didn't get chance to speak to anyone about the weird stuff that happened in the woods, and truth be told, I wasn't exactly sure what I'd say, anyway. Shaun had never said anything else about that day in the dungeon when I'd burned Ryan. Whatever answers he might have found, I suspected I was better off not knowing.

The following morning, we were summoned to the shifting room. It was time for our final exam, and the one I'd been dreading most. I mean, sure, the theory exams – Law, History, and Cultural Studies – had been no walk in the park, but at least I had a chance with them. Shifting? I was screwed.

If we were all being tested together – by which I mean, if Ryan was going to be there – I might have stood half a chance. But no such luck. Each student was to be tested individually. Plus side, I wouldn't have to watch literally everyone else ace the exam while I failed miserably. Downside, I was in fact going to fail miserably. And solo exams meant I had a whole lot of time to sit around contemplating how screwed I was. Which was very screwed.

The corridor had three other students in, and we all waited in silence, slouched in the seats that had been lined up there for us. All except Madison, who was incapable of keeping her mouth shut for more than thirty seconds, unless it was latched onto someone's face.

"Well, I'm not worried. My record speaks for itself. Oh, I can understand why you're nervous though, Jade. I mean, it's not like you've ever managed to really control yourself, is it?"

Mei glared at her, and I probably would have given her a snarky reply – if I didn't think opening my mouth right now was going to result in me vomiting all over my shoes.

"Leave her alone. It's nae any of yer business how she gets on."

I lifted my head to shoot Cam a grateful smile, but he didn't – wouldn't – meet my eye. He'd made it clear over the last couple of weeks that we were over, and nothing I said was going to change that. But it still hurt that he didn't even want to be friends. Worse, it had all been for nothing, because my little trip to the dungeon – my last – hadn't convinced Laura or Brad in the slightest.

The door opened, and Ryan shuffled out, his dark hair dishevelled. He glanced my way, and two seats along, Cam's jaw tightened.

"Jade Hart," a voice called from within. I swallowed and got up. This was it.

"Good luck, lass."

I glanced Cam's way as I trudged past him, and he met my eye for a quarter second before looking back to his feet. I nodded my thanks and stepped inside.

"Close the door," Brendon said, and once I had, he led me into the second chamber.

"This will be a timed exam," he said, "consisting of three parts. For the first part, you will have two minutes to shift into your wolf form. You may do so from within a cage if you wish, and you may use a privacy curtain if you desire."

Easy enough. That part was never a problem for me. Brendon shut and bolted the second door, sealing us in the shifting chamber.

"For the second part, you will have five minutes to retrieve that ball."

I followed the direction of his hand, where a football on a piece of rope dangled from a metal fixture set into the ceiling. It wasn't a particularly long rope, no more than two feet, and it was a very high ceiling. Mei's leopard form might be able to jump up and yank it down – maybe. But I didn't know any wolf who could jump that high. Certainly not mine.

"You will be marked if you show any uncontrolled aggression."

Great. That was me done, then.

"For the final part of the exam, once you have retrieved the ball, or when your five minutes have passed, you will have a further three minutes to resume your human form. Do you understand?"

I nodded. Shift, get the ball, shift back. Maybe find some flying pigs while I was at it.

"Excellent." He stepped inside one of the cages – which I thought was a pretty smart idea, all things considered, and picked up a clipboard, leaving the door open – which I thought was less of a smart idea, all things considered. My track record for controlling my aggression wasn't exactly stellar.

I sucked in a breath and put the thought from my mind. The more stressed I was when I shifted, the harder it would be for me to maintain control.

"Are you ready? You may begin."

I ducked into the nearest empty cage, pulled the screen across, and tossed my clothes aside.

Three more deep breaths, and a mental image of Madison's smug face – which I'd particularly like to thump right now, and I felt the bones move beneath my flesh as the change came over me. I gritted my teeth as pain speared through my spine, twisting and cracking it. My joints burst out of their sockets and I screamed through clenched teeth, willing the transformation to race through me and be done. My limbs thickened and my nails curved into razor-sharp claws. My jaw lengthened, my ears changed shape, and fur erupted from every inch of exposed skin, with slow, agonising precision. And then, it was over. I was in my true form once more.

A snarl burst from my throat and I stalked out of the cage. I could smell him. He was close. My head turned to the left. There. Sitting in his cage, watching me. And I was going to shred him.

No!

I shook my head, my slate-grey fur flashing in my eyeline. No. I could not touch Brendon. I had to get the ball. I twisted right and looked up at the ball hanging high above my head.

No. Fuck Brendon, and fuck his test. I didn't owe him a damned thing. I didn't have to jump through any hoops for him.

Not for him, then. For me. To prove I could. To prove everyone wrong. *Focus, Jade!* The ball was too high for me to jump, and–

Forget the ball. Brendon's scent was invading my lungs with every breath, and I could smell the blood pumping through his veins. Blood that I would spill before today was done.

I had to kill him. No. I had to get the ball.

My head flicked between the two a half dozen times.

And then I lunged at Brendon.

Chapter Twenty-Seven

I felt like I'd been hit by a truck.

I left the shifting chamber with my hair hanging lank around my face, and a defeated shuffle to my step. Was there any way that could have gone worse? Well, yeah, okay, I could have *actually* mauled Brendon instead of just trying, but the only reason I didn't was because he used his baton on my cuff, so I was pretty sure that didn't count. And I was damned sure I'd just failed my final exam.

I didn't spare a glance for the others waiting to go in. As I traipsed down the corridor away from their curious eyes, I heard Brendon summon Mei inside. I hoped she did better than me. To be fair, it was hard to imagine any way she couldn't. Shit. What was I going to do now? Failing my exams meant being held back a year – like I wasn't enough of an outcast as it was.

"Jade!"

I jerked my head up from my feet to meet Ryan's wild eyes. I shook off my self-pity. I wasn't the only one who'd just been through a gruelling exam. Maybe we could wallow together.

"Hey, Ryan. That was a bit shit, wasn't it?"

"What? Oh, the exam? Yeah, sure. We need to talk. In here."

He grabbed my arm and towed me into a storage room. I glanced around as he shut the door behind us.

"Uh, what are we doing in here?"

"Saving Brad, I hope."

I raised an eyebrow. I'd done everything I could to help him, and Laura, last time I visited. And they'd been pretty adamant they didn't want that sort of help.

"You know what, Ryan? It's been a pretty shitty day. Can you move, please, so I can go back to my dorm and feel sorry for myself?"

"Please, Jade. I heard Blake talking to Shaun. Draeven is coming tonight."

"Why?"

"Why else?" He slumped back against the door. "You told me there were only two ways I'd leave that dungeon – as a student… or a corpse."

I closed my eyes, exhaling heavily. "He's coming to pass judgement."

"Listen. I know what you think of Brad. But do you really think he deserves to die, just because he can't accept what was done to him? I can't let that happen. *We* can't."

It could have been either of us down there. It had taken me a long time to come to terms with what that rogue shifter had done to me, and I'd had a lot of help. We didn't have the death penalty in this country, and I'd grown up my entire life believing in the importance of giving a person the chance to reform. My views hadn't changed just because I was a shifter now. And it sure as hell wasn't right that someone should be sentenced to death because someone else had committed a crime against them. It was victim blaming at its worst, and it was bullshit. I set my jaw and opened my eyes.

"What's your plan?"

Ryan bowed his head for a second and pressed his lips together, then he met my eye.

"I've got the key for the dungeon door, and I've got the cell keys and the key for their cuffs."

"What? How?"

"I picked the lock to Blake's office after I heard him talking to Shaun."

"What the hell did you do before you came here?" I held up my hand. "Never mind. I don't want to know. We bust them out of the dungeon. Then what?"

"We get them out of the castle while everyone's busy with the exams, and to the wall."

"The warded wall," I pointed out.

"I've done a lot of research. That day you burned me? That was a druid power. Magic. And if you can use magic, you can bring down the wards."

"What? I don't know how!"

"Brad's been reading that book I took. He can tell you what to do. Please, we've got to try."

"Okay. Yes. Of course, I'll try. But we need a backup plan. There's no way of knowing if I can do this, not for sure."

"Fine. But we better think of it on the run, because if Blake realises his keys are gone, we'll never get them out."

He was right about that. And I didn't even want to think about what he'd do if he caught us in the act of freeing the prisoners we weren't supposed to know about. I shoved my head out of the door, checking the coast was clear, and then we hurried through the castle, making for the dungeon. We didn't pass anyone on the way. The instructors were all tied up carrying out exams, and the students were either taking them, or getting in some last-minute practice. The scents in the corridor leading to the sealed door were all hours old – we were the only ones here. For now.

"Hurry up," I hissed at Ryan as he slotted the key into the lock. He got the door open and we spilled through, pushing it shut behind us but not locking it. We weren't going to be here long.

"Brad first," he said, hurrying to the door at the end. I didn't object. If that had been Cam in there, he'd be my priority, too. I swallowed. Even if Cam didn't feel that way about me anymore.

We burst into the room at the end, and Brad jumped to his feet. He took one look at our faces and came to the front of his cell.

"It's happening, isn't it? Draeven. He's come to kill us."

"We're not going to let that happen," I said, grabbing the cuff key from Ryan's shaking hands. "I've got this. Get that cell door open."

I turned my attention back to Brad.

"Give me your wrists. Quickly."

He thrust his hands through the cage. The cuffs he was wearing were the same thick, silver-laced ones I'd been put in when I first arrived. The ones that had stopped me from shifting. Brad wouldn't stand a chance outside the walls with them on. But he also wouldn't be able to hurt any mundanes.

"Come on," he said. "Hurry up."

I nodded and inserted the key into the cuff. One twist and it fell away. He deserved a chance to be free. To find some peace away from this cage. I unlocked the second cuff and tossed it aside. Brad pulled his hands back through the bars and rubbed his wrists.

Ryan yanked the door, and it swung open with a loud creak. Brad eyed the open doorway for a moment, then eased forward, like he was expecting to walk into a solid brick wall. I watched him from the corner of my eye, trying not to stare openly. I could only imagine what was going through his head after months of being locked in this tiny cell.

"You okay?"

He grunted in reply, and stepped through the door.

"I know we haven't always seen eye to eye," he said, holding out his hand to me. "But I owe you for this. Truce?"

I nodded and reached out, accepting his hand. His grip tightened around me, squeezing my hand to the point of pain, then he wrenched my arm, yanking me off balance. I stumbled forwards and he drove an elbow between my shoulder blades. Pain exploded across my shoulders and my legs weakened under me. I spun round, trying to gather my wits in some sort of defence, but before I could even get my guard hand up, he planted a foot on my chest and shoved. I flew back, falling over my own legs and smashing into the wall at the back of the cell. Brad yanked the door shut.

"What are you doing?" I gasped.

"Sorry, darling. But I don't think you're going to be too keen on part two of our little plan. The part where we kill every bastard responsible for keeping us in these cages."

I lunged forward, shoving my hands through the bars and snatching at the key, but Brad turned it before I got there, and pulled it out. He dangled it out of reach, tutting.

"Nice try, but I don't think we want you getting in our way."

"This wasn't the plan," Ryan said, gnawing at his lip. "You said we were getting out of here. All of us."

"That's not enough," Brad said. "Not nearly enough. You can come with us, or you can stay here with her. Your choice."

"Ryan, you can't let him do this. Those are our friends out there."

Ryan shook his head.

"I'm sorry, Jade. We're nothing but outsiders to them." He touched a hand to Brad's arm. "And Brad is everything to me."

"And what are you going to do when Draeven gets here, huh? He'll kill all of you."

"Well, see, that's the thing, darling," Brad said, his lips peeling back in a feral smirk. He lifted his hand. The palm glowed red, and then a bolt of fire burst from it, smashing into the wall and leaving a scorch mark on the grey stones. "You're not the only one who can do magic. And now that my cuffs are off – thanks for that, by the way – there's nothing that can stop me."

He held up the cell key, cocked his head at me with a smile, and then tossed it into the far corner of the room.

"See you later, darling. Or not. Come on, Ryan."

He turned and strode through the open door into the hallway. Ryan gave me one last apologetic look, then hurried through after him.

Fuck.

Chapter Twenty-Eight

The door slammed shut, and then I was alone. Trapped.

I grabbed the cage door and gave it a rattle, but it didn't budge. I couldn't believe I'd been so stupid! Falling for that ridiculous 'truce' line. I should have known better than to let my guard down around that psycho for a single second. And right now, he was prowling Fur 'n' Fang's hallways, looking for victims. Because of me. I should have reported it the second Ryan told me he'd been visiting.

And as for Ryan... I stalked up and down the cell, scowling. I'd trusted him. I'd considered him a friend. Wanting to bust Brad out? Sure, I got that. But going along with this killing spree? Those were our friends he was talking about! Friends who had no idea what was coming for them. Because Brad hadn't spent the last months in denial about the strange powers that flared up when he was angry, or anxious. He hadn't buried his head in the sand when his hand burned hot enough to sear skin. He'd embraced it. He'd studied it. And the second I'd removed his cuffs, I'd unleashed a deadly power into my home.

And I wasn't going to let that stand.

I couldn't hide from what I was anymore. Not if I was going to stop Brad from hurting the people I cared about. I'd burned people who had been a danger to me – first Ryan, and then Jax. And what the hell was that thing that had happened in the woods during my tracking exam? Wind didn't blow from three directions at once. And Shaun had seemed just as bemused as I'd been. Because it had come from me. I needed help finding the scents, and the wind had brought them to me.

And right now, I needed that key lying on the other side of the room.

What was it Brad had done? I lifted my right hand and pointed it at the key, willing it towards me. It didn't budge. I squeezed my eyes tight, focussing with every fibre of my being on my desperate need for the key to move. My highly attuned senses detected no sound of movement: no wind, no metal scraping against concrete. I cracked one eye open, and sure enough, the damned thing hadn't moved.

This was pointless. Ryan's book said these were druid powers, and druids went to academies of their own, spending years to master their magic. It wasn't going to come to me in thirty seconds just because I wanted it.

I rattled the bars again, growling with frustration.

But Brad hadn't been able to practice, not with those cuffs on. I'd studied them in Law, and the symbols etched on them would hobble *any* magical creature, including a druid. Sure, he'd had time to read up on it, and train himself to focus, but he couldn't have used magic with them on.

I raised my hand to the key again. I'd been worried in the woods. Desperate. Scared I was going to miss Jax's scent and fail the exam. Well, I was a whole lot more scared now. What if Mei or Dean got in Brad's way? What if Cam did?

The dust in the corner of the room stirred. My hearted thudded. It was working. Blake, Shaun, even Fletcher – they were all tied up handling exams. No-one would be wandering the halls, keeping guard. The students were completely exposed. And everyone I knew and cared about wore a training cuff. The only advantage they had – their ability to shift – would be muted. Hell, half of them had never even sprinted on four legs. They would be easy prey for the rogue wolf.

The wind whirled round the small room, rattling the door like a coming storm. Yeah, there was a storm coming, alright. And none of us were ready for it.

I locked my eyes onto the key, willing the full force of the wind into it. It scraped an inch along the floor, then shot forward through the air, straight through the bars of the cage. I ducked with a yelp and it zipped over my head and crashed into the wall.

My stomach churned. I felt drained, as weak as a day-old kitten. But I couldn't afford to be weak. Not if I was going to stop Brad. I crouched down and picked up the key with trembling fingers, and carried it carefully to the lock. It took me three attempts to wiggle it into the keyhole, but I got it. One twist and the door swung open. I stepped out, then paused. Brad's cuffs lay abandoned on the floor, but the key was gone. Ryan must have taken it while Brad was overpowering me. For Laura. The three of them were going to carry out this crazy plan together. And whether they pulled it off or they failed, innocent people were going to get caught in the crossfire.

I hurried out into the corridor, pausing only long enough to sniff the air, but they were long gone. They hadn't locked the main door out of the dungeon, either. Guess they'd thought that cage would hold me. Their mistake.

I crept along the eerily quiet hallways. I needed to raise the alarm, and I needed to do it in a way that wouldn't cause mass panic. That meant finding Blake. I paused at an intersection. If Draeven was coming, then there was every chance Blake would be preparing for his visit. There wasn't time to blunder around trying to find him. I turned left and hurried in the opposite direction.

As I approached Shaun's office, a tingle ran across the back of my neck. Something wasn't right. I paused outside the door and sniffed. Brad. His scent was all around here. Ryan's and Laura's, too. I started to back away, but a voice froze me in place.

"I know you're out there, Jade." Brad's voice sent ice down my spine. "Open the door and come in, slowly – or people are going to get hurt."

"Don't do it, Jade!" Mei shouted. There was a thud and a muted yelp of pain. Shit. What was Mei doing in there? And what had that bastard done to her? I clenched my jaw.

"Don't make me kill her. You know I will."

"Alright!" I sucked in a breath, trying to calm my racing heart. "Alright, leave her alone."

I took hold of the door handle and eased it inwards, taking care to keep my hands in sight. Brad clicked his tongue in disapproval.

"I should have known. You used your magic, didn't you?"

I swept my eyes round the room. All three of the Bittens were in here – Laura gloating over Mei where she lay on the floor, glowering, and Ryan leaning against the far wall, trying to avoid everyone's eye. Brad was standing behind the desk, and Shaun was sitting in front of him, his hands bound at the wrists. The feral shifter was holding a blade to his throat, and even from here I could detect the stench of silver. And on the floor, in the middle of the room…

"Dean!"

I hurried a step towards him.

"Uh-uh, not so fast."

I stopped, turning my glare on Brad.

"What the hell have you done to him?"

"Ryan, shut the door," he said. "Wouldn't want anyone else interrupting us. The alpha's brat will be fine – unless I decide otherwise."

Dean's clothes were a smouldering mess, his t-shirt burned half away, and I could see pink splodges of healing burn tissue. His face was contorted with pain, but he was alive. His hands had been pulled behind his back and bound, adding insult to injury. I glared at Ryan as he shut the door behind me, but he steadfastly avoided my eye.

"You choose the wrong side, Jade," Brad said. "We're better than them. More."

"You're a psycho."

"Sticks and stones," he said with a shrug. "You've made your choice. Put those on."

He nodded to a set of cuffs sitting on the desk. Suppressor cuffs. I narrowed my eyes but didn't move.

"Now." He moved the blade, nicking the instructor's neck. A trickle of blood leaked from the wound, and Shaun's jaw clenched.

"Alright!"

I stepped forward and snatched them up. I snapped the first around my left wrist, but my right was already covered with the narrower – and less inhibiting – training cuff. I waved it at Brad. He smirked and pulled a key from his pocket.

"I already underestimated you once today. I'm not going to do that again. Switch the cuffs."

He tossed the key on the desk, still keeping the knife to Shaun's throat. The wound was still bleeding, and one glance at his bound wrists told me why. He'd locked him into a set of suppressor cuffs. I wasn't sure how he'd subdued the instructor long enough to get the cuffs on, but I was guessing it had a lot to do with what he'd done to Dean. Nothing like torturing a student to make an instructor compliant. Sick bastard.

I snatched up the key, unlocked the training cuff, and locked the second suppressor cuff in its place.

"See, that wasn't so hard, was it?"

"I'm going to kill you," I told him with a smile, keeping my voice relaxed. "The next time these cuffs come off, I'm going to rip your throat out."

He laughed, plucking the key from the cuff and sliding it into his pocket.

"You'll be dead long before that happens, darling. You, instructor." He touched the silver blade to Shaun's skin again. "I know Blake's bringing Draeven here. Where will they portal in?"

Shaun pressed his lips together firmly, completely still except for a finger that drummed anxiously on the desk. Brad pressed the blade harder against his throat, drawing another trickle of blood. Shaun's jaw clenched and the muscles in his shoulders locked up, but still he refused to answer.

"Fine," Brad said, raising one hand. His palm glowed red. "The girl this time, hm?"

He turned his palm to Mei, still glaring up at him from the floor, defenceless with her hands bound behind her.

"No!" Shaun said. His shoulders slumped in defeat. "They'll portal into the grounds, near the front gates."

"Do you think I'm playing?" His face twisted into a snarl. "Do you really expect me to believe the most powerful shifter in the country is coming here, and you're going to make him walk through the grounds?"

His palm pulsed brighter.

"He's right," I said quickly. "The castle is warded against portals. They have to come in through the front door."

"That true, instructor?"

"It's true."

"Fine. Get up. We're going to take a little field trip. Laura, you're with me. Ryan, stay here and keep an eye on these three. Bind her hands."

He hauled Shaun to his feet, and Ryan shuffled towards me, holding a piece of rope.

"And just in case you're getting any ideas," Brad said in Shaun's ear, "Laura's not coming with us to help keep *you* in line. If you try anything, she's going to get back here, and she'll make sure these three die slow."

"Alright. I get it."

"Good. Because you and the rest of my jailors, you're all dead. That's a given. But the mindless sheep don't have to die with you."

Ryan tied my hands behind my back, and I resisted the urge to claw his treacherous eyes out. Laura pulled a knife from her belt and handed it to him.

"Let's go," Brad said, shoving Shaun in the back. I glowered at him, but the instructor seemed unfazed, stepping calmly to the door. "We're going to Blake's office, where you're going to make a little announcement, and then we're going to meet the mighty Draeven. You'd best find us a quiet route."

"I will. No-one needs to get hurt."

"That's down to you, isn't it? Oh, and Ryan? If Jade gives you any trouble, make sure she's the last to die."

He bunched his fist in the back of Shaun's shirt and the two of them moved out of the room, with Laura following behind.

I waited until the sound of their footsteps had died away, as far as I could tell with my now-hampered senses, before I turned to Ryan.

"What the hell are you doing? You don't want this."

"Shut up."

"No. Shaun helped us. Both of us. Are you really going to let Brad kill him?"

"I said, shut up."

"Or what? You'll cut me with that knife?"

"Yeah." He glared at me, then his shoulders slumped. "No. I don't want anyone to get hurt."

"Nor do I." I stepped closer to him, watching his face. "I know you care about Brad, but what he's doing right now isn't going to help anyone. If he threatens Draeven, there's no coming back from that. Put that blade down and let me stop him, before it's too late."

"I can't. They'll kill him."

"They'll kill him if he goes through with this. He's no match for Draeven, you know that. Not even with his magic. I've met the man, and he's the Alpha of Alphas for a reason. Draeven will destroy him."

"He's just so angry. It's not his fault, he can't help it."

"None of us asked for this to happen to us," I said. "We're all victims. I'll do everything I can to keep him safe. You know this is his best chance. His only chance. I'll speak to Draeven on his behalf."

"You promise?" Ryan said, searching my face. I nodded.

"I swear it. Let us go."

Ryan nodded. "Okay. Turn around."

I did, and I felt a tingle of discomfort as the silvered blade touched my skin, and then the ropes fell away.

"I'm sorry," Ryan said. "I didn't want this."

"I know," I said, taking the knife from Ryan and crouching down beside Mei. She twisted round, holding her bound hands to me, and I started sawing at the ropes. I glanced back at Ryan. "You need to get Dean some help, both of you. Then you need to find Fletcher and tell him what's happening."

"Attention, attention." I jumped and spun around. Shaun's voice was filtering through the speakers in the corner of the room. Guess they'd already made it to Blake's office. "This is an emergency announcement. All students and instructors are to report to the main hall immediately. All students and instructors to the main hall, immediately."

I turned on Ryan.

"Why the main hall?"

"Brad stopped there on the way here. He put a spell on the threshold. Anyone who goes in won't be able to come back out again, not until the spell's broken."

"Shit. And you're just telling me this now?"

I gave Mei the blade and hurried behind Shaun's desk.

"What are you doing?" Ryan asked. I shot him a look.

"What, you don't think it was a bit weird that Shaun kept tapping his fingers on the desk from the moment these cuffs were on me? Have you ever seen him fidget before?"

I yanked open the drawer. Shaun kept a lot of junk in here, but after some sifting I found what I was looking for: a small key. I pulled it out and slotted it into the cuff on my right wrist. It fell away and I reached for my training cuff, then paused. If this was going to work, I'd need every ounce of my power. I left the training cuff lying there and unlocked the final suppressor cuff.

Chapter Twenty-Nine

Sheer, unadulterated power flooded through me, burning its way through my veins, setting every cell in my body alight with raw energy. Possibility. Feral magic pulsed in my veins, urging me to change, to embrace my true form and race through the hallways, slaying anyone who crossed my path. To prove my strength, my dominance.

"Jade?"

I turned to Mei with a snarl, then clamped a hand over my mouth. I'd just snarled at my best friend. Mei, who had stayed by my side through everything this year had thrown at me. Mei, whose life had already been threatened because of my mistakes. I needed to do better than this.

"Focus," she said. "Remember why you're doing this."

I nodded shakily and shoved the key in my pocket. I couldn't give in to the dark urges. If I didn't find a way to stop Brad, lives would be lost. Shaun's life would be lost. We didn't have time for my power to corrupt me.

"Do you want me to come with you?"

I hesitated again, but shook my head. I was having a hard enough time controlling myself. I didn't need to put Mei at risk again. The more shifters around me, the more of a danger I would be. And I didn't trust Ryan alone with Dean.

"Help Ryan with Dean," I said, and her eyes narrowed. My meaning wasn't lost on her. I hoped she'd have the sense to hold on to the silver blade, just in case. "Then find anyone not trapped in the hall and tell them what's going on."

I turned for the door. I'd wasted enough time here. Brad and Shaun would be on their way outside by now, and half the academy was probably already trapped inside the main hall. Obedience was a habit, and when they heard the word immediately, they didn't loiter.

I couldn't afford to, either. I took off at a sprint, covering the ground of the deserted corridors easily. The power flowing through my veins lengthened my stride until my legs were eating up the ground beneath them. I made it all the way to the back door without passing another soul – not a good sign. I didn't much like my chances if I had to take on Brad and Laura by myself.

I slipped through the door and out into the grounds. I had no plan, and I had as long as it took me to work my way round to the front of the academy to come up with one, because just throwing myself at Brad seemed like a good way to get myself killed.

I had to shift. Brad was uncuffed for the first time, which meant he was feeling everything I was. If I showed up in my wolf form, it would trigger that same primal fury in him that I'd had at just the sound of Mei's voice – times ten. And hopefully, it would force him to shift. Once in his wolf form, he wouldn't be able to use his magic.

I tugged off my hoodie and tossed it aside, then my t-shirt and my cargo trousers. A thought struck me, and I fished the key from my pocket and bundled it in a sock. If I could get it to Shaun – without my feral side trying to kill him – he could get out of his cuffs and shift, evening the sides. Except unlike us, he'd had decades of training.

I crouched down and thought about all the bad shit that had happened to me since that night at the farmhouse. And then I connected with the primal energy buried inside me. The change came over me faster and stronger than it ever had before, punching through my body. Fire burned along my spine, searing a trail of white-hot agony. I clenched my jaw and dug my fingers into the dirt, biting back the cry of agony that was clawing its way up my throat. I couldn't scream. If Brad heard me changing, there was no telling what he'd do to Shaun. Find some way to stop him becoming a threat, that was for sure.

My shoulders bulged and changed shape, and fur forced its way through my skin. I didn't fight it. For the first time since I'd been bitten, I wanted, truly wanted, this to happen. I embraced the wolf inside me and gave up the image of myself as human.

I shook out, settling my fur against my flanks. It was time to put an end to Brad. My lips pulled back in anticipation, and I prepared to launch myself into action.

No, wait. I shook out again, trying to clear my head. I couldn't just go blundering in. I needed to act smart. And I needed the key. I scooped up the sock in my mouth, then turned and loped into the trees.

I moved in near silence, twitching my ears and taking sharp breaths of the air, testing it for scent until I caught a noxious mix of magic, sweat, and rage. Brad. I recognised Shaun's scent, too. I'd tracked him often enough in class that it was branded into my senses. They were close.

I slowed to a walk, and stalked through the woods, peering out of the undergrowth. A flash of movement caught my eye – there! Three figures clustered near the front gate. Two standing, and one sitting, hands at an awkward angle – like they were bound. They were saying something, but I wasn't close enough to pick out the words.

I took a step from the treeline, and as I did, a gust of wind blew through my coat – towards Brad. Shit.

He spun around, and as he caught sight of me, I broke into a dead sprint. My four limbs devoured the distance, and I loosed a snarl around the small package in my mouth. Brad's eyes widened, and I smelled the sudden surge of adrenalin in his system, even at this distance. He opened his mouth to say something, but it came out as a scream and he collapsed onto all fours.

His shoulders bulged, shredding his shirt, and his spine started to twist and buckle beneath his skin. He howled again in pain, the sound more animal than human, and I faltered in my gait. My eyes twitched from Shaun to the vulnerable shifting wolf. He attacked me. He locked me in a cage. Forget Shaun. I was going to shred this pup, and nothing was going to stand in my way.

No! I had to keep to the plan. If I attacked, Laura would have time to kill Shaun. I could already see her hunting for Brad's blade. But what did I care if Shaun died? He wasn't important to me.

Yes, he was. I bounded past Brad without breaking my stride. Laura's eyes widened as she saw me coming and trembles wracked her body. I ignored her, shut out the compulsion to attack my would-be rival, and skidded to a stop in front of Shaun, putting my body between him and Laura. I spat the sock at his feet, then turned my snarl on the she-wolf, doubled over as the change tore through her body.

I sensed rather than saw Shaun's confusion, but he grabbed the sock between his bound hands and turned it inside out. The key tumbled to the floor and he groped through the grass until his fingers closed on it. I watched only long enough to see him take the key in his teeth and guide it towards the lock on the cuffs, and then my attention was back on Laura. I stalked towards her, my eyes locked on her half-human throat.

There was a snarl and a flash of movement – from beside me, not from Laura. I turned, but not fast enough. Brad smashed into my side, slamming me to the ground. His teeth snapped at my face. I kicked out at him, trying to gouge under his soft belly with my claws, but his russet fur was too thick for me to get any purchase from this angle. Yellowed fangs clamped shut an inch from my eyes and I twisted my head aside and kicked again, this time slamming my powerful hind feet under his back leg.

He staggered back, his teeth closing on air again, and I leapt to my feet. A sideways glance told me Shaun had the first cuff off and was working on the second. Laura's change was halfway done, and if Shaun didn't get the last cuff off soon, he'd be easy prey.

I snarled at Brad, snapping my teeth in his direction, and we started to circle, each looking for the other's weakness. Brad lunged towards me and I leapt back, but not fast enough. Teeth closed on my shoulder, sending a lance of white-hot pain searing through me. I snarled again and threw myself into him, snapping my teeth as his face and neck.

A new snarl rent the air. I twisted round: a sandy wolf loomed over Shaun, lips peeled back. I sprang from Brad and raced towards the pair. As I did, the last cuff fell away from Shaun's arm and his entire form erupted with a furious snarl, snapping the rope binding his wrists. He landed on all fours, crouched, and leapt at Laura in one smooth motion.

Pain shot through my tail and I spun back with a yelp. Brad's teeth were clamped around it, worrying at its base as he attempted to draw me back. I twisted round, trying to get to him, but my bulky form didn't have the flexibility to reach him. I yelped again and tried to kick out with my back legs, desperate to escape the pain. Brad locked eyes with me and his lips peeled back in what was unmistakably a smirk.

I roared my fury and twisted round, determined to wipe that look from his face, even if it meant ripping my own tail from my body. I howled again with agony, I felt flesh tearing, but I didn't dare look at the damage as I ripped free from his grip. My teeth closed over the russet wolf's neck and I clamped down, hard, clenching my jaw with all my strength. Another snarl erupted from me and pain and fury and fear and bloodlust all mingled into one until I couldn't think anymore. I worried at the flesh of the wolf's throat, searching for his jugular. His teeth snapped in my direction but each bite missed, closing on empty air, while I burrowed deeper into the thick fur protecting his lifeblood.

I heard whimpering from behind me but I couldn't look without releasing my grip on Brad, and if I did that I'd never get hold of him again. The whimpering changed from animal to human – female. A moment later, I heard Shaun's voice.

"Sit there. Don't move."

Brad redoubled his efforts to break free as the instructor came closer. I felt him slipping from my grip and clamped down harder.

"It's over, Brad," Shaun said. "Change back, and you won't be harmed."

Brad snarled his defiance, scrabbling at the ground beneath him, now slick with both our blood. His eyes swept the clearing, looking past us to Laura, and I felt the defiance drain out of him.

"Jade, let him go."

I rolled my eyes round to look at Shaun, because I was one hundred percent sure that was a bad idea.

"It's okay, do it."

I relaxed my jaw and worked it loose from his throat, then took a step back, eyeing the wolf warily. He stayed still as a statue.

"Change back, Brad," Shaun said again.

A sharp tang burned my nose, and instinctively I recognised it as magic. The portal. Blake and Draeven were arriving. I lifted my lip in a snarl, warning Brad not to try anything.

Light flashed to my side and then pain bit into my rear leg. I screamed in agony, spinning round and snapping my teeth at my own body. The silver blade was buried to its hilt in the muscle, and the pain was so intense it drove every thought from my mind. I could see Laura's triumphant face in my periphery, but it didn't matter. I had to get away from the pain. I had to make it stop. Someone had to make it stop, anyone. The movement drove the blade deeper into me, and it burned like acid was eating at me from the inside.

Brad darted out from in front of me, racing for the portal, but I could barely spare the focus to notice him, far less doing anything about it. I had to make the pain stop. It was killing me, I knew it.

Draeven and Blake stepped from the portal, and Brad raced straight past them and dived through it, Laura hot on his heels in her human form. I didn't care. Nothing mattered but the blade she'd wedged in my flank. I snapped my teeth at it, at myself, at anything that moved, the pain driving me into a frenzy.

"Jade, it's Shaun. Look at me."

Look at him? I heard his words but discarded them. Looking at him wouldn't help me. Wouldn't stop the pain, and nothing else mattered.

"Jade, there's a silver knife in your thigh, and I need to pull it out. But you have to calm down first."

No, I needed to bite and shred, I had to keep moving, keep attacking until the pain went away.

"Focus, Jade!"

Focus. I had to focus. Shaun could help me. He always helped me. I forced my jaws to stay closed, and my legs to stop moving. As soon as I did, they gave out from under me. I hit the floor with a thud that knocked the air from my lungs and sent fresh waves of hell through my flank. My lower jaw trembled, but I clamped my teeth together again.

"Good. Steady, now."

Shaun moved closer, watching me closely. I dropped my head onto the floor, rumbling deep in my throat. Every breath hurt.

"Good work, keep her still." Not Shaun's voice. Blake's. I rolled my head round to watch him as he approached, Draeven by his side. They crouched down beside me, and Draeven pressed both hands to my shoulder, holding me down. I could feel his strength, even in his human form. He looked at Shaun and nodded.

Fresh pain screamed through me as the knife slid free. My legs kicked out and a snarl ripped from my throat. I lunged, but the hands held me down, then I lunged again and this time broke free, teeth snapping at the air. My eyes locked onto Draeven. Draeven, who had pinned me down. Draeven, who had ordered me locked away. Draeven, who had failed to stop me being bitten and turned into this mess.

Draeven, who was responsible for everything that was wrong with my life.

I lunged at him, ignoring the pain that screamed through my hind leg. It didn't matter. What mattered was biting him, tasting his blood, destroying him and everything he stood for. My teeth yearned to rip flesh from bone, and every muscle quivered in anticipation.

"Jade, this isn't you," Shaun said, and my eyes snapped to him. He was guilty, too. He was one of *them*. "You can control this."

I didn't want to control this. I wanted to vent my fury. I wanted someone else to be the victim.

Shaun? I wanted *Shaun* to be the victim? No, that wasn't right. He didn't deserve that. A whine slipped from my throat. He was right. I had to fight back, get control.

I was more than just the crime that had been committed against me. I was more than the sum of other people's bad intentions. I was Jade Hart, and I *would* beat this.

I backed up a step, yelping as I put pressure on my injured leg. The pain sent a rush of murderous thoughts through me, and I shook my head, trying to dislodge them. I fixed my eyes on Shaun, the bloodied knife hanging limp by his side. He'd risked his life to pull it out, to stop me suffering. I didn't want to hurt him.

I backed up another step and lowered myself to the ground, keeping the weight off my injured limb, but the movement sent another wave of agony through it. Now I knew why my senses reacted to silver as strongly as they did. It was poison, and even with the blade gone, the damage wasn't healing. Couldn't heal. Not on its own. Not while the silver was spreading through my bloodstream. And no-one could help me while I was in my wolf form.

I cast the beast aside and sought my human-self. Human. I needed to be human. I felt my bones cracking and screamed, the tortured sound unrecognisable as human or animal. Muscles twisted and reshaped themselves, tearing at my silver-damaged thigh, and I dug my fingers into the dirt and screamed again.

Fingers?

I looked down. Fingers. I'd done it. I was human again. And my leg hurt like a bitch. Gasping, I sank back to the ground. Someone draped a coat over me.

"Alright Jade," Shaun said. "Just hold on. We're going to get you help."

Chapter Thirty

Ｉt would seem I'm making a habit of visiting people in hospital beds," Draeven said.

I peeled my head from the pillow beneath it to look at him, and Blake beside him. A few hours had passed since they brought me in here and left, and the resident healer had done something weird with his hands that had made the pain in my leg recede. I'd hoped that would be the last I'd see of the Alpha of Alphas. I didn't much fancy facing the consequences of my wolf-self trying to take a bite out of him. And that wasn't even the worst thing I'd done today. Which was presumably why Blake was here.

I sat upright, grimacing as the movement pulled at my torn leg. I took some solace from the fact they'd brought me here. I mean, you didn't bring someone to a hospital wing and have their wounds treated if you were planning on executing them, right? Although I was the first to admit that 'hospital wing' was a bit grand for what amounted to three beds, and a middle-aged shifter sitting behind a desk. I guessed there wasn't much call for more than that, what with shifter healing speeds. Too bad they didn't apply to silver wounds. How Shaun had resisted the ones on his neck for as long as he had was a mystery to me, but by the time the healer had attended to them,

I'd seen tendrils of grey spreading through his skin. But his wounds hadn't been as bad as mine, and no-one had insisted he be admitted. Maybe they just wanted me where they could find me, for when they decided to pass judgement.

Which, if the look on Draeven's face was anything to go by, was now.

"I want to talk to you about what happened today," Blake said. I took a slow breath and nodded, staring down at my hands.

"What you did today was incredibly brave."

I jerked my head up to look at him. That wasn't where I'd been expecting this to go.

"Had you not acted as you did, many may have been injured."

"But had you not assisted in Brad's escape," Draeven said, "there would have been no danger to begin with. It falls to me to decide whether your actions cancel each other out. You will explain yourself."

"What's happening to Ryan?" I asked, staring down at my hands.

"Worry about yourself," Draeven said, his deep voice gravelly and dangerous. But there wasn't much I could say to defend myself, and someone had to speak for him.

"It wasn't his fault. He'd been sneaking down to the dungeon without anyone realising. Brad manipulated him."

"We were well aware of his visits. And yours."

"You were?"

"Indeed. Have you forgotten, Ms Hart, that everyone here is capable of detecting scents that do not belong – such as two young shifters who had no business sniffing around prisoners they were not supposed to know existed?"

My cheeks reddened. I hadn't thought of that. We must've left a scent trail every time we went down there – and Ryan had been going a few times a week. That was hard to miss.

"Why didn't you say something?" I directed my question at Blake, because I couldn't quite force myself to question Draeven.

"I had hoped that seeing you and Ryan well-adapted and thriving would help sway them. But I was mistaken. I never imagined that the reverse would be true. Answer Alpha Draeven's question. Why did you free them, and why today?"

I lifted my eyes and pointed them in Draeven's direction. As before, I couldn't quite look at his face.

"You were coming to kill the others." His eyes bored into me and I bowed my head, because it never hurt to show respect when you were trying to save your hide. "Alpha."

"Was I, indeed?"

"I heard you were coming here after the exams. Why else would you?"

"My, Grandma, what big ears you have."

My cheeks burned red.

"Ryan was beside himself with fear. Not that I'm blaming him. I'm responsible for my own actions. I didn't think they deserved to die because of what happened to them."

"I was not coming to kill them."

"You weren't? Then… why?"

"Alpha Draeven visited Dragondale – the druid academy – yesterday," Blake answered. "He made an interesting discovery, which he was coming to discuss with me. The identity of the one who bit you has finally been uncovered."

My breath caught in my throat. Dragondale – where Leo had been hiding out. But if it hadn't been him, then, who?

"It explains much of your behaviour, and the other matter Shaun brought to me – your magic."

"You know about that?"

"I do," Blake said. "Though until today, we did not know the cause of it. The wolf who bit you was a halfbreed – half-shifter, and half-druid."

"I… I don't…"

"When she bit you, it would seem she passed on not just her shifter magic, but also her druidic magic."

"Is that even possible?"

"We did not believe so," Draeven said. "Indeed, we had no reason even to consider it. Halfbreeds are rare in our community, as are those reckless enough to break our most sacred law. I know of no other case where the two have converged."

"What will happen to her?" I wasn't sure why I cared – I mean, she'd completely torn my life to shreds, and half of me wanted her dead for it. The other half believed in the law.

"Nothing," Blake said, exhaling heavily. "It would seem she, herself, was under a spell at the time of the attack. A rage spell, cast by a powerful druid criminal. A rage spell she may have passed on with her magic."

I looked from one to the other, trying to process. "A rage spell? That's why I'm so angry, all the time? Does that mean you can fix it?"

"The spell itself has been broken," Blake said. "Whether you can be cured of its effects remains to be seen, though our own enforcers are consulting with druid experts in hexwork."

I sank back into the bed. My head was starting to swim. If Draeven was going to pass some sentence on me for letting Brad out, I wished he'd just get it over with, so I could get on with feeling like shit in peace.

"Your motive in releasing Brad and Laura," Draeven said, from somewhere out of focus, "was to save their lives, not to form your own pack?"

I sat bolt upright and stared at him, mouth agape.

"Our own pack? No! We had no idea what he was planning. He just said he didn't want to die."

"Well, he got his wish – thanks to you."

I ducked my head again.

"Not that his life was ever in danger. But I accept your intention was to prevent harm. You will be spared punishment. But I will be watching you closely, Jade Hart."

"And Ryan?" I asked, because apparently I didn't know when to keep my mouth shut. Draeven's jaw tightened.

"Ryan was complicit in Brad's plan *after* he learned of it. Threatening the life of an instructor cannot be allowed to stand unpunished. He returns to the alpha pack with me, to face judgement for his crimes."

Chapter Thirty-One

I limped into the main hall, leaning heavily on Cam's arm. I'd spent two days in the hospital wing – or what passed for one here – and though my leg hadn't healed completely yet, I refused to miss this.

"You dinnae need t' be here," Cam said for the third time – I'd been counting – as I hobbled towards our usual table at the back of the hall. I tried to make a dismissive sound, but it came out as more of a grunt, which did nothing for my argument.

"Dean, will ye tell the lass she doesnae need to be here?"

"Nope," Dean said, walking conspicuously close on my other side. No-one was giving *him* a hard time about coming down here – though maybe because his burns had healed within a day. Silver took longer, apparently. "I heard she tried to take on Draeven. I'm not about to upset her."

I rolled my eyes and ignored the banter, focusing on putting one foot in front of the other. The pain in my leg was bad – bad enough that I was starting to wish I'd done what everyone wanted and stayed in that hospital bed for another day. Not that I was going to tell them that. Besides, I was here now, and it was a damned sight further back to my bed than it was to that table.

It was crowded in the main hall, but people made room for us to pass. Apparently, my reputation had grown from outcast to badass outcast. It didn't hurt that Cam and Dean were glaring at anyone who didn't move fast enough. I wasn't fully sure why Cam was even here, but I wasn't about to question it. It felt good to be this close to him again, and with all the bad I was feeling right now, I latched onto the one positive thing.

"Do yer need tae stop?" Cam asked, his voice quiet enough that I was probably the only one who heard, even in a hall filled with shifters who had enhanced senses. I considered it for a moment, then nodded my head a fraction. It wasn't going to help my cause if I collapsed, and my head was already spinning. I hadn't left my bed in two days, and it had been a long way here from the hospital wing.

Cam stopped immediately and I eased my weight onto my good leg – which apparently hadn't got the memo it was supposed to be the one that still worked. My knee buckled, and I collapsed into the Scottish shifter. He caught me easily, holding me up with one arm wrapped around my body.

"Easy lass, I've got yer."

I leaned into him, letting him take my weight, and inhaling his scent and waiting for the dizziness to pass. I leaned my head against his chest – and then realised what I was doing. My cheeks flared red and I pulled away.

"Sorry," I said, looking up into his eyes. "I didn't mean to–"

He bent his head down and caught my lips with his, cutting off my apology. I hesitated, then reached up, embracing the kiss.

"Hey, you two, knock it off," someone called from a nearby table. Tyler, maybe. I didn't feel like turning to check. "Some of us are trying to eat."

Cam broke away and tucked a stray strand of my hair behind one ear.

"I don't understand," I said.

"I should have trusted you," he said. "I had no idea what you were dealing with. When you asked about Ryan, I thought it was because you wanted to be with him, not me."

"You," I said, leaning into him again. "Always you."

He lowered his arm around my waist, and the rest of the walk to our table didn't seem quite so painful.

"I still dinnae think ye should be here," he said, as I collapsed into a chair with even less grace than usual.

Now that I thought about it, he was probably right. I should probably be lying down when I got the bad news. Oh well, in for a penny, in for a pound. I put on my most glib voice as he settled into a chair next to me.

"Well, if you want to walk me back to the hospital room…"

"I'd carry ye if I thought ye'd let me," he said, a growl rattling inside his chest.

A scraping distracted me from that beautiful sound, and I jerked my eyes from his face to see Mei shoving a couple of plates across the table towards us. I frowned. It must have taken us longer to get to our seats than I thought, if she'd already managed to queue up and get our food.

"I'm glad you're feeling better," she said, claiming a seat opposite me.

"She should still be recovering," Cam grumbled.

"I needed a change of scenery," I protested. "Besides, lying there was giving me too much time to think about everything I screwed up."

Cam squeezed my shoulder, and I leaned into his touch. Whatever else happened today, I was glad he was back in my corner. We had some stuff to work through, but there would be time for that.

"There's one thing I don't get," I said, looking at Dean and then Mei. "What were you two doing in Shaun's office?"

They shared a look and Mei glanced down at her plate.

"What?" I pressed.

"Well…" Mei said, without looking up.

"Shaun told us your shifting exam didn't go well," Dean said, also avoiding my eye. "He wanted to talk about what would happen… if you got held back."

"He what?"

"He didn't want you to have to repeat the year without anyone you knew," Dean said. "So we said we'd repeat it with you."

"But only if you fail," Mei added quickly. "Which you won't."

"You guys would do that?" I looked from one anxious face to the other. "For me?"

"Well, of course we would," Mei said. "You're our friend."

Dean shrugged.

"It'd be dull without you around stirring shit up."

"I'll go see Shaun," Cam said, "and ask if I can repeat this year, too." He caught the look on my face. "Not that yer going to fail, lass."

I rolled my eyes. I was pretty sure that was a done deal. Trying to kill your examiner didn't tend to bode well for your grade, not even at Fur 'n' Fang.

"Before we make any decisions about who's repeating what, can we eat?" I said, nodding at my untouched plate of food. "Because I'm telling you, they don't feed us nearly enough up in the hospital wing. I think the healer was scoffing my share of the food."

For a while, the four of us said nothing, tucking into our breakfasts – because no-one made a full English like Mickey. We were half-way done when Madison, with Tiffany and Victoria in tow, came and sat next to Dean, giving me a filthy look first. I sighed and set down my fork.

"Look, if you've got something to say, just say it."

She sniffed loudly and turned her head away.

"Right, of course. Because you can't be seen talking to one of *us*, right? Not after everything that happened."

She scowled. "Don't downplay your part, cur. You let those freaks out."

"Yeah, I did. And I explained my reasons to Alpha Draeven himself, and he absolved me of any guilt. But if his judgement isn't good enough for you, then feel free to do something about it."

"I'm not about to risk being thrown out on the last day of the semester for your mangy hide. But if we meet outside these walls, all bets are off."

Cam glared at her, but I placed a hand on his arm and shook my head.

"Leave it. She knows she couldn't even take me right now, never mind when I'm not healing from silver poisoning."

"Just try not to put my future mate in danger next time you turn feral," she said, tossing her mane of blonde hair, and placing a hand on Dean's arm. I bristled, but my retort was cut off by Blake standing at the head of the hall, raising his hands. The entire room fell silent at once.

"Good morning, everyone," he said. "And well done for getting through another year without killing each other."

There were a couple of chuckles, but not from me. It had come a little too close to that for my liking.

"I'm not much one for speeches, as you know, but I want to thank you all for your efforts this past year. You should feel proud of yourselves as you go forward, upholding the ancient traditions of the Sarrenauth Academy of Therianthropy."

He paused, and nodded to several instructors standing behind him.

"The instructors will bring round your exam results. Those of you who have not passed all their subjects will be required to repeat this year. There is no room for failure. Should you find yourself amongst those who aren't progressing, spend your summer months wisely. Come back next year and apply yourself, and achieve the same success as your classmates."

The instructors started working their way round the tables, handing out sealed envelopes. I watched as Shaun worked his way towards our table, my stomach churning. I wasn't sure I wanted to open my envelope and discover just how many subjects I had failed.

"Portals will be opened from mid-day to return each of you to your packs. Please see the listings at the back of the hall for your departure times. The rest of the morning is yours to do as you please with. Enjoy your meals, and I look forward to seeing you again next year."

Shaun dropped an envelope in front of me, and I picked it up in trembling hands. He passed more envelopes out, to Dean, Mei, Cam and the others.

"You first," I said to Cam, dropping mine back to the table. He smiled, flipped his open, and pulled out the sheet. I scanned it over his shoulder, and then groaned. Maybe I should have found someone who wasn't perfect to go first.

"Nice work, mate," Dean said, leaning over the table and scanning his results. "Me next, then?"

He opened his envelope and read the letter inside. One look at his face was enough to tell me everything I needed to know.

"Well done," I said, a little grudgingly. Did everyone have to be so perfect? I wasn't looking forward to being the only failure in our year.

Mei scanned her results, and her mouth curved into a grin.

"I passed them all," she said. "My father will be very pleased."

"I'm glad," I told her. "You deserve it."

"Come on, Jade," Dean said. "Moment of truth. Are we repeating this year?"

I sucked in a breath and picked up my envelope. There was no point in putting it off. I ripped the flap and slid out the sheet of white paper. It scanned it, left to right, top to bottom, looking for the inevitable 'F'. Then I scanned it again. And again.

"I don't get it," I said at last. Cam leaned over my shoulder.

"Passed," he said with a smile. "All passes."

"Yeah, but how? I *know* I flunked the shifting exam. I tried to eat Brendon, for crying out loud."

"I think there's something written on the back," Mei said, squinting at the reverse of my results sheet. I flipped it over. She was right, something was written there, in Shaun's scrawling hand.

Jade,

Shifting back to human form while suffering from silver poisoning is more than equivalent to a first year shifting pass. Congratulations.

Slowly, a grin crept onto my face.

"I passed," I said. "I did it. We're moving up to second year."

Cam wrapped an arm around me and pulled me close to him.

"Congratulations. Now, I think you owe me an answer."

"An answer?"

"I asked ye something. On the, uh," he glanced away for a moment, and then back again. "On the day I acted like an idiot and dumped you."

"You weren't being an idiot," I said. "It looked like I was chasing after Ryan. I get it. But I'm pretty sure you didn't ask me anything."

He raised an eyebrow.

"Well, okay," I admitted. "I might not have been paying attention."

He rolled his eyes.

"Shocker. Do ye… Don't feel like ye have tae say yes, but do yer want tae spend the summer in Scotland… with my pack?"

I took hold of his hand and squeezed.

"That was what you asked me?"

No wonder he hadn't been happy I'd asked about Ryan. Scotland? With a real pack? I'd planned to go back to the farmhouse, but that place wasn't home to me, and I didn't want to spend summer alone. I wanted to spend it with Cam. And his pack.

"I would love to. Thank you. But I mean…" My heart twisted in my chest. "Is it okay for me to be there?"

What would they be like? What would they think of me, a Bitten cur? I didn't want Cam to get in trouble with his family because of me.

"It's a small pack," Cam said. "They raised me to judge someone by who they are – not what they are. They'll love you."

I leaned into his chest with a sigh. This year had been wild. I'd been so determined to hate this place, hate everything here. Every*one* here. But nothing about Fur 'n' Fang, hell, nothing about being a shifter, had been what I expected.

I spent half my time trying to get out of here. But now? With Cam by my side, and Dean and Mei – this place had become more than an academy to me. It was the home I hadn't known I'd been searching for.

I couldn't wait for next year, surrounded by my new family, and all because I'd been Bitten.

A note from the author

Thanks for joining me for Jade's first year at the Sarrenauth Academy of Therianthropy. I hope you enjoyed it as much as I did. Be sure to come back for her second year in Curse Bitten, book 2 in the Fur 'n' Fang Academy series.

Meanwhile, if you enjoyed this book, I'd be really grateful if you would take a moment to leave me a review.

Sign up to my newsletter by visiting www.cschurton.com to be kept up to date with my new releases and received exclusive content.

There's one thing I love almost as much as writing, and that's hearing from people who have read and enjoyed my books. If you've got a question or a comment about the series, you can connect with me and other like-minded people over in my readers' group at

www.facebook.com/groups/CSChurtonReaders

Printed in Great Britain
by Amazon

57328826R00190